D1474817

Joyland

Joyland

Emily Schultz
illustrations by Nate Powell

ECW Press

Published by ECW PRESS
2120 Queen Street East, Suite 200, Toronto, Ontario, Canada M4E 1E2

LIBRARY AND ARCHIVES CANADA CATALOGUING IN PUBLICATION

Schultz, Emily, 1974–
Joyland : a novel / Emily Schultz ; illustrations by Nate Powell.

ISBN 1-55022-721-1

I. Powell, Nate II. Title.

PS8587.C5474J69 2006 C813'.54 C2006-900293-2

Editor: Michael Holmes / a misFit book
Cover and Text Design: Tania Craan
Cover and Interior Images: Nate Powell
Typesetting: Mary Bowness
Printing: Friesens

This book is set in Sabon

The publication of *Joyland* has been generously supported by the Canada Council, the Ontario Arts Council, the City of Toronto through the Toronto Arts Council, and the Government of Canada through the Book Publishing Industry Development Program.

DISTRIBUTION
CANADA: Jaguar Book Group, 100 Armstrong Ave.,
Georgetown, ON L7G 5S4

PRINTED AND BOUND IN CANADA

"The house we hope to build is not for my generation but for yours. It is your future that matters. And I hope that when you are my age, you will be able to say as I have been able to say: We lived in freedom. We lived lives that were a statement, not an apology."

— Ronald Reagan

To Brian,
it's not ours to see.

JOYLAND

Gamebook

The things no one knows. Not even the best players.

Chris Lane stockpiles facts to use, like weapons, against his father, in a showdown that will never occur. He cruises through like a digitized arrow, meant, somehow, to represent a human. (50 points)

Tammy Lane is eleven and a half and she has already fallen in love many times. She does not yet know what love is, but the blue estuaries in her heart are large enough to have carried half a dozen devotions already. (75 points)

In 1984, Joyland video arcade closes its doors. At one time, Space Invaders was its most popular game — in spite of a dank row of boogers left anonymously along the machine's back edge. (100 points)

Unrequited love will almost always lead to violence. Some may know this, but in the heat of the moment, this information will be misplaced. (500 points)

Somewhere in the rustbelt of Ontario, there is a girl named Genevieve Cartier. You will never meet her. She is the key to everything. (1000 points)

In a few years, North America will undergo an economic shift. The factories will lock their doors. Only a faucet forging shop and a few dirt roads will remain. Every time Chris Lane washes his hands, he will feel his own imminent death, a closing down. (Lost player)

LEVEL 1

Galaga

PLAYER 2

The carpet frotteur knew cities of jacks, terrains of kitchen crumbs, the dumb wooden legs of furniture, and all that lay between them. The worn spot beside the right pedal her father's piano foot had stamped and thumped, and vigorously rubbed off. The catalogues and as-yet-paperless presents beneath her mother's side of the bed. The jagged letters of her brother Chris's name gouged white into an underlying beam of the playroom table (which had since become a study table), though he would not now admit that the letters had any association with him. The difference in vibration of footfalls — the hesitancy of her mother's, the severity of her father's, the singular triumphant stomps issued by Chris. The place to look for a lost Lite-Brite peg, a kicked Tinker Toy, a clumsy fallen Battleship, an elastic-shot chunk of Lego. The stretch of linoleum where a marble or HotWheels would stall. Whether or not a doll's shoe would fit beneath the door. First, second, third, and fourth grade accumulated between individual grains of shag. When Tammy rose up, she was halfway through Grade Five, she would soon start Six. She had witnessed the beginning of her life from this fixed, ground level. She teetered through the house off balance, unaccustomed to being vertical. By her eleventh birthday, she had found her footing. Eventually, she became addicted to height, learned to climb.

That summer, Tammy Lane was brave enough and strong enough to reach the very top of the maple tree in her backyard. From there, she could see the cars on St. Lawrence Street shooting past. She could see her brother flying away down the sidewalk on his BMX. She could see him flying away from her, away from everything she had ever known. Tammy watched afternoon lapse into evening and waited for him to come home.

Chris zigzagged through the grocery store parking lot, his butt in the air as the front tire cleared the curb and dropped him into the street. He disappeared through the branches. According to Tammy's *Big Book of Spy Terms*, he was "in the gap." When he reappeared, he was at the corner near the donut shop. Tammy lost him then — longer, "in the black" — and when she spotted him once more, he had doubled back through the grocery lot, riding hard and quick with his head down. Tammy pulled herself up by a branch she didn't trust, crooked her body onto a side bough that bent away from the trunk — at an alarming angle. The branch had been cut off and had veered, growing at a ninety degree angle from its sacrifice point, though not during Tammy's lifetime. She held tight, looking down, a thirty yard drop. She glanced back up just in time to catch Chris dodge into the string of back lots of the businesses on St. Lawrence.

Parallel, she located them: three shapes moving in the stretch in front of the donut shop. Bright blue track jackets and yellow hair bands. Girls.

To Tammy's knowledge her brother had only six fears. One, their father (though Tammy couldn't begin to fathom why). Two, J.P.'s older brother, who terrorized them on occasion (the same way J.P. and Chris liked to terrorize Tammy). Three, classical music (or anything other than hard rock and metal). Four, visiting their grandfather, but only because it meant being away from Joyland for days at a time (days, Chris said, that would make him "a total amateur again"). Five, ostriches (because he was once bitten while visiting an animal safari during family vacation). Six, clowns (due to too many viewings of the movie *Poltergeist*).

To this list, Tammy added number seven. Girls (an undiscriminating category including nearly all, except her).

Fears numbers three and four probably didn't count. Still, Tammy left them in. Chris's seven fears were a thumb-sized wedge in the pie graph compared to all of hers. The Seven Fears. Like the seven dwarves, fears were real and respiring, each with its own distinct personality.

She pressed chin against branch and let her lips trail over the grey, leaving a wide wet mark, the kiss of the bark on her lips like a hard, scarred thing. She dropped her forehead to the branch and closed her eyes. When she opened them again, Chris and the girls were both long gone. Tammy swung from one limb to another, carefully, letting her body hover in the space between just a fraction of a second longer than needed to obtain the exhilaration of floating.

On the outskirts of South Wakefield, on the other side of St. Lawrence Street, the building slouched like an extra baseball player on the bench: the disappointed V of eave, hands between the knees. Its back was covered in an emblematic tongue, the Rolling Stones' logo stitched to the concrete by an ecstatic spray nozzle held in a talented anonymous hand. Chris's paradise, Joyland, was scabbed with black paint, outside and in. He would come over as soon as Tammy jerked open the door of the establishment. He'd turn from the machine, as if he had caught a whiff of "sister" through the smoke; as if there were evils waiting to pounce, and then he would usher her out, all authority. This was their ritual. When the arcade had opened back in 1980, Tammy was seven-and-a-half and really didn't have any business being there. Alone, too short to see what was on the screens, she had looked for her brother between legs of worn blue jeans — cigarette packs bulging in back pockets, and obscenities falling off guys' mouths like ash off their cigarettes. And first, she had to cross the street. Cars gunned by at seventy, though the sign said fifty.

Today, Tammy had gone halfway and was waiting for the last two lanes to clear when J.P. Breton emerged from the arcade.

"Someone tell Chris Lane his sister's stuck in the

middle of the road," he yelled back through the door.

"Hey, just callin' it like I see it," J.P. laughed, not even flinching when Tammy slugged his skinny arm. He reached up and adjusted the strap of his ball cap, letting his corkscrew hair half-free before he matted it back under. He was one part Scottish and three parts French, with an Afro that rivalled Michael Jackson's and eyes as blue as Michael J. Fox's.

"Y'ain't never gonna get him to go home. Pffft — not today."

"Why not?"

"It's the last day." He snorted when he said it, as if surprised by the statement's hilarity. Then, scowling, he wound up for a kick, powerhoused a pop can across the parking lot. It hit the curb and fell. He squinted into the distance as if there was something there that was monumentally fascinating. "We're not supposed to know, but there's a rumour."

They stood there under the arcade's hand-painted sign. Edged red, gold jagged letters veered into one another like spaceships crashing. Above the black background floated a single floodlight that turned on at night. Now, five o'clock and June-bright, blue sky yawned behind the dark sign.

"Got any quarters?" J.P. asked. Tammy bit her lip for a second, reached into her pocket to fork them over. "You should play. While you still can." His hand fell on Tammy's shoulder as he ushered her inside.

As Tammy entered Joyland the smell of microwaved meat welcomed her along with a breathful of smoke. Below the pinging and powing of games came the low hum of hot dogs wrapped in paper towel, basking like babies in receiving blankets behind the pinhole plastic of the TV-sized oven. A dampness weighed the room down. The afternoon sun settled on the blonde forearms of boys, in motion at the wrists and elbows, their ball caps pushed back from glistening foreheads; the girls, just dark curving shapes streaming from the yellow jukebox. The microwave door snapped open and shut, plastic on plastic. Coins rang through slots. The bells on the front door rattled as it fell shut behind Tammy and J.P. He looped her shoulders protectively, salt and vinegar released from the skin beneath his mesh sleeves. Tammy was here for the first time to play. She'd just been born.

"Come on." J.P. gave her shoulder a squeeze before his arm fell away.

She followed him through the maze of games as if treading carefully through the secret garden that had grown at last, flower heads heavy with neon rain. Boys were bowed over the screens and other boys clustered around them. Their bodies branched away from one another even as their faces leaned close in concentration, cheeks illuminated.

At the end of the row stood her brother.

In the long line of boys in cut-offs and muscle shirts, a couple of them shirtless, Chris stood in a pair of full length brown cords, chalk-blue T-shirt tucked in at the waist.

Chris always stood with his weight more to one side, giving him an air of impatience. Today was no exception. He leaned to the left, palming the Fire button with what seemed like growing exasperation. Bottom lip curled under canine — Tammy watched the small stitch of white concentration she knew so well. He didn't notice them as J.P. loped up and stood beside him. J.P. said nothing. Tammy followed his example.

Her brother pumped the red Fire button. Green and

yellow space moths spun, a pinwheel on the left side of the screen, before forming a jet upward, the sorry remnants of their fleet lining the top of the disco-lit sky. Chris let his bottom lip loose of clenched teeth and his face settled into a placid dark cloud. One might expect his eyes to move back and forth, but he was almost meditative. Cool. Guiding his gunship with eyes that took in everything at once, rather than singular objects. Muscles coiled tight; the rest of him calm. Tammy observed the slight twitches at the corners of his lips, the orange explosions that were the result of his tapping fingers. Alien insects evaporated in puffs of pollen.

Her brother's face was smug, almost sullen, even in victory. His thick lips flattened in a tight sideways smile that held its true happiness back. There were always two of Chris — the one who protected her and ushered her out of Joyland, and the one who let his friends noogie the back of her head or drag her across the grass by her feet.

This was the latter Chris. Chris the champion.

His gunship glided across the bottom of the screen, dodging dive-bombing red butterfly ships. A train of tiny scorpions emerged, their curling tails trailing down the sky. Chris killed them with three successive shots. One of the gigantic moths swooped down. Hovering, it shot out blue cyclone-shaped rays, sucked Chris's gunship up in the beam, spinning end over end. Ominous music. FIGHTER CAPTURED. The enemy dragged Chris upward, tucked him behind its back when it reached the top. A new fighter was given and, biting his lip again, Chris avoided bullets, taking careful aim. The insect exploded. The captive ship fell to the ground slowly, joining with its saviour. A strong double force.

With the two ships steering as one and twice the firing power, Chris cleared the board quickly and advanced to the challenging stage. He nodded. "Ready to take over?" Glancing at Tammy for just a second, he made a move as if to step back from the machine. The first insects began to pour down the screen in a perfect line.

"No!"

"'Kay, okay." Chris picked them off without even seeming to look. "Next challenging stage then. There's nothing to it, see? They don't drop any bullets at this juncture. All you do is shoot."

Tammy nodded. *Juncture* was a conceited-Chris word.

The music chimed when CHALLENGING STAGE appeared in the centre of the starry screen a few minutes later.

"Ready?" As Chris said it, aphid crafts were already appearing, zooming in from either side of Tammy. She hit a bunch at the bottom and fired random shots up to the top of the screen.

At the end of the action, her results were displayed: 24 hits. From watching Chris she knew there were 40. He'd gotten all 40 and the word PERFECT! with an exclamation mark. Tammy knew about percentages. She'd hit 60%. If it had been a test, barely a C.

"That's respectable," Chris tried to reassure her. Her expression had given her away. "Keep playing." She got killed in all of two seconds. Jumping out of the way, she let him take over again.

J.P. was still there. Tammy's face grew hot. She shook her hair back, feigning confidence, Pam Dawber to the intended Brooke Shields.

"Should've played third round 'steada seventh." J.P. readjusted his ball cap again. "Prob'ly did as well as I would've." He peered over Chris's shoulder at the game for a couple seconds. "I got your back," he said to Chris, then headed off.

"You can't compare yourself to him," J.P. said over his shoulder as if he expected Tammy to follow him. They wandered toward the far wall, where J.P. stood in front of the air conditioner, flapping his shirt up and down off his belly. "If we all did that, we'd feel so bad we'd never play."

The black mesh shirt swung back down over the pucker of J.P.'s belly button, the white circle of skin confessing the fact he never went shirtless. Three years older, he was nearly as skinny as she was.

"What's your favourite?"

"Aw, whatever," he said. "It don't matter. I don't play to compete. You know, it's all a game."

Across the room, a bell shrieked and something went *splat!* A sputter of boy-laughter scrambled its way across the surface of the noise. The microwave rang. Pengo plinked out its theme.

At the opposite end of the arcade, through spaces between machines, Tammy noticed the yellow jukebox light and the stray parts of the people collected in front of it. Jean pocket details stretched so tight, the corner rivets resembled tacks stuck directly into the wearer's behind, as if to restrain the skin from pushing right through the material. A plastic purse the size of a gym bag was being swung about. Blush brushes and compacts tumbled over a pack of Players Light. Several blue-line notebook pages had been folded into exact two-by-two squares. A full-size can of hairspray clunked against the jukebox. The debris of combs and picks and hairclips shone, proud possessions encased behind the plastic. Two of the other purse straps were thin denim, decorated with clunky Twisted Sister buttons and feather clips. Behind the plethora of purses and makeup bags, beaded crop tops exposed brown skin. An orange tube top suctioned to triangular breasts. They jutted unapologetically from the chest of a girl wearing hot pink lipstick. These five or six girls circulated, passed in and out of Tammy's line of vision, just parts of them, like jigsaw puzzle pieces, their odd shapes somehow fitting together. If they saw Tammy standing there with J.P., would they mistake her for his sister instead of Chris's? Would they mistake her for his girlfriend?

Laughter. A pair of snapping fingers as one of the girls began to dance. She wriggled behind the black frame of a game and then all Tammy could see were the bruised legs of a skinny girl in a pair of pink and white pinstriped shorts. Her bum rested against the starburst of the jukebox panel, one knee thrust out, her entire kneecap the size of a silver dollar, and on it a black mark the size of a quarter. Tammy couldn't see her face. A crop-top girl was moving in front now, a freshly lit cigarette held at waist level. Expert fingers dangled, short square nails with chipped pink polish. The cold that the air conditioner hissed out hit Tammy's back with a wave of pleasure.

She wanted to argue with J.P. It wasn't a game: it was a world.

The Frigidaire swirled up her neck as she gathered her hair into a ponytail and held it for a second before shaking it out over her shoulders. When she glanced up at J.P. she saw he wasn't paying attention to her, but to the same thing she had been distracted by: the girls weaving and dancing between the cracks.

"You like Pat Benatar?"

Tammy nodded.

"Good." J.P. launched his body away from the wall toward the jukebox. White strings straggled from his jean cut-offs and trailed his thighs, catching in the thin puffs of his leg hair. He took long steps and Tammy had to skip to keep up. He sauntered past Chris, who was still pounding out space bugs. Just before they reached the end of the aisle, J.P. turned around.

He hunched down slightly. "So when I give you the quarter, you think it over like it's your idea. Then pick 'Love is a Battlefield.' They totally love that song but I don't want them to think I would play it." J.P. looked at her earnestly, his breath hitting her face. Sweet, like Grape Crush.

She swallowed and nodded.

The jukebox girls had a smell about them; it hovered there like a nimbus. Tammy had noticed it before, at school, whenever gangs of Grade Eight girls passed by her, trailing fragrance like a ribboned kite-tail of colours. Soap and smoke and confidence — she'd wondered if she would ever carry that scent, if, when she reached a certain age, it would roll from her skin the way it did from theirs. She didn't know if it was natural or chemical — some combination of hairspray, perfume, and powder — or less contrived, seeping out of pores as easily as sweat, something undefinable. Femininity. Its essence. Their laughter washed over Tammy as she approached. She looked at her feet. She looked at J.P. She didn't know how to look at them. They were all protrusions and nubs and tucks and foreign flesh betraying the confines of their clothes. Even their eyelids were alien: swollen purple and white, ringed with blue mascara. They were like extraterrestrial angels.

"Tammy," J.P. was saying. "What'dya wanna hear?"

She looked up at them all then. Just looked.

"Tammy?" J.P. repeated.

The girl with the orange halter began to laugh. She poked the one with the bruised skinny legs and skinnier arms. "Fuck," said the tube top, her pointy boobs jiggling with giggles. "She's just like her brother!"

"Yeah, she don't know how to talk!" hooted the chunky blonde with the plastic purse.

A chorus of laughter.

"Kitty cat got your tongue?" asked Cindy Hambly, who Tammy knew from Chris's grade at school. Nice-ish, but not really.

"She is Chris Lane's sister, isn't she?" the tube-top girl asked.

"Oh puh-leeze. Look at her, of course she is!" Cindy leaned toward her, fingers straying to Tammy's head. She pulled the hair back into a ponytail, as if there were no boundaries. "Just imagine if Chris had longer hair."

"He'd look like Boy George."

"Trans . . . vesta-tite!"

"You idiot — trans-ves-tite."

"What's . . .?" Tammy didn't get to finish the question before they all exploded. Their bright faces turned brighter beneath their blush. Their bodies swerved, knocking into one another as they giggled and snorted.

"Oh geez," said the brunette with the drinking-straw arms. "It means your brother looks . . ." she wrinkled her nose, ". . . a little too much like us."

"Yeah, but maybe he'll grow out of it," said Cindy, a note of sympathy in her voice as she looked down at Tammy. "You know . . . when he grows another foot or so!"

"Short Fry!" they all chorused, like it was the most hilarious thing.

Tammy peeked over her shoulder at the Galaga game. Chris's head turned, just for a second, in response to the outburst. His mouth clamped into a tight line and he looked back into the game. Between Tammy and her brother, two other guys — maybe Grade Nines or Tens — swayed against the machines, knocking things dead with their index fingers. Their massive thighs were covered in squiggly dark hair. Tammy looked up at J.P., who stood taller than her dad. At the far end of the arcade, Chris leaned further and further into the screen, as if he could escape into it, become a wheeling, firing, two-dimensional object in a graphed-out universe, trying to jam things up and override the system like Tron.

J.P. was still extending the quarter. One hand came to rest on Tammy's shoulder. "'Kay, don't spaz. C'mon, chill. What do you want to hear, Tammy?"

She only had one line, and she'd forgotten it.

The girls stopped and looked at her, waiting. Tammy held power over the whole arcade, could subject all of them to her choice.

"Maybe Pat Benatar?" J.P. prompted.

The girl in the orange tube started to smile, shook her hair back from her shoulders joyfully. Her lips were greasy with colour, wet all over, like she'd been sucking on a cherry popsicle. She looked positively thrilled with J.P.'s offer.

Tammy shook her head. "Scorpions."

The girl's lips fell flat, her face emptied. The rest of the group exploded. The skinny girl leaned over, clutching her ribs. The plastic-purse girl and the beaded-crop-top girl banged into one another as they laughed, the can of hair-spray in the bag smashing once again across the glass of the jukebox.

J.P. crisscrossed hands over Tammy's shoulders, around her throat like he would strangle her — then pulled her back against him in a half-hug. She felt his warm chest ridged with ribs against her back.

"Tammy Lane, you little fucker." She'd never heard the F-word spoken with such affection. "I shoulda known you'd do your own thing just to piss me off. You don't even like the Scorpions, ya spaz."

"She is just like her brother," the girls were saying, in self-congratulatory tones. "Just like her brother."

"I just want you to know," J.P. said, clutching one hand to his heart, his head bowing toward the face of the orange tube-top girl. "I was fully preparing to sacrifice my quarter for Pat Benatar. But now . . ." He spread his hands wide ". . . due to no fault of my own, I am forced — *forced*, I tell you — to play 'Rock You Like a Hurricane.'"

The quarter went in and the buttons were pressed. The song blasted out over the whole arcade. Guys looked up from pinball and foozeball, nodding their heads in appreciation.

Tammy wandered off. She hated the Scorpions. They were Chris's favourite.

"D'you meet the girls?" Chris asked.

He'd been growing his hair all spring, eyes barely visible under brown bangs that parted in the centre and trailed thick off his cheekbones. Beneath them his eyes flicked nervously back and forth, checking that none of the beautiful creatures were about to walk by at that particular moment.

Tammy nodded.

"They're asswipe dumb," Chris said, though he never cursed at home. He closed the conversation by flipping a quarter heads/tails from his thumb to his palm, as if it were of infinite interest, as if he could distract either of them from what they both knew Chris felt. "Burnouts," he said. The coin flew up. He made a swipe and caught it in his fist. "Druggies." His voice dropped lower. "Don't ever be like them."

He paused.

"You wanna see something?"

Tammy nodded. Anything.

"On Galaga, they can bring out your own dead ships and turn them against you. But it also means you can win them back." The quarter sailed up again, spinning.

"Call it."

"Heads."

Chris lay the quarter on his wrist without looking. He pulled his hand away, exposed the silver antlers of a Canadian caribou.

"Tails," he said.

"But it's the *head* of the deer," Tammy pointed out.

"It's a caribou. And don't be a brat. The queen's always the head and the animal's always the tail." He feathered his hair back through his fingers, swaggered toward the machine, Chris the champion again, leaning to the left with that air of impatience as he stood before it, continuing to pontificate.

"Even if it were an American coin — a bald eagle — it'd still be the tail. Doesn't have anything to do with whether it's coming or going. You can be player number two. Besides," he said, "that way I can show you."

"How are South Wakefield girls like bowling balls?"

J.P. leaned back against the machine, self-righteous and satisfied after a half-hour by the jukebox with the tube top. Chris had been showing Tammy the nuances of the Galaga game. Namely, that if she shot the bugs before they dive-bombed, they were only worth half as much, so if she was playing for points, it was better not to attack until they went on the offensive. Sometimes, Chris had explained, he played for points, and sometimes, he just played to survive.

"How are South Wakefield girls like bowling balls?" Tammy repeated. Even as she parroted J.P., her head felt huge on her shoulders. She stared at her running shoes. Blue and white suede. "How are South Wakefield girls . . ."

"You can fit three fingers in them."

J.P. leaned back, grinning. Chris erupted into the machine, shaking his head and losing their last player.

"Oh man!"

"She doesn't get it," J.P. said with a mocking glance at Tammy.

"Of course not, she's eleven!" Chris sucker-punched J.P. and J.P. doubled over. "Don't talk that way around my sister."

"Yeah, well, you laughed." J.P. faked a jab.

"Tell me, Chris."

"No way."

J.P. leaned down, cupped fingers confidentially around Tammy's ear. She arched into his hand.

"Tell me," she said, this time to J.P.

J.P.'s voice was husky as he hissed, "It has to do with s-e-"

"Don't!" Chris yelled, ineffectual as Tammy usually was. J.P. held him off with one elbow.

J.P. threw his head back and yelled: "S-E-X!" The whole arcade swivelled slowly, looked over with disinterest — the kind of gradual, obligatory head turn Tammy's mother did whenever she yelled, "Mom, look! Look!"

"They say that incest is best," the pinstripe girl called over.

"You would know!" someone yelled back at her.

"Yeah, your mother showed me."

They all turned back to their games.

That night, as Tammy ran home, the concrete blurred beneath her running shoes. White flecks flashed like constellations embedded in the dark asphalt. A universe spun away under her footsteps. Spirograph pictures passed beyond her recognition. The starburst on the jukebox panel. Things she would never see again. She closed her eyes and imagined the air pushing past as J.P.'s breath when he whispered *"s-e-x."*

Closed, the world around her became bits. Its sounds and its smells. The cut grass of the Scotts' lawn. The indent of the sewer that clanked when she ran over it. The lopsided lurching of running blind. Open, Tammy took in the world and stepped over the curb, across the grass clippings (which stayed on her shoes). She continued on the sidewalk — over squares that had been newly paved — a pancake paleness in comparison to the street. Her calves jolted with every step. An X mark had been made with a fingernail overtop of a mosquito bite to stop it from itching. Short thin hairs stuck out over the elastic of tube socks. All down the street, houses shimmered lit eyes, windows still open, only the hum of an air conditioner or two breaking the pinging that lingered in Tammy's head.

She stood in her driveway, looking up at the Little Dipper. A line of crabs inched its way across the night sky. She locked her fingers into the shape of a pistol. Raising it above her head, she watched the streetlight throw her shadow into the silhouette of a Charlie's Angel. Tammy angled her body away from the house, where her mother had just flipped on the porch lamp.

"*Pow,*" Tammy whispered. "*Pow,*" and she shot at the stars before she heard the door open, and her mother calling her in.

LEVEL 2

Frogger

PLAYER 1

After Joyland closed, the youth of South Wakefield had nothing to do but concoct ways to kill each other.

Until that point, the world Christopher Lane had lived in held a faint glow, like a vending machine at the end of a dark hall, a neon sign blinking OPEN again and again. Fear was the size of a fist, and the town where Chris lived was little more than the smell of manure and gasoline, the sound of breaking glass and midnight factory whistles, a series of houses he had or hadn't been inside. Permanent items disappeared in an afternoon, and Chris would later wonder if they had ever existed. A lost street-hockey ball, its lonely green fuzz languishing to grey in a thick lilac bush in some backyard beyond penetration. An incarcerated swingset whose legs had always kicked off the grass with their enthusiasm. The dog who couldn't stop humping, though Chris didn't even know what that was then, the mangy beast seeming only excitable and overly affectionate toward him until the older kids clued him in, pausing their whoops for a minimal parcelling of information. Chris shook his leg and the dog wrapped its paws Chinese-finger-trap tight. Chris shook, then kicked, the dog's butt scuttling across the cement. These other kids moved out of the neighbourhood gradually, like cranberries falling off a nostalgic half-dried Christmas string — two and the thing was drooping, four and the neighbourhood seemed on the verge of decay. A set of sisters too old to bother about. A pair of grape-juice-lipped brothers, one with a motorized go-kart, the other with the unnatural ability to recite the entire alphabet while belching. Chris and Tammy stood on the curb and sang, "Na-na-na-na, Na-na-na-na, Hey Hey, Goodbye!"

But the Lane house didn't change. Nothing changed except the television commercials, and the things Chris wanted. A bitty grey woman growled, *Where's the Beef?* A long-eared cartoon bounced between two blonde child actors, his shape stitched immaculately to the screen somehow, above or behind their blood-and-bone figures, the point nothing more than brightly coloured breakfast cereal: *Silly Rabbit, Trix Are for Kids!* The ongoing inanimate argument between solid, dependable Butter and the sneaky-lipped dish of *Parkay.* A bear knocked on the door, proferred a cereal bowl: *More Malt-O-Meal Please!*

Meanwhile, in other corners of the household, a ten-year-old set of toenail scissors stood guard, in their usual station on the second shelf of the medicine cabinet. They donated their opaque moon-shaped testimony to the Lanes' normalcy.

Like all children, Chris felt his parents mysterious — their joint and sudden chorusing into songs he had never heard on the radio, their individual smells, the way they would fuse occasionally at the lips or fingertips as if drawing power from one another, recharging. His father's accent lifted around the other kids' parents and eventually cologne-faded from dense to faint, American twang settling into something flatter, something Canadian. Mr. Lane's brown brow hid a machine of knowledge. Mrs. Lane's polyester pants had the miraculous ability to turn into a folding chair where Chris could sit for hours. Days smeared under his palm like eraser guts (Pink Pearls and Pink Pets, Rub-A-Ways and Arrowheads, Unions, a bright green Magic Rub, the Sanford Speederase made in Malaysia, the godly Staedtler Mars Plastic); they blew away leaving only a faint grit. Chris seemed to age in three-year increments, passing from three to six (before three was thumbsucky and didn't count), six to nine, nine to twelve, and twelve to fourteen, an age that, fittingly, broke the cycle. Running Creek Road was the world, and the world was big and small simultaneously, easily forgotten.

Joyland opened in the midst of the third trimester. Chris underwent a delivery, in reverse, leaving the outside world behind as he clamoured into the dark.

He found a just-across-the-street understanding of the opportunity for pleasure. The constant presence of temptation smoothly transformed into something less like sin and more like human experience. Holy mechanics comprised a system that could be predictable and random simultaneously. This was the world of the video game. In this universe there was no guilt, no darkness to the daylight. With twenty-five cents Chris experienced explosions of colour, the graphics on the screen somehow representative of all the beautiful, violent things he did not yet know.

He crossed this street again and again. The candy-coloured cars flew by him and he proceeded with minimal caution toward his destination, as if drawn by a homing instinct.

Joyland was located three blocks down from the one-level house where he lived with the people who had emerged into reliable unmysterious figures: Mom, Dad, and Tammy. South Wakefield lay like a plain white dot on a large dark screen — population 9,000, situated in Southern Ontario. As minute and unremarkable as a fly on a lily pad. Beyond Running Creek Road, there were six factories, five churches, four elementary schools, three sports stores, two arcades, one strip mall, and a movie theatre that had been turned into a "gentleman's club." Chris was fourteen years old and Joyland was the only place where he felt himself shine.

During the day, the road was like a fluorescent tube, sunlight thrown from it, blinding. A rumble of transports and supply trucks thrummed from one end to the other, heading on through, down into the States. At night, the hose of the highway lay silent, turned off. Only the occasional truck, trying to make some time, threw up grey dust in its wake. Joyland sat on the other side like a small black hole in the pocket of the night.

The stunt in the road hadn't been Chris's idea.

Tammy sent home long ago, J.P. and Chris sprawled on the curb opposite the arcade, leaning back on their hands, drinking grape pop. Over the course of the night, the misplaced patch of boys grew in the stretch of cement in front of the Twiss's Gas 'n Go. In addition to Christopher Lane and John Paul Breton, gathered a standard post-Indian-Creek-Grammar-School group: David White, Kenny Keele, and Dean and Rueben Easter. Pinky Goodlowe had been too steamed to stay. He'd jumped on his BMX and ridden away, massive knees hitting the handlebars.

"Man! I dunno, we got this sort of, like, bottomless summer now. Eight whole weeks of nothin'. How many days of pure street hockey d'you think you can stand? In a row, I mean?" J.P. spoke specifically to Chris, the others oblivious to the gravity of the situation. Chuckling, David had pressed his crotch against a gas hose, pretending to pump the pump. Between his legs the nozzle hooked in — blank tin body and glass face — the machine reduced to the simplest notion of female, something entered.

Chris shook his head. "The crescent's good for it, I guess."

"Yeah, but my folks hate it. They'll beat my ass." J.P. stretched his legs out in front of him, bent slightly at the knees. "Straight days of hockey, draggin' the freakin' nets back and forth every time a car wants in or out. The neighbours'll be over yellin' at my mom before the week's out. What else we got?"

"I don't know." Chris tilted his head back and let the last swig of pop ripple through his throat. "Swim, bike, TV, soccer, baseball, the usual . . ."

"Pffft. Boring, bo-ring." J.P. squeezed his bicep, the muscle bulging up around a mosquito that had landed there. He watched its back end fill with blood. When it burst, J.P. wiped the residue off with two fingers and leaned over to rub them on Chris, who lurched up and away a few feet. J.P. reached round and rubbed them on the ass of his shorts.

"I don't know why you do that. You still get the bite, ya know." Chris scrambled back down, settled on the curb more upright.

"'Sfun," J.P. shrugged.

David dropped to the curb beside them, followed by Kenny, Dean, and Rueben. Behind them, Johnny Davis had claimed a seat atop the mailbox in mute sixteen-year-old oblivion, with the exception of the odd fartish exhalation.

The side door to Joyland opened, rapping across the concrete night. They all stilled, watched Mrs. Rankin reach up to unhook the bells. In one hand she grasped the chip carousel from the counter, yellow plastic pouches still hanging from it. The other fist fumbled with the string of chimes, which warbled through the dusk with ecclesiastical melancholy, until Mr. Rankin appeared, a thick ring of keys hanging from his thumb. He reached up — the woman's stubby white fingers still groping — and unjangled the bells with a click into his silent hand, the other closing the door and poking the lock.

They waddled to their truck to stash their things. She got in, sat staring out the windshield at the boys across St. Lawrence Street. She had trout-coloured eyes, visible even from that distance. Mr. Rankin returned to the door and fastened a heavy chain across its handle.

The boys sat with the final snap of the padlock clamping down on them. Mr. Rankin turned his back to the blotted black building and walked slowly to the vehicle, opened the door, and got in — no sudden movements — as if he could feel bullets in the boys' gaze. The potato chip rack, shoved between them in the front seat, waved little cellophane wings, rotating when the truck reversed. A scatter of gravel. But before the headlights had disappeared down the highway, the boys had begun a eulogy, recounting their greatest Joyland moments.

Upon entering, there had always been a moment of disorientation. Although the arcade was at street level, it had small, raised windows like a basement, which gave it a watery underground aura. Walking out of daylight into the dim hull, the eyes always needed time to adjust. This second was a pure assault of sound. The noise of bells and bombs as they dropped. Of hearts beating and alien life forms detonated. Slowly, sight returned. A pulsing room came clear, streaking and glittering in the dark. Chris would begin scanning the place for the first available game.

Rows of machines lined up to meet him. Passing through the door, he was greeted by Pac-Man, Pitfall II, Centipede, Tempest, Tron, Dragon's Lair, Gorf, Pengo, Defender, Mr. Do!, Mario Bros., Frogger, and beyond these two rows more — all of them humming, singing, shrieking, bleeping, burping, and whistling. Staring into their plastic faces, Chris perceived whirled light plotted into some decipherable map. He plunged inside that space and became a swivelling, pivoting hero, with a simple twist of his hand and the ability to remain focused. In Donkey Kong, he climbed up ladders, he climbed out of himself and became the person he had always wanted to be: the kind other kids grouped around to watch play. To admire.

For two years, Chris had paid his dues, leaning carefully over shoulders, trying to see the patterns. He learned from the masters of South Wakefield: Johnny Davis, Mickey Newton, Pinky Goodlowe, among others. Joyland was full of competition, good-natured fuck-yous, two-for-flinchings, and the occasional well-placed jab. A scrawny, intellectual, preteen boy will receive his fair share of pounding, so it was not without fear that Chris had entered Joyland each day. A ten-year-old pipsqueak when the arcade opened, it was there that he had first been dubbed Short Fry. He had learned by observation. Behind the gangs of twelve-year-olds, Chris had clutched his quarters in a sweaty fist, waiting for a machine to come open, the coins heating in his hand. Older guys — fourteen or fifteen — swaggered about the place with the confidence they would not have to wait long for a machine. The true video game gurus held a rank all their own. As if they had absorbed luminosity from the screens, they emanated it from their very hands. In the unspoken pecking order, those first two years, Chris had always been last in line.

Pulling rank more than once, Pinky, the twice-held-back kid from Chris's class, had given him the chance to play. Two years older than Chris but miles taller and wider, Pinky walked a very thin good-guy/bad-guy line. Pinky was the fifth of five brothers, each of whom had virtually disappeared from South Wakefield by the ages of sixteen or seventeen. The first was killed in a car accident before Pinky was even born. The second went to jail for a knife fight, did his time, then landed back inside almost immediately. The third had gone into the factory early and never emerged again, "making good money on the line," Pinky said. Chris had never met this brother, though he knew the house on the edge of town with a car graveyard in front and a legend of pot plants in the back. The fourth brother was a free man, but no one knew where he had gone. Pinky said he had left town after knocking up his girlfriend. Other sources said he just didn't get along with their father. Pinky was famous as the last-chance child. He claimed it was right there in his name, which was his father's: Peter Goodlowe. But his family just called him Pinky. Maybe his mother was trying that one last time for a girl. Pinky was anything but.

For the number of times Pinky's fat knuckles reached out to jerk Chris clean off his feet by his collar, they were also used to clear a path for Chris. Pinky had a strange sense of justice that couldn't be held against him — even if he hadn't been five-foot-nine by Grade Six.

"Time for Short Fry to play," Pinky would say, yanking whoever had hogged the machine out of the way. "Okay, Chris, do your stuff," he'd add, hovering to watch Chris's moves.

While Pinky acted as sentinel, Johnny Davis was Chris's true mentor.

From across the room, Chris scrutinized the earnest way Johnny leaned into the machine. The eerie darkness of the arcade emphasized the reflection thrown into his glasses. From a certain angle, Chris could see a pure square of blue-green light wavering overtop Johnny's eyes: an exact replica of what was on the screen before him. Through the fast-rushing traffic and river logs in Frogger, Johnny bowled forward, pumping the controller, his icon edging upward. The froggish green patch of colour bounded toward home, safety — onscreen and off, the shapes caught on glass in miniscule. He was not just the master of the game. Johnny Davis *was* the game.

Johnny Davis was about five-ten, one hundred pounds. At age twelve, Chris hadn't even topped five feet, so it was awkward and obvious whenever he tried to look over Johnny Davis's shoulder to watch him play. Mainly, Chris stood to the side and looked under his armpit. Chris assumed this post for over an hour one day while Johnny was on the Pac-Man game, forcing the yellow mouth through the maze. At one point, Johnny couldn't outrun the ghosts, and his man spun around and dissolved. He abandoned the machine even though he still had two players left.

"Take over for me," he said. "I need a smoke break." He shook the cramps out of his hand and walked away, leaving Chris there to play for him.

Witness to this event were both Kenny Keele and and J.P. Breton. Also nearby was Mickey Newton, second only to Johnny Davis as a player. Chris saw in Mickey's face a kind of jealousy that should not be permitted to pass from an older guy to a younger one. Chris had been handed the controls to the master's game. Immediately, Chris felt like Mickey Mouse in *The Sorcerer's Apprentice*. He prayed he wouldn't make such a mess of it.

When Johnny had come back, Chris had earned him a free man and was still going.

"Good moves for a geekboy." Johnny shook his head and lit up another cigarette right then, dropping the match into the metal ashtray affixed to the machine.

"You always stand there looking under my armpit," he'd said, watching his disciple eat up the board. "Good thing for you I don't have B.O."

Chris had registered his first high score that day, courtesy of Johnny Davis. The rest Chris would get would be his own work.

Now there were a handful of players without games: a circle of smart-mouthed friends and a few clumsily told stories. Johnny kept lighting one cigarette off another and not saying a word. He stared at the building as if he was telekinetic, could tear the chains from the door with his eyes.

"What are we gonna do?" Kenny Keele snivelled. He bobbed his bowl-like feathered haircut. Chris glared at it, though Kenny's small hawkish face was turned in the other direction. It was about the fiftieth time the question had been voiced in an hour.

"I don't know about you," David White said, "but I'm gonna lie in the middle of the road. Over my dead body can they close this arcade. I mean, what the fuck? We can't play at Circus Berzerk, it's in a mall! Our moms are there buying groceries and lottery and sweaters and shit. There are little kids climbing all over. You can't even smoke there." David flicked his cigarette across the gas station parking lot toward the closed booth. Chris eyed it warily. Red sparks flew up and disappeared.

David had a point. The only other arcade was lame. They had to walk into it through a huge open-mouthed clown face. There was a helium balloon stand in the front. The owner sold ball caps with fake turds on the brims under lettering that read *Shithead,* not to mention squirting flowers, joke birthday candles, sparklers. In Chris's estimation, whoopee cushions were all right, but not when his best friend's dad was there buying them.

David stood up. He removed his John Deere cap, his Playboy necklace, his digital watch. He dropped the chain and the watch inside the cap and handed it ceremoniously to Kenny.

"I'll take that belt buckle off ya," Dean said. It was as huge as a Harley, equally eagled.

"If I die," David said, a sudden Southern twang to his voice, "give my mama my love."

"What about Cindy Hambly?" J.P. snickered, half under his breath. Everyone knew she'd made out with David once, but was dating a high school guy now.

Kenny blinked behind his glasses, and accepted the cap and its contents with a constipated expression Chris recognized as alarmed devotion, vintage Keele.

David stalked to the centre of the road and crouched down, spread-eagle across the centre line, legs waiting for northbound traffic, head and arms waiting for southbound.

"Come on, White," Chris yelled. "Don't be such a martyr."

David held up one hand, middle finger extended, no intention of moving.

"It's a peaceful protest," Kenny insisted, and the next thing Chris knew, Kenny had spread himself across the northbound lanes, the John Deere cap carefully folded and clutched atop his chest.

"What the hell," J.P. said, and left Chris sitting on the curb.

The Easter brothers followed J.P. out, Dean first. Rueben rolled to the pavement after him, propping his head up on his brother's shins.

Across the street, Joyland glared morosely, the reflection of one streetlight caught in the small high window. Chris had a feeling somewhere inside, coiled like some long sticky thing waiting to snap loose.

"Come on, Lane, show your love!" J.P. yelled.

Chris glanced up at Johnny Davis, Video Game God. He didn't even bother looking down at them, just stared into the dead-eyed windows of Joyland. The circle at the end of his cigarette glowed orange, made a small perfect hole in the night.

Chris crawled on his hands and knees. Under his palms, the concrete had tiny gritty teeth that left marks in his skin. Rolling slowly onto his back, he lay in the middle of a lane looking up. Waiting.

Gazing up into the night, he willed himself into a different headspace, a time before Joyland, and a time ahead. Suddenly, Chris knew why all the sci-fi series were about searching for a half-extinct human race and trying to get home. He was trying to formulate a theory, distill it from his brain and put it into words — when Johnny Davis jumped off the mailbox.

"What is *this?*" Johnny yelled, as if he had just noticed what they were doing. "It's like you're playing chicken without cars. Kid shit," he said. He turned, kicked the mailbox three times hard. Chris raised himself up on one elbow, watched Johnny lurch all ninety-five pounds into it, the slim tendons in his forearms popping as he rocked the red metal off its legs. In slow-motion the box tipped, then landed on its back, the arrow-like Canadian Postal emblem pointing suddenly skyward. The sound thundered across the gas station parking lot and echoed on the empty highway. Chris could feel the vibrations jolt through him.

The boys in the street sat up on their asses, stared. No one said a word.

Johnny Davis plunged his hands deep into his pockets and walked away slowly, looking nothing like a guy who'd just lost it.

David snorted, and Kenny lay back down, the rubber grip of his running shoe facing Chris. A red bull's eye of rubber.

Chris turned and watched Johnny Davis trek the entire length of St. Lawrence Street. From a distance, Chris knew they must look like they'd parachuted out of the dark and landed there — arms and legs thrust out haphazardly across the cement, sneakers pointing at the heavens. But Johnny Davis did not glance back. He walked the four blocks up, and when he reached the fork in the road where the downtown intersection began, veered left and passed from sight. It must have taken at least ten minutes. Still, not one set of headlights.

Chris paused another minute, looking up at the sky, willing something to happen.

Nothing did.

When Chris got home, his father's face was like a blank television.

Mr. Lane hunched in front of the TV, staring at it as if he had only just turned it off. His grey head sunk into his shirt collar. A thirty-eight-year-old force field, emitted invisibly, sealed him inside, determined to make him ancient. Uncanny static crept into his silences, as if the radio broadcaster in his head had run out of things to say at exactly the point Chris passed out of range. Mr. Lane had a remarkable ability to sit for long stretches, doing nothing. When he did speak — as he did now — his voice was gruff.

"Should've been home a goddamn hour ago." What he said was "goddamn" but what Chris heard was Q*bert-ese: *@#*!*

"They closed it down," Chris said, the defence sounding weak as it hit the air.

"Couldn't use one of those quarters for the phone?" Mr. Lane got up and left the room.

Chris had, of course, been spectator to the goings-on at his friends' houses when they were getting it. He knew he had nothing to complain about. Had once, in fact, witnessed a whole house constrict with smoke as voices pitched — a result of J.P. having brought him home without asking after ball hockey — the argument hurtling into a chin-to-chin faceoff, hard-ribbed and tense as sexuality.

Yet, Mr. Lane's words were chosen with great deliberation. A well-placed piece of profanity — even one of the mild swears — carried enough force to knock a tooth out. The Lanes were a family of respect, pride, patience. A family of bullshitters. Chris yearned for a great bloody brawl. Even the kind of daytime television drama that began with innuendo and ended with sobbing. Anything that might breech the barriers.

Any number of elements could, possibly, have shaped Chris's parents. He had seen pictures of his mother as a seventeen-year-old — before her father died, before she had left the farm because she "didn't get along" with her mother, repeating only that she "couldn't stand to stay." From a young age, Chris played a game of interview, and this was always Mrs. Lane's answer to that particular line of questioning, no matter how Chris found new ways to phrase it.

"Why did you move to South Wakefield?"

"I couldn't stand to stay out there. Coming to town was like moving to a city."

"Did you come here to meet Dad?"

"I met him later."

"So you came here to go to school?"

"No, I just came. Because."

"You came and you lived here all by yourself?"

"Go play with your sister."

Chris had seen the farmhouse, once, though it wasn't more than forty kilometres away. However ambiguous the "couldn't stand to stay" answer, it was, in itself, an admission of passion. His mother fled grave sadness, suitably outfitted with a Samsonite makeup case, and a Jackie O. coat with big buttons, clomping down the stairs of the bus like Marianne Faithfull off an airplane, desperately searching for something *far out* — desperate enough to drop out of school at seventeen and work in a factory for it. But neither Mrs. Lane nor Mr. Lane would admit to ever having used the phrase "far out." They claimed to be too old by the time the '60s hit though, using proper math, the answer did not compute.

Chris backtracked and dropped his parents into more traditional settings, occasionally Al's Diner or the Bunkers' living room. Once, when Chris had shown a brief interest in motorcycles, Mr. Lane had explained the row of old-fashioned bikes and scooters pictured in Chris's library book. He casually tapped the ones different friends or acquaintances had owned.

"Gas tank in this model's right here . . ." *tap, tap*

". . . meant guys were riding around with a hot tank of gas right between their legs."

In the boy's mind, Dad was soon outfitted *Sha-na-na* style and had owned each of the vehicles consecutively. When Vietnam hit, Chris's father had crawled belly-down through mud in the middle of the night to get across the border to safety in Canada, the sky glowing eerily behind him as if the war were actually occurring within the U.S. instead of far overseas. In truth, Mr. Lane had arrived with a machinist's qualifications. Canada needed cheap labour — non-union — and Nam had absolutely nothing to do with it.

In the lives of Chris's parents, there were two things of utmost importance, so far as Chris could see: 1) which of them would drop the kids off; and 2) what they were going to eat for supper. There was also 3) money, but that was not discussed openly. In this way, Chris's parents functioned as a distinct force, sharing the same concerns, their actions made with deliberate unity. Kentucky Fried versus the local fish & chips. It was a decision of enormous gravity.

At fourteen, this is what Chris knew of his mother and father: on Sundays his mother wore tan sweater vests and white blouses with big bows at the throat; his dad wore wide-collared shirts that had gone out years ago, stiff brown polyester slacks, and brown shoes; Mom smoked menthols; Dad, duMaurier; they sat in the same chairs every evening in front of the television; Mom preferred Dad to drive on any trip beyond town limits, or at night, but she was otherwise quite happy to run Tammy and Chris here or there; Dad was obsessed with weight, and Mrs. Lane had dwindled over the years; Chris's father was, in most matters of consumption, frugal, yet every day, even in winter, ate a single scoop of chocolate ice cream after supper.

At age ten, Chris and Kenny Keele had finished off the carton one afternoon, promising Mrs. Lane they'd go to the store to buy more. They promptly forgot. After supper, Mr. Lane had gone to the freezer. He rummaged behind steam breath, face hidden by the open door. Clearing plates, Mrs. Lane didn't say anything. Shut-door, Mr. Lane walked from the room without glancing at any of them. In the mudroom, he put on shoes (he never wore them in the house, though Mrs. Lane did). He removed coat from hook. The zipper toothed out a *pffft* that could be heard from the table. Leather gloves snapped softly over wrists. Tammy gaped all fish-eyed.

Mrs. Lane did not look at Chris at all. She turned a blast of water into the kitchen sink. Dad went out. The door closed with a civilized *foooom* behind him. Chris sat gazing down at the plastic lace cloth on the table. He traced taupe eyes on white plastic with his finger — no hole or height difference between the eyelet pattern and the rest of the cloth. His mother turned off the taps, and Chris knew there were wide, white letters ringed with blue, ringed with red, tight beneath her palms — faucets fashioned at the factory there in town. Sometimes, Chris imagined them, shipped all over the continent, ringing under the dirty hands of strangers, the steel name of his hometown brand emblazoned under their palms, as close as he could get to being somewhere else.

Tammy continued to stare at Chris. He stood up and pushed his chair in hard so that its back slat landed a wooden slap against the table edge.

"So?" he railed, arm shooting out vaguely at Tammy

as if it weren't attached to his body. He swaggered out of the room. By the time he'd reached the hallway to their rooms, that swagger was a half-sprint. He chunk-clunk-slammed his door, threw himself down on the bed. A bubble stretched across the back of his throat and he pushed his head down into the crook of his arm, as if the suture between mouth and stomach would disappear if only he thrust his body into the bed further. Chris cried. Through his skull, the house was silent. He willed the tears down, until they too were completely inaudible, even if someone were to enter the room. Guilt: a silent song of stitches sung into himself. Three hours later, the front door opened. Dad sang "The Gambler" at the top of his lungs.

By fourteen, Chris knew all he could know. He did not know, for instance, whether his father owned any pornography. Certainly Chris had looked for it, in all of the usual places (sock drawer, underwear drawer, under mattress, in closet, in garage). A decrepit shed decked the backyard — "Dad's space" — but was bolted padlock-stiff at all times. One afternoon, both parents at work, Chris had jimmied the lock with the help of Pinky Goodlowe. The red semi-rotten door yawned, boards scraping their teeth across the concrete floor as Pinky pushed inwards. Fingernails combing blackboard, the little hairs raised on the back of Chris's neck as they broke the November-thin musk of the shed. Inside, they found an exercise bench and some free weights, a hundred odd pin-ups of men from the '40s and even as early as the '20s. In outdated gym clothes, they stretched from the darkness, bent in low leg lunges, squats, weight training. Abrupt veins erupted from their forearms and foreheads. Displaying double-pipe flexes, nineteen-year-old knuckleheads grinned Eddie-Haskell-ish. Charts of old wrestling techniques wallpapered the damp, knotty walls. Yellowed smiles stretched across faces that evoked another era so completely, it was as if their genetics had died out with them. Now they were locked up in the place Chris's father came to be outside his life — to be with them, one of them.

"Can I have this?" Pinky asked. He held up what appeared to be one of several extra sets of handgrips. Chris tried, but couldn't wrap his fingers around them. He shrugged. The grips disappeared into the back pocket beneath Pinky's plaid shirttail.

Chris did not know if his father had other obsessions, did not know if his father might have been *his* age, for instance, the first time he consumed liquor, the first time he thought of girls. Chris did not know if Mr. Lane, in his youth, had been the sort of person who picked on others, or the sort who was picked on. In short, Chris could not imagine his dad being any different at any point in his life than he was now — at this very moment — stalking from the room, his ice cream spoon left in the bowl on the coffee table rather than taken to the kitchen, where a small blast of water would have saved the milk from hardening in thick muddy streaks.

Flicking through the stations, decisions were made: the best news, the best game show. But after nine, stillness stretched, reflected in the murky face of the unemployed TV (26 inches, wooden frame, RCA, *Made in U.S.A.*), the couch with its brown-and-orange afghan, the two armchairs, and one pair of his father's shoes placed always to the left of the doorway. Chris did not know what bearing any of these items had on his father's personality or the lives of his parents as a couple. Did not know if his mother was flirting with the jeweller when her voice rose at the end of a sentence like that. Did not know if Mrs. Lane enjoyed her job at the cannery, or if she wanted more out of life. If there was more, Chris hadn't the slightest idea what it might be.

His parents were without history, without future. Chris imagined the farmhouse down the dirt road with the invisible old woman inside it, the past like a three-dimensional postcard. A snapshot of something still in existence but slightly out of reach. Like a picture on a faulty television, perpetually rolling, a zigzag of colour and a black line seemed to prevent Mr. and Mrs. Lane from interacting. Their conversations swept through the room, yet their faces were always bent out of shape, so that Chris could not see the expressions that went with the words.

Had it always been this way? It hadn't. They had been exciting, funny, fusing arms around one anothers' waists, making big productions of little things like Yahtzee shakes and throws.

His father's shoulders tensed as he turned at the end of the hall with a backward glance.

By way of answer, Chris sniffed back. He didn't bend to undo his laces as he toed off his shoes.

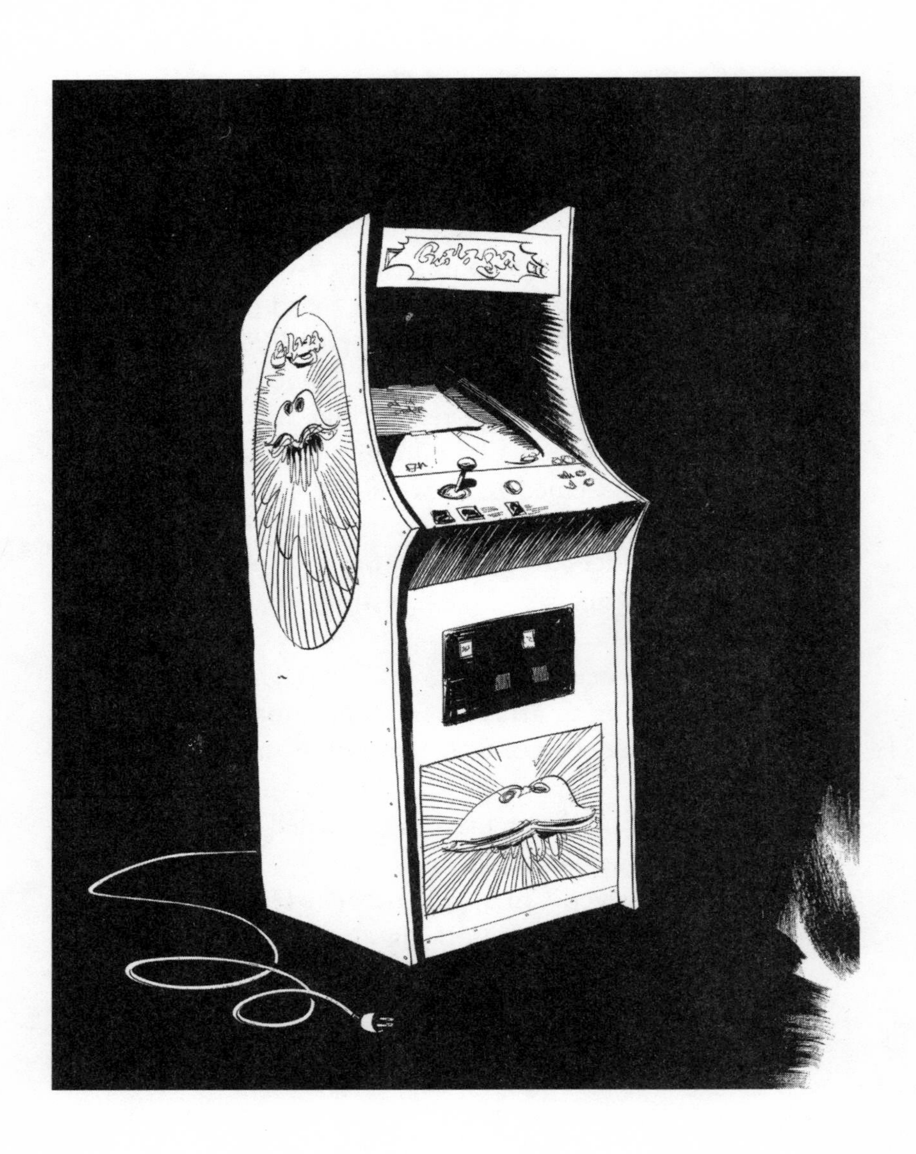

LEVEL 3

Galaxian

PLAYER 1

"Get outside with your sister." Mr. Lane poured milk over his Corn Flakes (Kellogg's, packaged in London, Ontario) and left the carton on the table, lumbered into the living room. Mrs. Lane crossed the room and picked up the container of milk, flicked the triangular lip shut with her index finger. *Neilson*, the carton declared in red script. *44% Vitamin D. Pasteurized. Since 1893. Halton Hills, Ontario. Ottawa, Ontario. St. Laurent, Quebec. Meets and/or exceeds all Canadian Dairy Standards — guaranteed!* Its contents were boring, but its birthplace exotic.

Halton Hills. Chris rolled the words around his mouth without opening it. His mother left the table with them.

Chris pushed the Sunday comics page aside. Beneath it, Minnesota's Mondale was winning the battle of words against the Gipper. An arms race put on pause for a flag-waving race across America, while outside, down St. Lawrence Street, the high school band was beginning to assemble — among a series of half-decorated flatbed trucks and a tub of McDonald's orange drink — to squawk out "O Canada!" on dinged French horns and barely sucked clarinet reeds. Born in Illinois, February 6, 1911 — the same month and same state as Chris's grandfather — Ronald Wilson Reagan certainly wasn't being billed as a Hollywood informer to the FBI during the Communist bedlam of the '50s. Read here: champion of the Iran hostage crisis, Reaganomics, a system of strategic defense, "Peace Through Strength," and on and on. But the American smudge of politics, thick as Charmin, went unread under Chris's elbow. In a border-town rag, what was Mulroney but a big chin? The fourteen-year-old's view of the world was in cartoon. Better yet, pixelation.

"Don't you want to watch the parade?" Mrs. Lane asked, but she wasn't looking at Chris. He shrugged, but her back was to him as she opened the refrigerator.

"I don't understand how you could spend all that money there," she said, but when she came over to the table again she lay a folded purple bill next to Chris's elbow. The bulbous chemical tanks of Sarnia, Ontario stared up at him. He examined the industrial wasteland on the back of the ten-dollar bill.

Outside, kitty-corner to their house, came an onslaught of shattering glass. The VanDoorens were at it again. They scoured the town with a pickup truck, nimbly picked up broken glass, later transferred the toothy sea to a flatbed trailer, and — when they had accumulated a sufficient amount of it — sold it back to the factory to be melted down and reformed. Sometimes the crunch of it came as early as 5 a.m. By comparison, the Lanes were lucky today.

Chris's mother cringed. "I don't like this borrowing money from your friends. You pay John Paul back. But don't ask for anything more for fireworks tonight."

Chris folded the bill carefully in half lengthwise. He folded it in half the other way, then in half again.

"Thanks," he mumbled, looking up for just a second before he bent beneath the table and shoved it into the top of one of his tube socks.

J.P. called less than a minute later. Mrs. Lane picked up, handed off the phone. She hovered, like she was waiting for something. Chris shuffled sideways, away from the china cabinet, but Mrs. Lane made no move toward its drawers, and instead stayed, suspended over him. He coiled the cord around his body and faced the wall so that the line wrapped all the way around him.

"Whad'you want to do tonight?" J.P. asked. "Cuz there's this guy I heard about . . . Doyle. He can get you anything. You just show up."

Chris nodded and didn't say anything. In his chest, his heart flickered and buzzed. He ran his tongue over his lips nervously. Mrs. Lane picked up a cloth and began wiping down the kitchen table. Chris turned round again, uncoiling himself to watch the trail the dishcloth left behind — side to side — as it dried, its easy rhythm slowing things down inside him.

"I have that ten bucks I owe you," Chris said finally, just before he hung up.

Chris watched his most recent recruit skitter away from the stick that had fallen, like an act of God, across its path. It was one of those little red ants — mean buggers — and it reared back and squiggled around, as if in a state of shock, unsure of what its next action should be. It proceeded on a new track, rushing into it decisively, as if called by a collective consciousness back to the mound. When Chris dropped the stick again, the ant reacted immediately, no disorientation. It pivoted and changed direction, branching away from the stick entirely, a wide-angle turn. Chris blocked its path.

Tammy came running down the street, a pink plastic skip rope trailing behind her.

"I jus' talked to Jen," she panted, "and she's marching with her dance class, and —"

The brown twig came down in front of the red ant again, and Chris laughed. He had this idea of a cartoon insect, rearing up with large white eyes. An invisible sound bubble of what the ant might say if it could talk. The collective consciousness cursing.

"— she says there's a frog race again this year. Downtown. After the parade."

"Uh-huh."

"D'you 'member when you entered, and your frog just sat there, until almost the end, and by then all the other frogs had jumped out of bounds?"

"Yeah, I remember."

Tammy had developed this annoying new habit of

saying, "Remember when . . ." about almost anything. As if it hadn't been just a couple years ago. As if Chris had a tumour in his brain and had forgotten everything.

"We should get us a frog, huh? I think we could catch one if we went on our bikes down to the crick." She spoke fast and Chris looked up, hunched his shoulders at the word — *crick*, he hated it, like a bug scratching its legs together, *crick, creek* — squinted into the sun to see her. Tammy's hair had scrunched its way half out of its ponytail, and she was wearing a pair of his old Adidas shorts. They looked funny on her, the little upside-down V's at the sides stretched open to accommodate her. Even though she had a basic eleven-year-old stick figure, nothing fit. Skinny skin expanded the second she put it under clothes, like one of those miniature foam monsters from the novelty store. Sunk underwater, they swelled like tongues. Tammy wasn't large, just awkward. The fact that she kept trying to wear his old clothes probably didn't help. It simply reinforced the fact that she was a girl. She was an embarrassment.

"Tammy, why don't you —"

"We could go get one right now, Chris. If you don't want to enter, I could. If you'll help me catch one, we can —"

"Tammy. Sit down for a minute."

She dropped onto the grass like she'd been shot. Her face was as red as her T-shirt. His old T-shirt.

"You're gonna wear yourself out before the parade even starts," he told her. "Whad'you do, drink Coke for breakfast?" Chris looked down, realized the ant had long ago escaped. He snapped the stick in half and tossed it into the gutter.

"What time is it?" Tammy asked for about the thousandth time.

"Ten after ten."

"Fifty minutes until the parade. We could —"

"Did I ever tell you what happened after the frog race?"

She shut up, rolled onto her side. One hip jutted up from the grass like a bike tire, the white stripes on the dark shorts making her somehow rounder.

"Do you have your period yet?" It was one of those questions Chris hadn't considered asking. It just popped out, because he had suddenly thought of it and wanted to know. Tammy flipped onto her stomach and put her head down on her arms, as if by turning that part of her body away it would deflect his question.

There was a long silence. Chris stared at her but she didn't look at him or answer. She picked at the grass, pulling individual strands up by their roots before flicking them away. Her hair fell across her red face.

"You know I don't," she said finally, flicking the grass in his direction. "Why are you being mean?"

"I'm not."

The sky above them was a clean, clear blue. Chris lay back and gazed up into it. Clouds burst open like big white peonies. Two were exchanging foam, underneath, just at the corner. Chris could see they would eventually morph into something else. He could hear Tammy, about a yard behind him, kicking one running shoe against the other.

"You should be careful," he said, without looking at her. "At the arcade yesterday —"

Clunk, went her running shoes. He closed his eyes.

"J.P. —"

Clunk.

"Guys are going to —"

Clunk.

"You don't look like those girls yet but —"

Clunk.

Their parents hadn't told Chris a thing about sex. It was as if it didn't exist as long as they didn't talk about it. The idea of extruding some new kind of substance was so strange, almost like communicating with outer space. The blue sheets, especially, were the perfect backdrop for his message. The lines of lust were obvious as paper airplanes. On the patterned sheets — thin blue and green stripe — his testament was more discreet. There, even the smallest drops clung and would not let go. Like dots of braille — if one wasn't looking for them they weren't noticeable. Once, Chris had been able to transport the fluid all the way to the bedside table and across the digital clock. Dried, like candle wax, across the red stick numbers. It remained, however faintly, over a year later, a lingering streak of this substance his body was constantly producing. Chris imagined it as a dispatched satellite, video footage in outer space: a living thing removed, projected, a flickering replica of human existence. Like starlight, it stayed long after the actual heat formation had dissipated or burned out. Chris waited to see how much time would pass before it was discovered, until it began to have meaning. Without any consultation, he had joined the leagues of boys across the nation engaged in the employment of socks. Socks were excellent resources. He could leave them crumpled and crusty beneath the bed, casual clues. If anyone noticed, they didn't say a word.

Of course, his employment had begun much earlier, gradually, before building to full-time occupation. At the age of ten, Chris's body had Barbapapa-ed out from underneath him, formed its own confused shape in his hands. Rollercoaster first-cart fear rumbled low in his guts. He held it tight as the crossbar, waited for it to go down, and eventually realized it wouldn't. The thing stuck there, immobile. When it melted all over him, vomit-warm and candy-apple-sticky, he realized he was sick — really sick — that he needed to go to the hospital. He swabbed himself clean with terry cloth — his nearby bathrobe — and lay shivering in bed all morning. A cartoon conversation converged between his shoulders, angel on one, devil on the other, to tell or not to tell. Thankfully, not to tell won out and Chris was chicken-souped by lunchtime and back to school, furiously head-ducking the usual *Where-were-you*s. As if this indignity wasn't enough, until Grade Six Sex Ed., he mistakenly believed a tampon was something a girl used to apply makeup. He felt it was his duty, somehow, to make sure Tammy knew things before they happened to her. Meanwhile, she naively shrugged her hair back and panted "Tell me," to his friends in dark arcades.

But what Chris had just said was all he could manage. Neither of them spoke for a long time. Then her shadow pitched across him as she sat up.

"What about the frogs?"

A lone Galaga game stood inside the doorway of Jorge's Pizza, splintered linoleum peeling out from underneath it. Someone had used Liquid Paper to change the last "a" to "oober": *Galagoober.* The sight was enough to make Nolan Bushnell cry. But the Pong pioneer would never see it. Chris Lane was the only one to bear witness.

He walked up to the counter to ask for change. Sad curtains had been stretched back and pinned on either side of fat windows using flat gold thumbtacks. A fleet of dark woodgrain tables stretched, waiting, their lone occupants precision-centred twenty-five-cent vases. From these, plastic rosettes erupted on dust-furred felt stems. Seven or eight of them surfed the moatish light between the counter and the windows looking out on the street. The counter was tall, the space behind it raised so that the proprietor would have towered over the establishment had she not been a woman of minimal height. She emerged reluctantly, wiping her hands on a dishtowel. A brandy-coloured EXIT sign burned behind a wooden hallway of doors labelled with figurines of pants and skirt. Chris proffered the purple ten with the factory smokestacks face up. Wilfrid Laurier, two red two-dollar bills, and four shiny silver caribou replaced it.

Waiting for J.P., Chris dropped into the deceptive repetition of the machine. The switch had been set to run fast by the owners, probably to clear kids like him out of the foyer quickly. He was not thrown off balance by the difference. He rammed his ship from side to side, picking off insects, though he longed for a Galaxian machine rather than this sequel, most often considered superior. Galaxian had a sameness he enjoyed, with its chunky graphics and unchanging board. Its insects fell leisurely, rhythmically. Space was its own silent music. The Galaxian bullets had a delay, were almost impeded, chug-chugging their way through the sky as the enemy armada broke formation to leaf their way down. Chris could fall into a kind of stupor and meld with the game, changing his speed as he advanced steadily through levels, never needing to adjust his tactics.

CHALLENGING STAGE, the present machine chimed.

There was a Galaga at Circus Berzerk in the mall, but no Galaxian. Already Chris was mapping, mentally tallying the (limited) resources of South Wakefield post-Joyland. No Galaxian anywhere. Space Invaders had breeched the divide between arcades and restaurants, its popularity granting machines access to new venues; Galaxian was a glorious follow-up, the first full-colour video game. Yet the donut shops were now rationed with Ms. Pac-Man table games, a lone Donkey Kong Jr., and one old Football table with a Trak-Ball. Defender guarded the lobby of the Metropolis Diner. The bowling alley ought to have been a thriving base, but its agents had clung to pinball, refusing to accept a new plan of action, eventually stocking with a meagre five machines — by that late date, not one Galaxian among them.

Chris traced a family tree of games backward: Galaga, Galaxian, and Space Invaders, the grandaddy of alien gatecrashers. He imagined them in Texas, rows of ten-gallon hats bent into the cabaret containers of the machines, brushed felt bending beyond the wood-grain lips, a protest of Bible-belters mouthing, *Space Invaders ARE SIN!* , the machines slowly scooping out their march of destruction in ice cream parlours: Farrell's and DQs across the Lone Star state, across all of America. Mesquite residents, mad as hellfire, had taken the matter all the way to the Supreme Court in an attempt to ban the video game from their community. Chris always envisioned it like that, people on two sides suddenly in the same room, as if the corridors of law offices could be lined with the games and their gamers to make the illustration complete, horrified Christians in suspenders, a pack of judges' robes joining the play. A crunching, tinkling panel-sized Taito-licensed-by-Midway drawing of conflict. A knob stationed in the centre for Control.

Meanwhile, Tokyo was all lights, yen falling like rain, the music of space plinking down narrow streets until the coin shortage forced the government to quadruple its supply. Chris leaned back and shot this third wave of third-wave Invaders — oh Galaga! — his ears echoing with the singing of coins across an ocean, six years after the fact. Tokyo had really had them: whole buildings dedicated to one game. He stood before the gleaming mouth of an arcade filled exclusively with Space Invaders, Space Invaders, Space Invaders, Space Invaders, and more Space Invaders. Then, as the blue moth craft swooped down, Chris shot and it evaporated. There was only South Wakefield, a lousy pizza parlour. Japan was a calligraphy of vector lines, another language, a two-dimensional icon from another game. It didn't even exist. South Wakefield was a flock of ships above Chris's tapping fingers, the broken flooring under his soles, and the Portuguese owner-lady staring at him with eyes of brooding boredom.

When J.P. arrived, Chris committed suicide. He'd used up two quarters. He dumped the remaining $9.50 into his friend's outstretched hand.

J.P. scoffed, annoyed.

"You're late."

The South Wakefield Canada Day festivities had not

changed since 1975, the first year Chris remembered them clearly. That day held the newness of a crisp dollar bill in comparison to today's sweaty quarter. As Chris and J.P. left the pizza place, they were caught in a surge of sunburned moms, complaining toddlers in tow.

"You should've seen us try to get the car here this morning."

J.P. dodged ahead. He didn't mean just any car. He meant *the car*. Mr. Breton's crash derby special. "Had to get Marc to help get it down here. Son of a bitch." Even as J.P. swore, his voice rose like a high school girl's. Chris watched him wipe sweaty palms on the ass of his shorts. The day Mr. Breton had brought the old Dodge wagon home, he'd demonstrated, using ether to bring it back to life. It made a violent *clack clack clack!*, like a baton dragged across jail bars. J.P. and Chris had painted it black and white, like a police cruiser. OPP, J.P. had hand lettered the sides, and instead of *Ontario Provincial Police*, he'd painted *Optimal Playing Power* in tiny script underneath.

They took off, swerving through the post-parade crowd. All the while, Chris kept eyes peeled for girls his age, girls who might be in his classes come September. Jostling between tank-topped bodies, there was the instant mental sorting: too old, too young. A fresh-looking blonde covered her mouth as she laughed. Sweet, but seventh-gradish. Chris squeezed past a gang of confident smokers — chubby legs announcing themselves to the world in cut-offs. Fifteen. The one in the sparkly lettered T-shirt glared as Chris's shoulder grazed her chest.

J.P. followed, smirking. He made a sucking noise when they were safely through.

"You wasted that one."

Chris didn't look back. He could feel a pack of angry eyes on him. Unconsciously he touched his fingers to his shoulder, as if it were holy now, as if it had touched the robe of Jesus. In truth, her breast had felt like anything else under cotton: elbow, shoulder, stomach.

"I didn't mean it," he said, fingers jerking away from the spot. He walked away fast through the crowd.

"Pffft. That's your problem," J.P. laughed.

Scanning the people in the street, Chris hoped for a glimpse of Laurel Richards, the one and only girl who had ever played worth a damn at Joyland. Her thin limbs were called to the forefront of his brain by the smell of suntan oil rising around them, Piña-Colada-prevalent. Laurel hadn't been there yesterday, and that seemed to Chris more tragic than anything he could imagine.

From the moment Chris first saw Laurel in Joyland, he began to construct a timeline in his mind of the direction their lives would take. It began with her peering into the game, followed by his exponential masturbation. From that point on, however, there was one major problem with the timeline: Chris's tendency to revise it. Always, it started at the same moment, but the hinges in the line and the words relating to them became erased so many times, as Chris's daydreams expanded and exploded, that eventually Chris stopped his mental erasing. Their timeline became a 3D figure, similar in shape to a molecular compound. It began as a simple nucleotide, maybe an adenosine, with several bulbs and branches, then double-helixed and spread until it was as complex, as astral, as DNA.

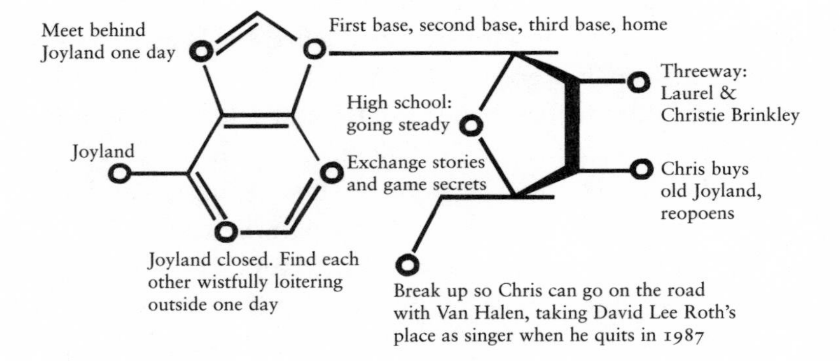

FIG. 1: *Timeline of Chris Lane and Laurel Richards' Relationship*

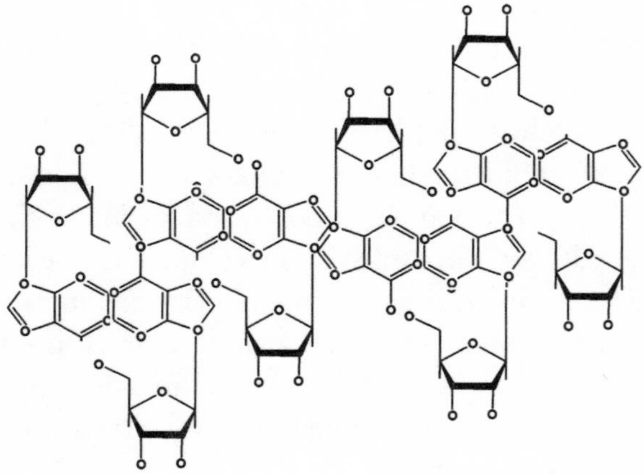

FIG. 2: *Timeline of Chris Lane and Laurel Richards' Relationship*

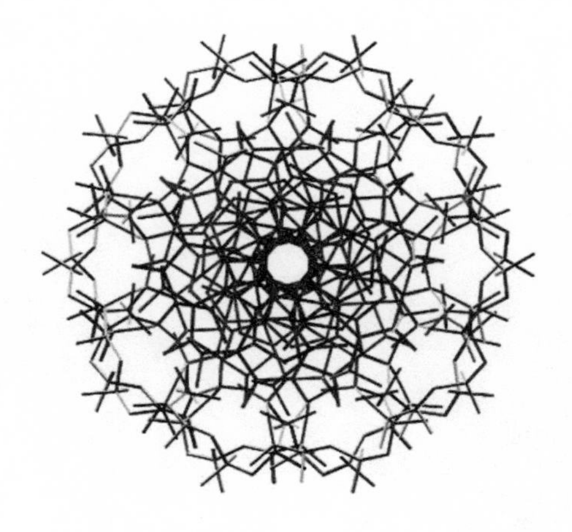

FIG. 3: *Timeline of Chris Lane and Laurel Richards' Relationship, Three-Dimensional View*

LEVEL 4

Centipede

PLAYER 2

The purse pitched back and forth like a pendulum, harder and harder, until the contents grew heavy and nearly forced Tammy forward.

"Mom!" she hollered, stopping the motion abruptly with her left hand. The strap wrapped around it, quickly cutting off circulation. She untangled herself, pulled the zipper back, dug around for her mother's car keys. From the bathroom, running water. Tammy twirled the keys around the ring on her thumb: leather tab key chain, engraved "No. 1 Mom." Tammy stared at it in her hand.

The key ring was the diameter of the mouth of a pop bottle, she realized. The mouth of a pop bottle . . . About the same size, her best friend Samantha Sturges had said, of Samantha's thirteen-year-old cousin's wiener, which she had seen last summer while changing in the back seat of the car to go swimming.

"He'll be there again this year," Samantha had said last week, about going to the beach for fireworks night.

"But he's your cousin," Tammy had pointed out.

"So? He's still *gorgeous*." In Samantha's book, being *gorgeous* was all anything was ever about. She wondered if Sam had seen it by accident or on purpose. Tammy hadn't thought to ask. She had seen Chris's before, but that was years ago — she hardly remembered — before she even knew about s-e-x. When she'd asked Sam tentatively what it looked like, Sam had confided, "*Weird*. Like the neck of a pop bottle covered in Silly Putty."

Mrs. Lane came into the living room, where Tammy was standing staring down at "No. 1 Mom." Mrs. Lane put out her hand and the silver ring with the leather tab fell from Tammy's palm to hers.

"Don't dig through my purse," she said, taking the strap and looping it over her shoulder as they walked out, one behind the other.

On the ride over to the Sturges's, Mrs. Lane rolled a cigarette between filament-thin fingers, and placed the end tentatively in her mouth. She seemed to nibble at it, as if considering whether to spark it up or not. Tammy watched the end bounce up and down as her mother contemplated. She took the cigarette out and, rolling it once more between her fingers, as if she could consume it through her skin, placed it in the ashtray. The end was wet now, like a lipstickless kiss. The paper clung to the things rolled up tight inside it, showing through, vaguely, brownly. *Gross.* Tammy turned to the passenger window. She pushed the shoulder strap of the seatbelt down beneath her arm and leaned back against it, leaving only the lap belt in effect.

They inched out onto St. Lawrence Street, traffic all stops and starts, the town rerouted around the stretch of Canada Day game booths. A gigantic, purple balloon head bobbed behind the Kentucky Fried Chicken. Tammy watched it — the inflatable jumping booth — wondering if it was dumb to want a ticket. *Under Twelve,* the sign said. Tammy knew this, though she couldn't see it from where they idled. She remembered from last year that she'd had one more year left.

Mrs. Lane put her blinker on, started to edge over.

"Damn," she said softly. She paused, signalled again, and eased over, waiting.

Samantha lived in what Tammy secretly called the "left ovary" of South Wakefield. Everyone else called it Forest Hill: a new maple-bricked subdivision with double driveways and pencil-thin trees. Sam had arrived four years ago, joining Tammy's class at school with a package of Magic Markers, as if she'd sprung, miraculously, half-grown from the dirt mounds that would gradually transform into her neighbours' foundations. St. Lawrence Street branched into a triangular subdivision and two more main streets (King and Jamison) heading in opposite directions, ends extending into cul-de-sacs. The left (northern) ovary was Forest Hill. The right was not fortunate enough to have a name, called only Southside or south South Wakefield. In pink-on-pink-on-white glossy, Tammy had traced the contours: a sex-ed. booklet given by Samantha's mother to Sam.

Chancing upon an aerial photograph of the town in the library a week later, the analogy came clear. Located toward the bottom of Ontario — at the very bottom of all of Canada in fact — South Wakefield was the sex organ no one ever talked about.

The idea implanted itself in Samantha and grew to proportions beyond Tammy's timid brain. "*Va — gina,*" she would mouth to Tammy, across the room at school, for no reason but to see Tammy turn bright red and bend over her desk, hair hitting the blue lines of her notebook. "You live in the *va — gina.*" Dirty words were a wonderful thing to Sam. She saved up a list of them for every situation. A year dangled between the two girls like a spider on a thread. Sam had been held back in kindergarten due to poor attendance. A sinister case of pneumonia, or so she said. But Samantha said a lot of things. She was a reference queen, from Terrabithia trees to dictionaried profanity. She said that she could go out with any guy she wanted, *just like that,* as she snapped her fingers.

Tammy let her arm fall casually out the car window. The air resisted her cupped hand with a muted *whoosh-whoosh*. Keeping the hand low, against the door, so her mother wouldn't see, Tammy closed her eyes and felt the motion of the car, tried to gauge whether they had passed the pharmacy or the post office yet. Tammy knew when the car was crossing the bridge, between the incline and the *thruuuuum* as the tires found traction. She felt the sting of a bug in her hand, and opened her eyes, yanking her arm back through the window. Mrs. Lane glanced from the cigarette in the ashtray to Tammy. Then her eyes flicked quickly back to the road. She turned somewhat too sharply onto Sam's crescent.

The Sturges's house had a For Sale sign pounded into the front lawn, exactly centred between the two trees that still hadn't grown large enough for climbing.

"He's not going to be there, is he?" Mrs. Lane asked. By "he," she meant Mr. Sturges. Tammy shook her head.

"So it's all finally going through?"

The sun fell into Tammy's lap through the windshield, sealing her thighs to the vinyl seat with sweat. She didn't look up.

"I guess so," she said as she chewed on her lip — something she knew, even as she did it, had been picked up from Chris. "Can I have five bucks?" she asked. "Just in case?"

Her mom picked up the white leather purse and opened the car door.

"I'll walk you. I want to ask Kathy a couple questions."

Tammy pulled each leg off the sweat-sticky seat individually, using her hands, as if to emphasize the family's poverty to her mother, the way she made Tammy look in front of others. Everyone else had upholstery. Her mom was the only one who still insisted on giving the money directly to the chaperoning parent. All of her friends got to hold their own. Tammy had an aqua-green velcro wallet with a white grid pattern across it, but what good did it do? With the exception of last year's class photo of Samantha, and a couple of Scratch 'n' Sniff stickers, the wallet was always empty.

She stood behind her mother as Mrs. Lane knocked on the frame of the screen door. It was Joyce, Samantha's seventeen-year-old sister, who came and stood on the other side of the screen. Through the black mesh, her perfect face was cut with lines. A dark half-circle rose above her left lid, but not her right. Not a bruise, but Maybelline.

"I was just doing my face," she said. She reached out and unlocked the screen door. "They're in the backyard," she said to Tammy's mom, but she opened the door anyway. Her arms grew out of her waist, a glut of baby blue material, silver snaps glinting like eyes up and down her shoulders.

"We'll go around then," Mrs. Lane said, nodding emphatically — something she always did when she talked to strangers or mere acquaintances. Even for those four words, her voice had risen half an octave.

A wavering sheet of heat vapours hung in the air above the grill. Through it, the lawn chairs seemed to fold up on themselves and the sky became a mushroom cloud. Tammy's dad always wound up half cursing, lighting and relighting matches, saying, "God —" and "Holy —" always biting his breath back, cutting himself off before he got to the second syllables. Mr. Riley ("Warren," he insisted) said the trick was the lighter fluid — lots of it — enough to fry a pig in the pen. Samantha crossed her eyes. Tammy saw Warren notice and pretend not to. He blinked and went on without another glance at Sam.

"They say the way to a man's heart is through his stomach," Warren began. "But with your mother —" He pointed the pronged fork at Samantha before pushing it into the steak and flipping it onto the grill "— it was the other way around."

They had always played darts together, Sturgeses and Rileys, but the gang had broken up a year before when Warren's marriage did. Sam's dad was on his way out too, in an unrelated toss of events, coming and going, never staying at the house more than a night in his six-month attempt to move out. By now, he was way off the board: a scud.

Sam had said she was glad, but Tammy knew she cried a lot more now, even though the fighting was done. In a moment, with a word, Samantha's face would constrict and turn colour. Of course, Sam never cried over her parents; it was always something else.

Yet when the hollering had been at its height, Sam had never cried. Tammy had stared anxiously at the hinges of the tri-sectional door between the Sturges's living and dining rooms, as if she could peer through the cracks, see whether Mr. and Mrs. Sturges were twenty paces from each other, like cowboys in a showdown. Were their elbows bent and ready, fingers twitching at their hips, itching to grab, if not their pistols, the nearest blunt objects or breakables for throwing? But all Tammy had seen was the yellow light, obscured by the pattern in the frosted plastic panes.

"Never mind them," Samantha had always said, leaning forward to turn up the volume on the gigantic television set. Even when it sounded like Mr. and Mrs. Sturges were about to fall through the doors, her eyes never wavered from the blue flicker of images. The Saturday Shocker. *Twilight Zone* reruns. A magic stopwatch, dropped; a man trapped forever in a timeless world.

Warren was Mrs. Sturges's white knight. He looked about as heroic as a Playskool figure, cylindrical and shapeless.

The static sound of steel frames on concrete announced their presence before they appeared in the backyard. Dusk had arrived, along with Mrs. Sturges's relatives, friends, town neighbours, all of them dragging nylon lawn chairs across the driveway.

With them was Rodney, the now-fourteen so-called *gorgeous* cousin. Upon introduction, he was dismissive, a curt nod and a cooler-than-thou dodge away. His coolness soon wore off, and he became instantly more interesting. He glided back and forth across the grass, pelting his younger brother with a squirt gun. They yelped and hooted, and every once in a while Rodney would look over at the girls like he was waiting for them to watch. Rodney did an army roll through the grass, staining his white jeans, but bringing up the transparent orange plastic, catching his brother in the back with the stream. A dotted, dark curlicue of wet bloomed from the pale blue cotton.

"They got here pretty late," Samantha whispered, "I don't think we'll get a chance to go swimming."

Tammy felt an unrivalled sense of relief.

Shelly was a hand-me-down friend, the daughter of one of Mrs. Sturges's neighbours, the Peggs. They lived around the corner from Sam in Forest Hill, and had everything: trampoline, swimming pool, CollecoVision. Everything but brains. Everything about Shelly Pegg was stupid. Even her name was stupid. Shelly looked like a lollipop. A very large head perched atop her scrawny body. She had a nose like a mushroom and a heavy chin which was engaged in a constant struggle to pull down her flat, broad cheeks. She always looked as if someone had given her a piece of bad news.

Smelly Shelly's shoelaces were lined with friendship

pins, though in truth, she had made nearly all of them herself. Small red beads, opaque, beside transparent yellows. Miniature copper pins and large silver ones. If she jumped too hard while skipping double dutch, pins would pop open and big orange beads would scatter in all directions. But she couldn't skip double dutch anyway. She could hardly do Blue Bells Cockleshells, Eevy Ivy Over. "Poor Smelly Shelly," Sam would say, and turn the rope even harder, so that it whipped against the side of Shelly's head. Tammy had to admit that even she couldn't jump to that speed.

Being dumb was a fate worse than death. Tammy saw the assignment of fortune as an enormous fist, the duke of life held out, an offering. Sometimes there would be a Bazooka Joe or Swedish Berry in one hand but not the other. Sometimes a person would pick right and get to blow bubbles. Other times, she got nothing. Shelly got the kind of nothing that never afforded any other choices. No one was ever going to offer Shelly a free ride. No one was going to say, "Pick a hand." No fifty-fifty chance. Sam played that joke all the time. Holding out her fists, smiling and waggling her eyebrows. Neither hand ever had anything in it. Tammy fell for it once or twice when she was about nine. Shelly fell for it every time. Trust was a terrible thing. "Poor Smelly Shelly," Sam would say again, shaking her head.

"I've got some more friendship pins," Shelly said now, dragging her lawn chair to where Tammy and Sam were sitting cross-legged in the grass. Sam leaned closer to admire them, pointing to what was obviously the centrepiece of Shelly's shoelace — a gigantic silver pin with alternating beads in hot pink and baby blue.

"You can have it if you want it," Shelly said eagerly.

"Okay," Sam said, grinning. She gingerly removed the pin and clipped it to her own shoelace.

The last time Shelly had given the girls friendship pins, Sam had worn them happily for an afternoon. Then at school on Monday, she'd taken hers off, watched the beads bounce across the tiles, and used the pin to torture the boy who sat in front of her. "Friendship pins are dumb," she'd said, even though everyone in the class was wearing them. Sam and Tammy hadn't — wouldn't. They *were* dumb, if only because Sam had said so. She'd held the pin, hovering it at the back of the boy's neck, about a centimetre from the skin, waiting to see if he would lean back. Technically, her hands were still on her desk, she could claim. He was invading her space. His name was Martin Stevens. Samantha said he was dumb, that all people with last names for first names and first names for last names were dumb. But that if she wanted to, she could go out with him, *just like that.*

At recess, he and the other boys would offer to play Kissing Tag with the girls, then all the boys would concentrate on Sam, chasing her around until they headed her off and got hold of her. She would dig her fingernails into their arms and always get away. She was so cool like that, Tammy thought. The boys would all rub their wrists and forearms, swearing "Bitch!" But back in class the small cresent-moon marks were an honour — akin to the hickies older kids sported around town. "Look what Samantha Sturges did to me," boys would hiss across the aisles, trying to top each other with their pain. "Mine go deeper."

The Pegg children went to a private Christian school, where they didn't play Kissing Tag. Shelly said the boys thought it was gross.

"Maybe the boys just think you're gross," Sam said. Tammy flinched at the meanness that time. No one had ever tried to catch and kiss her either.

This evening, Shelly was wearing a Garfield sweatshirt and carrying a Cabbage Patch Doll — two items Tammy noted immediately as "issues" they would need to discuss with Shelly before the night was over if they were ever going to help her "improve" herself. Shelly was dumb, dumb, dumb. To prove it, Sam and Tammy gave each other knowing glances whenever Rodney raced by.

"What, do you guys like him or something?" Shelly asked.

"Or something," Tammy said.

"We're psychically communicating," Sam said. "If you can't say anything in our language, don't say anything at all. You'll break our concentration."

"Rodney!" Shelly hollered across the yard.

"Shut up!"

"These girls like you!" Rodney didn't turn. A stream of water flew from his gun and zipped across the dead air. Shelly cupped her hands to her mouth. "These girls — Owwww!"

Sam caught Shelly by the ponytail. The bobble on top tilted with the strain, and then snapped. Shelly clutched at loose strands and eight or nine falling bobby pins. Shelly's hair wasn't really long enough to wear in a ponytail anyway. Or so Tammy told her, as consolation.

Mrs. Sturges lay a blanket across the seven or eight feet of sand Warren referred to as the Beach. The sand was cold, almost comforting, as Tammy dug her feet in, let the granules spill between her toes. A small grey spider inched its way toward her. She quickly pulled her toes up onto the blanket. All down the Beach, neighbours from the other houses were sitting together in rows, getting ready to wait. Another hour until the fireworks would start, a long ways away, down the river, but still, they claimed, better from here, with the reflection falling into the water. A couple of girls younger than Tammy and Sam were playing hand-clapping games, with a more complex diagonal crossover than Tammy remembered from the last time she'd played. They began singing faster and louder. Their voices wobbled out over the water and bounced back as if they were singing into tin cans . . .

Miss Molly had a steamboat. Her steamboat had a bell.
When Molly went to heaven, her steamboat went to hell — o
operator, please give me number nine,
and if you disconnect me, I'll kick you in the be —
hind the yellow curtain, there was a piece of glass.
When Molly sat upon it, she hurt her little ass — k
me no more questions, I'll tell you no more lies.
The boys are in the bathroom, pulling down their — flies
are in the garden. The bees are in the park.
The boys and girls are kissing in the d–a–r–k dark.

Somebody shushed them — and people began to settle in more closely, shoulder-to-shoulder, a strange sense of family among strangers as hems of blankets touched. Warren brought out some Mason jars with holes punched in the lids.

Across the yard, Shelly squealed, screwed the jar lid on, and ran over to show her mom and little sisters. Shelly was actually good at something. The first catch. Not a firefly but something rarer: a sleepy white tuft of caterpillar curled in a green leaf.

Inside Sam's and Tammy's jars, the fireflies lit up sporadically, and only from their back ends. Tammy studied her insect as it crawled over the glass on eyelash-thin legs. She thought of the story Chris had told her that afternoon. Even in the dark, her head grew hot, as if from the sun.

After the frog race, Chris's fellow entrants had lined up along the dock. Frogs had been returned to the massive pickle jars that had been used to transport them — seven jars in a row stood in direct sun. The boys stretched out on their bellies, watching. A roll of silver duct tape braceleted David White's wrist, the air holes in the lids Xed over. From a distance, Chris too had watched as the frogs jumped up against the glass more and more slowly until eventually they fell backward and died. Laughing, the boys pushed the jars one by one into the water. When they got up, they loped away silently — shoulders hunched, like dogs who've been caught pissing on the floor, tails between their legs. Except, Chris had said, no one had caught them. He didn't even think they knew he'd seen. Where he'd stood on the bridge, Chris had watched the jars float by beneath him. Inside them — bloated and brown — rubbery carcasses he wished he could forget.

Tammy tapped the glass with her finger. Its hollow *tink*. The firefly fell backward, then buzzed up again. *Bees: kaleidoscopic vision*, she remembered. The words appeared in her brain as if on flashcards. *Bees see simultaneously from several different angles . . . Almost,* she told herself, *like seeing everything at once*. Tammy wondered if the same held true for fireflies. She watched its rear end glint once more. Then she unscrewed the lid and let the bug flit away, a dark speck on the dark, until it had reached a safe distance again.

When the first fireworks hit the sky, Samantha's hair slipped from Tammy's hand in a half-finished French braid. With the sudden flash of aqua light, Sam reared forward. Coloured dots *Plinko*-ed down the night. Grey-white streaked the sky like a gone-to-seed dandelion.

"Awright!" Samantha said when the bang travelled the distance and broke.

Far back, Shelly Pegg sat on a lawn chair, little sister in her lap, another in her mother's. Shelly leaned against Mrs. Pegg's shoulder in a way that made Tammy suddenly jealous. When the firework burst, the one lumpy figure they made in the night clapped with the enthusiasm of a crowd.

Rodney put two fingers in his mouth and released a long shriek of a whistle.

Bits of fire and ash broke apart from their compact shells, where gunpowder and chemicals — dioxides, Chris had told Tammy — pressed tight, waiting to distribute this formation of colour. As flecks of orange rained down, lighting upturned faces, Tammy glanced over to where Rodney was sitting. She tried to imagine what he looked like underneath his clothes, to see him the way Sam did. He gave no indication of being watched, and Tammy looked away. In front of her, Samantha was absently unweaving her half-braided head. Behind her, Tammy could feel Mrs. Sturges and Mr. Riley pressing closer together. She knew they were holding hands.

Between the inevitable smashing and trickling down, there was a sense of hovering, gapping. Suddenly, Tammy's throat felt stretched and raw. It was from standing too close to the barbecue earlier, breathing in the lighter-fluid fumes and the air streaked by charcoal. When she ran her hand across her eyes, she was sure it was because the fireworks had a double impact, stretched out as they were, reflected in the water. It was because they were so bright.

She wondered what her parents were doing right now, whether they had joined the crowd downtown, or were watching on the local cable channel, or were just creeping around in the dark of the house — which was how Tammy always imagined the house after she had left it. *Where was Chris?* she wondered.

PLAYER 1

Chris shot the mushrooms. He killed the spider for 600 points before it could brush against him. He loved the crueller, less-apparent elements of such games, the fact that so often, touch could kill. Zapping the centipede on the screen before him, Chris revelled in its breaking — down and down into smaller and smaller bits, each of them alive, inching its way downward.

"Could you hit a few more mushrooms?" J.P. oozed sarcasm, completely bored by Chris's burgeoning score. He leaned back against another machine, flexed the brim of his ball cap. Circus Berzerk was a far cry from Joyland.

The plaza offered the comforts of air conditioning, but little else.

"Technically . . . they're toadstools." Chris jerked his player away from a falling flea. At a certain point, shooting became a natural extension of breathing, as though Chris wasn't playing the machine but simply existing in it. The boards passed from green and red to pink and blue to orange and yellow, his man moving to and fro in a rainstorm of colour.

"Jesus." J.P. snorted. "I thought you wanted to go to Doyle's. Would you just get yourself killed already?"

And so it ended; there was little choice for someone like Chris. High scores were lost to the whims of others. The game could go on indefinitely — infinitely, if he let it.

Below Chris, corroded green metal opened to flashes of grey: moving, shape-shifting water. The old railroad bridge was still in use, though Chris could not fathom how. Even a few years ago there had been more gaps than bridge. He stepped carefully. J.P. was doing a play-by-play sportscast of the entire crash derby though if Chris had had any interest he would have gone himself that morning to watch. He pussyfooted one running shoe in front of the other, edging alongside a crater. With shorter legs than J.P.'s, the holes seemed to open wider beneath Chris every time he glanced down. He squashed the fear with a laugh — the briefest, most private tactic available for convincing himself he could get used to this feeling, as easily as any other annoyance. Camp pranks had once induced the same queasiness: flashlights held to illuminate the face from below, casting up a ghoulish glow, lengthening the shadows of the eyes and emphasizing the sulphurous yellow tone of human skin.

Through the hole, the water thrashed. It ran fast for such a small river, as if it could compensate for its narrowness with its force. In less than a minute they would be on the other side. Chris could see the row of houses already. Shingles stood out from the trees on the riverbank like blackhead zits. One among them, he guessed, would be Doyle's.

The boys approached from the back, unable to tell whose house was whose. The yards pressed together without fences, only red cedars or unkempt raspberry bushes lining the property. In all likelihood, kids bikes lay half in one yard and half in their neighbours'. Toys — plastic shovels and naked Barbies — were thrown here and there, half-sunk in mud. A car's viscera lay out on a picnic table. The loving owner had wandered off and left it for the afternoon, mid-surgery. Willow whips from the trees tangled Chris's feet as he and J.P. climbed the bank, trekking away from the railroad tracks. They headed around front, where the numbers would help them determine which house held the thing they sought.

It was no different than its neighbours: a two-storey farmhouse holding its ground in the middle of town. The entire facade was nailed over with Insulbrick. The step up to the porch was an unsteady mason block, the porch barely wide enough to accommodate Chris and J.P. A much larger verandah hugged the entire side of the house. Chris wondered if they should try around there, but J.P. had already rapped on the metal frame of the screen door.

Chris turned to him. "Are you sure . . . ?"

The door nearly broadsided Chris as it swung open.

He fell backward off the porch and landed on his ass in the grass.

The man in the open doorway slouched, shirtless. He looked to be about twenty-five. Or forty-five. Chris couldn't tell. Looking down at Chris in the grass, the guy gave a high-pitched titter — a sound young enough to have come from a fourteen-year-old, though the face it snaked out of had hard, thin lips and harder thinner eyes above them. One hand grasped at the low waist of his jeans, as if he had just pulled them on before deciding to open the door. A trail of black stitches ran down the centre of his stomach toward his groin. The pink head twisted away as the guy jerked his fly up.

Averting his eyes, Chris scrambled to his feet.

"What do you want, man?" His gaze drifted from Chris to J.P. without seeming to focus on either one of them. The guy leaned against the door, and J.P. jumped backward off the porch as the screen swung open farther under the weight.

J.P. shot Chris a quick glance. "Well, we heard . . ."

The guy in the doorway — obviously Doyle — began to laugh.

"Aw shit," he said, pulling his hand through shoulder-length liver-brown hair. He buzzed his lips in an abrupt, juicy fart. "You crack me up, kid. What are you, like, twelve? Whad'you and your *girl*-friend come for?" Doyle shot out suggestions. The names dribbled down at Chris — tiny taboo nuggets of vocabulary.

"Awwwww, come on," Doyle groaned, "don't look at me like that. You're too young to be a narc."

J.P. answered, his voice dropping an octave, his chest instantly convex, bursting with authority. "Just booze, man."

Doyle offered them weed instead.

Chris shook his head. The offer might have been more tempting had it come from someone capable of holding himself upright.

"Fuck. Ing. Hell," Doyle said, each syllable a sentence, his brown head doing a slow, annoyed dance. He leaned against the door, which forced it wide. "Gonna have to wait while I go get it. C'mon in."

J.P. went first and Chris followed, ducking past Doyle. He reeked of smoke.

"I was just in the middle of something," Doyle muttered holding up a finger. He lurched past them into the living room. J.P. and Chris stood politely in the hall, as if they were visiting a distant relative. Faded Mom-style yellow wallpaper with flowers plastered the musty hall. Overhead, a stained glass lampshade cast bright-coloured triangles into a spiderwebbed corner. Through the doorway, at the far end of the living room, Doyle's back was to them. A white flannel sheet with wide pink stripes on one end flapped as he unfolded it. Chris looked carefully at his feet as Doyle twisted around.

Suddenly Doyle seemed in less of a hurry. He began to offer advice on every kind of alcohol and how it would "make your frickin' head spin . . . like a twelve-year-old girl chugging wine at a wedding." Interwoven with his personal escapades, his expertise was wasted; the stories never reached conclusion, twice sidetracked by who had been present before he could tell the boys what had been consumed or what effects it had. After about forty minutes, he stood up as if he had just remembered why the boys had come.

"How'd you hear about me anyway?" he asked, snagging

his keys from the table. Chris and J.P. exchanged worried glances, as though Doyle might back out if they gave the wrong answer.

"My brother, Marc Breton."

At seventeen, Marc Breton was all shaved head, hulking shoulders, the rest of him hambone and hair, skin corrugated with zits. He was the kind of guy whose retort to any put-down was still, "I know you are, but what am I?" not out of some kind of mental defect, but out of lack of necessity to find a new comeback, pipes more honed than brain. The dumbfounding irony, Chris had discovered, was that Marc was an honour student, squeaking in at 80%. On the floor of his bedroom his yearbook lay open to the honour roll page — constantly, as if Marc were also trying to convince himself — and Chris had seen it when he and J.P. snuck in there to play the Atari.

"Aw shit." Doyle spread one hand on the glass top-portion of the screen door. "He's practically old enough to buy for you. I don't see why he couldn't do it." He shook his head and went outside, leaving a sweaty hand-print on the door where he'd been. He hadn't bothered to put on a shirt.

On the other side of the window he swung up into his pickup and backed it half-down the pebble driveway and half-across the yard.

"You'd think he wouldn't drive when he's so stoned," J.P. laughed.

Chris poked him in the ribs and nodded to the couch at the far end of the room, where the white flannel sheet covered a human shape. One that hadn't moved, he'd noted, since Doyle had covered it an hour ago.

LEVEL 5

Combat

PLAYER 1

J.P. pulled the sheet all the way off her, exposing the oversize Mickey Mouse T-shirt she wore. A pair of pink underpants were visible through the well-loved white cotton shirt. A few small bruises dotted her legs and ankles. Strands of drool hung between her teeth and the pillow, colourless as fishing wire. She didn't move.

Chris and J.P. could only guess that the girl was sixteen or seventeen. Her skin was like a boiled egg. She was smeary-eyed, black eyeliner Halloweening beneath her closed lids. She had baby-fat cheeks. Under Mickey's smiling face her breasts seemed larger than those of the girls they knew. These were their only clues. They didn't know her. All of this they determined quickly and without speaking. Her body was bent half-sideways and half face-down. They couldn't tell if she had collapsed there or been thrown.

"Touch her," J.P. said, his chest rising and falling quickly under his T-shirt.

"You do it."

J.P. didn't move.

"*You* do it," Chris said again.

J.P. stared back at him.

Tentatively, Chris reached out. The distance between hand and girl became immense as the two boys watched its journey. Chris made contact, brushing the bangs back from her forehead.

"She's warm."

J.P. let out a low whistle.

Chris stared at the petal-shaped bruises on her thighs. She was dark-haired. Short black shoots flecked her skin, pricking out like thorns — especially the top inside of her thighs, along the neat pink seam of her cotton underwear — as if she'd shaved them, but not today.

"You think they were doing it?" Chris whispered, barely daring to force the words out.

J.P. pulled a face.

"Should we cover her back up?"

Humidity poured the night out, cherry-cough-syrup thick. The image of the girl's body burned in Chris's throat like whisky. The boys hung their feet over the edge of the railway bridge, watched their sneakers kick back and forth over the water as it got darker. Even thinking of her made Chris dizzy. He could still feel the warmth of her skin on his fingertips.

Rueben and Dean Easter showed up from selling beadwork chokers and armbands at the festival downtown. Rueben had just buzzed off all his hair, perhaps to differentiate himself from his twin, and J.P. and Chris passed their fingers over it, rattling their lips until the joke grew tired. In exchange for feathered roach clips and beaded soft leather, J.P. and Chris shared their stash — a glorious forty-ouncer, because Doyle hadn't been coherent enough to remember what they'd paid him.

"Make sure they don't ask for the stuff back later," J.P. said under his breath.

Technically, the Easters weren't Native — "Indian." Their mother had lost her status when she left the reserve five miles to the west, married her second husband — a Whitey — and settled in town. But it made no difference. In South Wakefield, you had only two options. You were white or you were Indian. And if you looked it, you were it, no matter where else you'd been. Everything shuttled back and forth between town and reserve: love, hate, babies, school buses, racial slurs, cheap cigarettes, knife fights — a border relationship equal to any existing between two trading countries. For about thirty seconds, Chris contemplated pushing J.P. off the bridge. Although Rueben was twice J.P.'s weight, he pretended he hadn't heard over the first flock of fireworks. Dean was sitting farther away — Chris silently thanked God, because Dean was even bigger and never would have swallowed something like that.

Back and forth they passed the hooch, bright liquid inside a dark bottle. "To Joyland." Coca-Cola Vicks Vapor Rub. They managed about six slugs each before Chris became completely jumbled, with each gulp feeling a little more possibility that the fireworks would spray down and knock him in the forehead, leave a glowing mark. When he closed his eyes, all he could see were the bruises on the thighs of the girl on Doyle's couch. But neither J.P. nor Chris said a word about her.

"What're ya gonna do now, Lane?"

The question came out of nowhere. Chris passed the whisky bottle on to Rueben, almost dropping it into his lap. J.P. and Dean snickered.

"What?" Chris tipped his head back. The night had gotten as smoky as he was drunk, the fireworks' final shootout already lapsing into a memory.

"With your summer."

Chris shrugged. "What're you gonna do?"

Dean threw his arms back-forward in a strangely graceful slo-mo, casting an imaginary line across the thin river. What was Joyland to him?

"Catchin' three-eyed fish," Rueben qualified, practically singing. "You should see 'em! Holy . . . Covered in tumours! You dunno what they dump in that river up there."

"Yeah, go on."

"Kill us all," Dean nodded, his face a disgusted fraternal twin to Rueben's animation. "Poison their own fucken workforce."

"Yeah?"

"Yeah."

"I'll prob'ly get a job," J.P. said, to Chris's surprise.

When Chris asked him about it again at the end of the night, on the corner where they parted ways, J.P. shrugged before he stumbled off.

Three days later J.P. was doing the six-to-ten shift at Twiss's Gas 'n Go, the self-serve directly across from the dormant Joyland building. Legally, he wasn't old enough to work alone, but after his first two shifts, he did anyway. Through the chrome frame of the cubicle, his skinny limbs floated out of a ghost-white T-shirt, an oversize Hanes of his dad's. The red regulation windbreaker hung on the hook behind him, the white thread of logoed letters folded up on themselves.

Chris parked his bike against the booth, out of view of the street. In the lit Plexiglas cube, the two of them sat, passing a pocket game back and forth. Epoch Man. J.P. took a pack of smokes off the shelf, unwrapped the cellophane. *Players' Light. Montreal.* He used a lighter from the little plastic sales bin, and then put it back. The open pack flipped in Chris's direction, but his thumbs were busy. J.P. picked up a different Bic and lighter-flicked in quick succession, watching the blue-gold flame's instant growth. It rose and vanished, rose and vanished, leaving behind the smell of a gun. A couple of cars pulled up and J.P. took the money. They didn't need change. They didn't want receipts. Chris watched bugs gather beneath the station lights like grey haphazard stars. Across the road, the eave had come further loose, and Joyland seemed to have sunk into itself even more.

"If Mr. Twiss thinks you were in the booth, I'll get in trouble," J.P. said, holding the smoke in for longer than a half second this time. He blew it out the cash window. "You should get out of here before we close. Twiss comes back for the float."

J.P. may have been the first to have a job, but Pinky Goodlowe was the first to have a girlfriend. Chris found them sitting on a parking block together outside the variety store where she worked, Pinky's legs spread wide around the bulge in his Adidas. She leaned her crimped head against his shoulder, one of her flat eraser thumbs casually trailing the area inside and above his knee. The phallic swirl of Nike bounced up and down on each of Pinky's long white basketball shoes. He'd never committed fully to either brand, had apparently been saving all commitment for her, this large and sudden girl named Donna Jean Tripp.

From a distance, Chris could see her licking his neck, a raw hamburger tongue slipping out of her mouth. Chris's insides did a slow rotation between revulsion and fascination. As he drew closer, he brought his bike to a slow cruise and waited for Pinky to put a halt to her molestation. A signature of acne scrawled across her sunburnt face. She was one of those girls with skin the same colour as her lips. She looked like she could be the older sister Pinky didn't have. As Chris approached them and stopped, he saw there were two distinct blue cables on the underside of her tongue. He would think of them long after. Pinky put his arm around her and pulled her closer to him, her head into the crook of his neck, until she became little more than a red mark upon him and Chris couldn't see her face anymore.

When the gang asked Pinky later what he was doing with her, This Donna, Pinky said she had let him masturbate her with a pencil. He had gone in to buy a Coke, and they had just been talking, hanging out. She had asked him for his number. She handed him a pencil. He told her she had to put it down her shorts, if she wanted his number so badly. He said he wouldn't write with it unless it smelled like her.

"I dunno," Pinky sputtered, "I was so *totally* kidding, and then she like, *did it*, man. She did."

Chris bit his lip. "That's vile." He snickered anyway. He closed his eyes and thought of Laurel Richards, but the pencil only fit behind her ear, or the end of it tapped against her teeth, pausing between her lips.

"Was it wet?" David asked, authority and skeptic simultaneously.

"Dripping."

"Love built to last," Kenny had scoffed.

But it did last. The next day Pinky was still hanging out with This Donna. The whole gang of them, including the girl, stood around outside of the booth at Twiss's until J.P. yelled at them to get the hell away before they got him fired.

They distanced themselves by forty feet at most, taking up residence on the curb. With a doggish grin, David pulled a pencil out of his jean-jacket pocket and slipped it under Donna just before she sat down. She didn't notice it. Her pink thighs pulped beyond garbardine seams.

"Hey," David said, "you're sitting on my pencil." Giggles. She lifted up one of her sweatpocked legs, ruby pinpricks where she'd shaved. The yellow wood rolled away in two pieces. David snorted into his palm. Even Chris tried not to laugh, his head ducking against his ribbed shirt collar.

This Donna's face didn't blink.

"What are you on?" she said to David, seriously, nostrils flaring. Pinky flamed silently, thick ears scarlet. This Donna stood up.

"Your friends are really — really — *juvenile.*" She stalked off. Synchronized to her pace, Kenny's lips exploded with the puffed air of elephant footsteps. They looked at Pinky, laughing, but instead of joining in, he got up and followed her.

"I better catch up with my old lady," he mumbled before he went. It didn't matter that his old lady was only sixteen. Chris could imagine what she would look like in three or four years. Already a wall of acne separated her from them. At any rate, the words *old lady* sounded natural when they fell from Pinky's tongue, like he had a history with a girl he'd just met, like the future was already fixed.

"You think she did the pencil trick?" Kenny asked when they were long gone.

Chris glanced over his shoulder at J.P. in the booth, arms propellered over the inside glass with a spitty Windex bottle. When he told him about it later, J.P. just shrugged.

A. J. Mitchum Fabricating, the door said in black-and-gold Lettraset. The office smelled of tuna fish and solvent. A woman got up from a desk behind the wood-panel reception counter and peered at Chris with exasperation. Huge gold barrettes stapled into a bush of red hair. On the desk behind her, a half-finished sandwich waited wordlessly on waxed paper.

"I'm interested in summer employment," Chris said.

"I don't know nothin' 'bout what they want," the woman with the squirrel eyes and squirrel hair told him. "Y'over sixteen?" He nodded. She gave him a knowing look. "We already took a buncha students, so I don't know if we're hiring any more. We got an application I can dig out for you," she said. She glanced back at her desk, but there was nothing on it except for the sandwich. "You're better off just go round back and ask. Check the tables. Ask for Mr. Abell."

Across the parking lot, Chris could make out the picnic tables embedded in a patch of green grass spotted with white petals. One short bulky man sat there, a paper painter's cap atop his round head, a can of pop in his hand. When Chris got closer, he saw that the man was actually a woman, and the confetti on the ground, cigarettes. Chris kept walking.

A couple of guys in ball caps were smoking at the top of a concrete ramp outside a huge rollback door. A gust of heat heaved out into the summer afternoon. It was dark inside, and Chris could see dirty coveralls moving around. A guy inside the dark square gazed over, a pair of dark eyes underneath glasses underneath safety goggles. Then something sparked — followed by a whole shower of sparks — and his face burst bright for a second as he quickly looked back at his hands. Chris physically jumped as metal on metal clanged.

The two guys outside the door eyed him.

"Are you Mr. Abell?" Chris asked the less dirty of the two. The guy held his cigarette like a joint. As soon as Chris asked, he realized the stupidity of the question.

The guy shrugged, shook his head, took another puff

from the cigarette cradled between thumb and forefinger. He dropped it at his feet but left it burning. The other guy just smirked.

Chris walked away from the noise in the hole. He headed back past the picnic-table woman. A scrapyard yawned at the other end of the lot. It had been studiously scoped out on previous excursions with J.P. Climbing over railroad ties, scrap wood and metal, they'd entered illegally from the back. They'd planned to lug home materials, build something. Once they'd been yelled at to get off the property. The other time, they'd abandoned a couple of half-rotten wooden flats in a field when they grew tired of dragging them. This time, Chris could say he was looking for Mr. Abell.

Beyond the fence, wood and metal pronged out of the half-dirt half-asphalt yard: misshapen molds, tubs, gears, gigantic packing crates, boards, poles, and wires. A big guy was dragging flats back and forth, stacking and restacking them. Chris froze, hovered three inches from the corner of the building. The wooden flats made a fat *smack smack* when thrown atop one another. The guy bent to grab one of the skids. He hefted it above his head, then slung it on top of the others. The pile wavered, and the guy reached out and steadied it with one hand before it could topple. In profile, Chris could see it was J.P.'s older brother, Marc.

Slouching against the building, Chris tried to decide if he should go over. He watched Marc reach up, pull down the flat he'd just stacked. He lugged it across the yard and lay it where it had been — against the building with a bunch of others. Chris ducked back. Marc went and pulled another flat, carried it, leaned it. Pulled, carried, leaned. Pulled, carried, leaned. When he'd unstacked the entire group, Marc began again. Unleaned, carried, heaved into a stack. Unleaned, carried, heaved into a stack. *Smack, smack. Smack, smack. Smack, smack.*

Chris had known the tedium of folded newsprint, its smudges and its weight, especially in gruesome rain when bike tires vomitted against his back, wetting him twice-over. He had known the two-dollars-an-hour-to-not-kill-his-sister also known as babysitting. But with these exceptions, Chris had never had a job before, had never drawn a regular paycheque or clocked in. Within one cycle of unstacking and restacking, he could tell what Marc was doing. He only had a certain amount of work to do in a given day and he'd obviously run out. Either he was incredibly bored, or he kept moving to protect his livelihood. It didn't matter that he wasn't accomplishing anything. He only had to look as though he were useful.

A couple of the flats in the pile were rotten, and Marc pushed on the boards, testing them as if it were of great importance that the flats in the scrapyard be of absolutely the best quality. He retreated a few steps, then flung himself forward, pseudo-karate-kick style. The board snapped. Marc grabbed the broken skid and launched it over his head into the big blue dumpster. When he returned from the dumpster, two mismatched pieces of pipe smacked together intermittedly. He was singing. His voice fumbled across the cement as he picked his way between stacks and dumpsters. Sunlight glinted off the pipe as Marc began to beat it against the slats of one of the skids. Not hard enough to break it, just hard enough to make a dull *thwack thwack, thwack-thwack-thwack*. He stopped and looked around.

Chris plastered himself against the building. He glanced over his shoulder, but the rest of the lot was vacant. The dark hole at the end of the building had swallowed the man-woman and the smokers.

Proximity brought with it a scrambling for memory; panic at being caught, and an immediate rationalizing of fear, why Chris wasn't just singing the song of the chicken shit even though the brick at his back scratched with breaths going all the way through him. Illegally in Marc's room, more familiar with his ripe smell than his erupting face, Chris and J.P. had snuck a thousand times to sit cross-legged on the bed, corded to Combat and Air Sea Battle. They kept the volume low to listen for sounds from downstairs. If they got caught there using Marc's things, going through Marc's stuff, J.P. said they could say goodbye to their nuts, that his brother was fully capable of extracting a pound of flesh without spilling a drop of blood. Chris doubted somehow that Marc was sharp enough in spite of the ten-point type in the open yearbook. Grade Eleven honour roll: a joke. Thumbing through the black-and-white panorama of student faces, Chris had also noticed that one or two girls' heads had been removed in perfect circles with an X-ACTO blade, and when he had asked J.P. about it, he'd waved his hand like it was nothing.

"Oh yeah, he likes to do that. Pastes them in his porn mags to make them more real." Why it seemed juvenile or creepy, Chris couldn't say. It smacked of JCPenney-underwear-model masturbation, but who was he to judge? At least Marc was able to buy them.

Metal on concrete filled the air. Chris peeked around the corner. Two steel tubs stood together silently. Marc currently hunted in a corner of the scrapyard, his back to Chris. He returned, a plastic pail under one arm. Placing it upside down next to the tubs, he began to beat the pipes across them. The pipes twirled, Sheila E. style. Marc resumed his slow thwacking. He bobbed forward and back, nodding his head, grooving with his eyes closed. "Owner of a Lonely Heart" cracked across the concrete. Marc's arms continued to swing their rhythmic masochism. Why would he expend all his energy in a pretense of work, then be so completely self-absorbed three minutes later? He stuck his lips out, degenerated into some kind of drum solo of his own invention.

"Loser!" Chris hollered. He took off before Marc could figure out who had yelled it.

Chris had to double back through the A. J. Mitchum Fabricating office to get out of the back lot. The squirrel woman gave him an inquisitive look as he passed through, but didn't get up from her desk. At least the sandwich was gone. Chris said nothing, just gave her a thumbs-up sign, and walked out fast, the glass door falling between them. He would never work here.

PLAYER 2

If-I-Die-Before-I-Wake had awoken. She practically jumped from her bed, eager for the day. Tammy prided herself on quick response time. Even before she had washed her face, she was aware of her actions.

The ease with which she awoke pleased Mr. Lane. Even in summer, he insisted they all rise at a regular hour. He left for the factory at seven, and appeared consistently in her doorway ten minutes before that. She never moaned or pulled the covers up over her head the way Chris did. After all, she was a spy in training.

A fleet of three planes now drifted across the purple sky, exiting at the top of the screen and reentering from the bottom, almost as if the world were so small, Tammy had flown all the way around it. Chris caught her with a barrage of bullets that streamed from the opposite side. Flying too close to the edge of the screen, Tammy was picked off — burned — her fleet sent reeling. She'd thought she had been chasing Chris, but now it seemed he was chasing her. That was how quickly things turned.

He was up by fifteen games. They'd set out that morning to play all of the twenty-seven versions on the Combat cartridge, the first Atari game they had ever owned, a giveaway that came with the console. Beginning as chubby tanks, they'd chugged through the green field, hide-and-seek behind obstacles and blocks. They shot each other — as many times as possible within the allotted time. Tammy's favourite was number six — invisibility — the green playing field empty, yet them still on it, as if in some alternate universe, giving away location only as they shot or got shot. Their tanks would suddenly appear, drilled from one area to another, sometimes bouncing clear through the borders of the screen with the impact.

"'Member when we got this game," Tammy said, pressing her joystick hard to the side, "and I could barely make the tanks change direction?"

"I *remember,*" Chris enunciated and shot her again.

The scores at the top of the screen began to blink, time almost up.

The second they finished the set, Chris threw down the

controller and flipped the on-off switch, dissolving the television into static. He went to the kitchen to call J.P. who, it turned out, had just been fired from the gas station for smoking too close to the pumps. Chris gave the back door a jubilant slam, grabbed his bike, and sailed down the Lane driveway. Tammy carefully wrapped up the cords and stashed the controllers under the TV stand. Even after she watched the screen shudder into darkness, she could hear a faint hum.

When she left the room, it seemed to follow her. When she closed her bedroom door, the hum remained, hovering, invisible. The whole house was flickering, buzzing with it. Tammy put her cheek against the wood panel as she switched the overhead light on-off, on-off, on-off. She couldn't feel the electricity, she decided. That was impossible.

There was nothing specific she could put her finger on as having changed. The days started and ended the same. Chris snapped like an elastic band thumb-shot in any direction he chose, but even his randomness was expected. The only thing that was different was the direction of Mrs. Lane's lawn chair as she sat in the fenced backyard, watching the mosquitoes emerge from the hedges. So where did the buzzing come from?

Out in the yard, Mrs. Lane was listening to the plastic chatter of talk radio. Tammy wondered if it might swat down the invisible thing she sensed hovered here inside the house. This microscopic, misanthropic organism. The itching silence that swivelled and circled, waiting for blood.

In spite of the heat in the room, Tammy pulled the curtains to practise her moves. It had not yet occurred to her that Tina Turner's "Private Dancer" could be a song about anything except dancing alone in one's room. Tammy lifted the needle, switched albums. The Police. They were the cutest, with their mirrored shades and spiky hair. Sting's square jaw was like an anvil weighing down her heart.

In the chunk of light that fell through the curtains, she watched dust motes flickering between the windowsill and the Rice-A-Roni-coloured carpet. Flecks of light floated, stirred like gnats when she reached out and swatted her hand through them. Out the window, her mother sat stiffly in the lawn chair. White squares of shirt and shorts bubbled between the nylon chair's green lattice. What did her mother think about, sitting there staring at the bushes, listening to the Scotts next door? If Tammy was thinking about her mom, did that mean her mom was thinking about her?

They were flesh and blood. It only made sense they should be psychically connected. Tammy decided to send her mother an ESP signal. If she got the signal, she would turn and look at Tammy's window. Tammy moved closer. She stood to one side of the gap. The nylon curtains that hung over the sheers were scratchy and ropy with smoke. From behind, her mother seemed small, almost as small as Tammy, one knee pulled up, shoulders hunched with nervous tension, even though the very act of sitting and doing nothing should have cancelled out such a thing. Tammy couldn't know that in another two summers she would grow from four-foot-eleven to five-foot-four — make up the five inches that separated them. She concentrated on the back of her mother's head, zoomed in, took aim with her eyes.

Mrs. Lane stared straight ahead at the garden.

Tammy never meant to spy on anyone. She hated to think of someone spying on her. Yet she couldn't seem to stop herself from doing it. Was it so terrible? *If you were a blind person,* Tammy reasoned, *everyone would see you, but you wouldn't see them.*

LEVEL 6

Dig Dug

PLAYER 2

Tammy put her hands together, tucked her chin, bent her knees, took a breath, and jumped.

With a rush, the surface was broken. Bubbles spurted past her ears. She opened her eyes. Yellow gaseous light wavered above her, drifted languidly down like food-colour droplets dispersing in a vase of water. Tammy saw herself at the bottom of the vase. The rest of the world, a beautiful flower up there, out of sight, ready to suck her up.

She propelled herself along the fat blue lines that striped the bottom of the pool, marking the deep from the shallow. On the incline, she let a small amount of air escape from her mouth, bit by bit, slowly, slowly as she continued through the shallow end. When she reached the far side of the pool her lungs would be empty, but not before. If she could make this underwater lap consistently all week, only lifesaving and mouth-to-mouth would stand in the way of her receiving her Blue badge.

She heard the barrage of bubbles as another swimmer followed her into the pool. She watched the concrete beneath her. Not looking ahead made the journey seem shorter. If she didn't know how much farther, she simply rationed her breath and kept going until her fingers bashed wondrously into the wall.

When Tammy made contact she sprang up, mouth yawning open for that first flood of air, head huge with the weight of water. Sound surged. On-deck clapping. Screaming. Feet slapping on tile. Of the seven different levels of instruction, each was intent on its own group's exercises. The echo of human voices bounced up, clung to the long fluorescent lights and metal beams. Indiscriminate noise. Noise without words to it. Tammy breathed in. Oxygen swelled her lungs; she had made it.

The swimming lessons were Mrs. Sturges's idea. Now that they were spending more time at Warren's, Sam needed to become a more advanced swimmer. Mrs. Sturges didn't feel comfortable leaving her alone on the Beach. According to Sam, swimming lessons were *dumb dumb dumb,* but if she had to do something dumb, there had better be a best friend to suffer through it with.

Except Sam would be leaving before the lessons were

over. The object was not to obtain her Blue badge, but to become a stronger swimmer. The course was four weeks. By the end of the third, Sam and her mom would be moving out to Mr. Riley's, leaving Tammy to find another partner from the pool for the lifesaving portion. When, exactly, this decision had been made, Tammy didn't know. She assumed Mrs. Sturges had known for some time, but that Sam hadn't. Then again, Tammy couldn't guess how long Sam might have waited to tell her.

They had been riding in the car with Sam's older sister, Joyce, who had offered to take them to get French fries at the Drive-Thru.

"Want to see my apartment?" Joyce had asked. "I move in next week."

"You're getting your own apartment? How will you pay the rent?" *Three's Company* sprang to mind. Tammy lived under the mistaken impression apartments were only for people in cities. Their town was short and fat with one-level houses, the two-storey high school a bizarre phenomenon on the flat line of horizon. Tammy and Sam had made plans to move to the city together and get an apartment one day. Tammy wanted to move to Chicago, because it was close to Milwaukee, but bigger. She felt they would be most like Laverne and Shirley there. Sam wanted to move to Los Angeles. She liked the name. Movie stars lived there and she thought they should date actors so that they could "get discovered."

On the south side of South Wakefield, Joyce pointed out a plain white house with baby blue shutters. Smurfette-sized, the structure barely surpassed the Lanes' garage. The grass was taller than the tiny porch. Parked on either side of its rusted railing were two black cauldrons bubbling with dry red geraniums. Beside the driveway, a lawn jockey held an empty lantern aloft. There was bird crap on his shoulder, a white splatter against his bright red jacket. A clown-lipped smile permanently creased his faded black face. Tammy bet he hated having to stand out in front of that place all day. It looked nothing like An Apartment.

"So there's no buzzer?" Tammy asked.

Joyce laughed. "There's a stairway around back. Up to the attic. That's my part of the house."

Now that she'd pointed it out, Tammy could see one round window up next to the roof, right in the middle like a small Cyclops eye. With little blue shutters on either side.

"You don't have the whole thing?"

"No, I *don't have the whole thing.*" Joyce's head did a nasty little dance on her shoulders. "Mrs. Fields lives downstairs. She's, like, sixty-five or something, so I can't have parties. But she's charging next to nothing." Joyce worked at Jorge's Pizza, but she still had another year of high school.

"Is your Mom going to give you money to take care of Sam?"

Joyce hooted. She put the car in Drive. "Are you kidding? If she left Sam with me, by the end of the summer she'd be smoking and going out with college guys. I can *not* even be trusted with myself."

When Tammy looked over at Sam, she gazed out the window, peering at the houses as if it was L.A. and she might spot the home of someone famous, like Matt Dillon. The unrolled window tossed Sam's hair around her face so Tammy couldn't see her expression.

"When are you moving?"

"A couple weeks," Sam answered, without looking.

Joyce turned the radio up and began to sing along to the Cars' "Good Times Roll."

On the bridge between the south and north sides, Tammy spotted a green Volkswagen Beetle coming toward them.

"Punch Buggy!" She leaned into the front seat and landed one on Sam's shoulder.

"Ow!" Sam yelled, whipping her head around. Freckles stood out like little flecks of blood on her vitreous face. "It's not my fault," she hissed, and Tammy could see immediately she'd been crying silently. "Mom says I can come back in the fall for school if I don't mind bussing in." Sam reached around herself to rub the bruise that Tammy knew would come.

Tammy nodded and nodded, as if it would make Sam's statement come true.

Above the pool, the sounds lingered, amplified between the fixtures. Tammy lifted herself out backward, plopped her wet butt on the concrete edge.

She watched as Sam passed into the shallow end and came up about fifteen feet short. Her red ponytail spread out like a thick round hood on her shoulders. She snapped her goggles up into her hair. Sam liked butterfly stroke best because, she said, you didn't have to put your face in the water. She coughed. Water lapped around her pelvis. Her hips were like handles beneath the gradient green to mint-green spandex. In her bathing suit, Sam was all angles, white elbows and collarbone. Under the water, her thighs were twice as white, even though Tammy knew they were covered in sandy freckles. Sam wrapped one hand around her ribs. The other trailed behind in the water like a kite-tail as she waded toward the ledge where Tammy sat waiting. Even coughing, Samantha was graceful. Tammy didn't know if it was a trick of the bleach, but an hour into the lesson, the lights overhead always seemed to take on small white and blue halos. She tipped her head back and stared up at them as Sam climbed onto the deck. The combination of frailty and boldness made Tammy squishy with affection, as though she had swallowed too much water.

Sam stretched out full-length on the tiles behind Tammy, put her head down on crossed arms until her breathing regulated. On the deck in front of her, her goggles lay like the unseeing white outlines of a second set of eyes. Two more of their group were underwater swimming the lap now. They looked like blobs of gelatin. *If it were ever quiet here,* Tammy thought, rubbing a hand across her eyes, *I would hear the lights humming.*

Three more days of laps, then they would begin mouth-to-mouth. Tammy could only rub her eyes and hope Samantha wouldn't leave her to do it with someone else.

In the dressing room, Tammy held the towel around her, shifted it down to her hips once she had her T-shirt on.

"Hurry up!" Samantha hissed. "My mom's waiting outside."

Tammy tucked one end in at the waist, sat down on the bench. Underpants were difficult. They always twisted halfway up her leg, wet skin and cotton not a winning combination.

Sam zipped up her gym bag, went and took a quick look out the change room door.

Tammy stood, pulled underwear past her knees before she felt the towel loosen and slip. She made a mad grab at it.

"Don't be such a prude." Sam snatched it away completely, exposing the perverse crimped black swatch between Tammy's legs.

Two girls from the Lifesaving Two group looked over and laughed behind their fingers.

Tammy yanked up her useless Fruit of the Loom, followed by her shorts. She pulled her tube socks up as high as they would go. After being wet, the hairs looked darker, and stuck to her calves at odd angles. As she followed Sam out, floor tiles flashed past.

On her knees before the instructor and a semicircle of ten other girls and boys, Tammy tipped the victim's head back and reached inside the mouth to clear the passage. The moisture stayed on her finger. Samantha had three freckles at the bottom left corner of her mouth. They formed the triangle where Tammy focused as she leaned over a closed-eyed half-drowned Sam. One hand was positioned under Sam's neck, the other cautiously clamped Sam's nostrils shut. Tammy kept her eyes open, leaned forward, placed her lips all the way over Sam's. She blew, firm, puffing up Sam's cheeks, Sam's mouth slack, but sticking to hers nonetheless. Sam smelled sweet and astringent — strawberry jam and chlorine. Her body was warm, the baby hairs on her neck, damp. Tammy's own air gushed back at her as she took her mouth away. It puckered out of Sam's body in an exhalation — warmer coming back than going in. Tammy crooked her head and counted, watched Sam's diaphragm for signs of breathing. She sealed her mouth to Sam's again, and blew.

When Sam came back to life they traded places. Tammy felt the heat arching above her. Sam's face poised over hers. Tammy visualized three distinct freckles. She let the sounds float to her from far away, wavering, otherworldly. Sam's fingers burrowed under Tammy's ponytail, coaxed her throat upward.

"Hey, you, in the blue bathing suit — call an ambulance!" she yelled for help as they'd been taught. Tammy had forgotten. One finger thrust between Tammy's lips, pushed her tongue down. Sam pressed her lips deliberately around the perimeter of Tammy's, melding. She let out a heavy gust. It rode past Tammy's teeth, hitting the back of her mouth like something solid. Tammy let her body bloat with Sam's breath.

When they had both returned to life, the week was over.

In the girls' room, Tammy pressed the towel across her crotch and struggled into her shirt quickly, so that no one would see that her nipples were like cold, clay-coloured pepperonis on her chubby chest. She fastened her bra around her waist and shimmied it up underneath the shirt. Sam leaned over in her T-shirt and underwear. A white terry-cloth towel rubbed up and down the damp length of her fiery hair. Her bum thrust out, two bony nubs under the white cotton. A sprinkle of green and yellow daisies across the material. Two unrestrained points jutted beneath the yellow T-shirt. A strange lick of fire passed under Tammy's towel from her forehead down her neck and farther — down the backs of her arms and legs, stopping someplace in the middle for just a second. Tammy struggled quickly into her underpants, elastic tangling and untangling. She stepped into the legs of her shorts and let the towel fall on the floor at her feet. The wet weight of it was like rock. *Plunk,* against the tile. Samantha turned and smiled over her shoulder.

"You're quick today," Sam said. The elastic on her shorts snapped as she pulled them on. "Let's go." She stuck her toes through the loops of her yellow flip-flops.

Tammy knew her only option come Monday would be to do it with Colleen, the last girl their age left in the group. A quiet, coke-bottle-eyeglassed girl from the Catholic school across town, she was also a redhead, but smelled like peanut butter and potato chips.

The only thing Tammy could do now was grab her stuff off the floor and concentrate very closely on the backs of Sam's heels rising off the foam bottoms of the flip-flops as she led the way out of the change room. Her heels were wrinkled pink, and one had a small white spot on it, as if it were about to peel.

PLAYER 1

The field stretched before Chris, immense and impenetrable. In a moment, the green would be broken into rows by their yellow-slicker bodies. J.P. wore a garbage bag over his T-shirt and shorts. Even Chris had given in, resigned himself to the afternoon heat before it happened; under his plastic sheath, he wore shorts for the first time since grade seven. His spare leg hair mocked him. He miserably watched his peeled-potato knees descend the bus steps. Mud instantly embraced his running shoes. With an ecstatic *squish,* it fastened itself around his feet. The stench of wet corn welded to his nostrils the second he hit the ground. The smell of it made him queasy as cheap rye.

For $3.25 an hour, farm work was the only option available to the enterprising South Wakefield fourteen-year-old. The boys fanned out, each taking a row, corn tassels opening paper cuts in their palms as they yanked them from stalks. The leaves submersed Chris's skin in 7 a.m. dew. By two o'clock, he'd be sunburnt dry.

Pretend it's Dig Dug, he told himself, shoes heavier by the moment. *In Dig Dug there are no patterns laid out for you. You're just a person underground with a shovel, making tunnels, moving dirt out of the way.*

"Lane," a ferric voice cut through the leaves.

Chris halted, glanced behind him, down his row. Nothing. He knocked his shoes together. A melon wedge of mud tossed aside.

J.P.'s brother emerged from the folds of the field, a red bandana flaming above his green garbage sack, outlaw-style over his nose and mouth. He wore aviator glasses to prevent slicing his eyes on the sandpaper edges of the plants. In the dim, mirrored lenses, Chris watched two miniature versions of himself waiting.

Marc wasn't their crew leader. Only the farm kids wound up as crew leaders. Marc was a trailer, the hall-cop position of the field. A. J. Mitchum had obviously tossed him aside on a skid. But the ruined body of a fifth-hand Barracuda sat on cinder blocks in the Breton driveway, in permanent pause mode until Marc earned its restoration in dollars and cents. His personal deadline:

September. The six-foot-tall cornstalks surrounding them were a testament to Marc's desire for a senior year on wheels. He held aloft a fistful of green whips, the pull that Chris had missed.

"Are you blind?" Opening his hand, the tassels dropped in a pile on the earth. He walked over them, their leaf-blonde bodies milled into mud. Marc turned, climbed through the cornstalks into another unsuspecting detassler's row.

Fygars are underground dragons that breathe fire, even through what you might think of as a solid wall of dirt, Chris told himself. *But you can drop rocks on them. When Fygars come for you, their eyes float like white outlines before they magically appear in your path. Your shovel doubles as a pump you use to blow them up like puffer fish, until they deflate and die.*

Chris began pulling tassels again, the *pop pop pop* as the green wicks exited the stalks.

The corn crew lounged in the dirt, drink boxes and white bread sandwiches between them. A sun-demolished Chocodile oozed in its wrap, and Rueben laughed, pounded his fist upon it. The chocolate sponge envelope farted its creamy contents out onto the ground.

"It's not far to Doyle's from where the bus drops us," J.P. said, reaching into his pocket. "I got five bucks. What've you got?"

Rueben abandoned the smeared cellophane, dug in his pocket. He came up with a fistful of change. Dean had a dollar. Pinky had two, and everyone exchanged impressed looks, because Pinky hadn't joined them in anything since

This Donna had happened.

J.P. glanced at Chris, who balled waxed paper and stuck it back in his bag.

"I thought you said Lane wouldn't go there again." Rueben arched googly eyes in J.P.'s direction, and Dean snorted, pulling at the elastic on his ponytail as an obvious means to lower his face, brown strands looping and relooping at the back of his head.

"What?" Chris glared at them.

J.P. smirked and wouldn't meet Chris's eyes. He pulled his ball cap off and poured water from a jug across the back of his neck, sopping it up with his T-shirt.

Rueben burst: "J.P. said Doyle calls you his squaw."

"That's not why I don't want to go back there," Chris said. He let the sentence hang like a threat, though stacked next to a word like *squaw*, his ambiguity seemed only more incriminating. He picked up a stick and swiped it through the dirt, drew tight little circles with it, didn't look at any of them. He had masturbated over the girl and then felt guilty about it, the end result heavy as willow bough falling across his lap, the remembered outlines of her bruises swimming up at him reluctantly from the slough. Squirting in one's own lap over a messed-up — possibly abused — chick wasn't noble, Chris didn't need to remind himself. He had wiped it up with an old T-shirt and alley-ooped it — *two points* — into the wicker hamper. The sound of the tossed shirt landed like a sack full of spit, sunk to the bottom and stayed there for days.

The only girl he had ever seen in her underwear. The little hairs on her thighs, her clogged mascara eyelids, spidered the back of his throat, fissured it with flame. Her story hovered in the shade pattern of the overhead light of his bedroom just after his mother had come and switched it off. Blobby and misshapen. The girl who slept on Doyle's couch. The girl who slept with a dealer twice her age.

"You know why," Chris said eventually, impatience puffing the words. He tossed the stick aside and stood up, walked away, heat surging up from his body into his face. He turned his back quickly so they wouldn't see, tried to inject some swagger into his walk as he headed toward the trashcan at the corner of the field to dispose of the remains of his lunch.

When he glanced back, J.P. was twirling his finger in the universal symbol for crazy.

Behind the boys, up by the barn, an unexpected figure had appeared. Chris bit his lip, forehead furrowed, held his breath. The horizon vacillated with veins of heat, as if Chris peered through warped glass.

It was his dad.

Mr. Lane's stocky figure was unmistakable. He was wearing jeans and steel-toes, a none-too-clean white T-shirt, like he had driven directly from the factory. When he spotted Chris, he used his whole arm to beckon.

The field trudged beneath Chris. Then the field tore. *You don't find someone in the middle of nowhere unless it's crucial,* Chris thought, but the thought didn't have words. The thought was nothing but dirt.

Individual stones of gravel. Chris's forehead rattled against the glass.

"Yep." Mr. Lane said it from the back of his throat. He gestured vaguely but Chris didn't look over. In Chris's peripheral vision his father's jaw clenched. Stones drilled the ditch as the car accelerated over the dirt road.

"'Fraid I didn't drive out here to take you for ice cream. . . ."

The replay of words slogged back and forth through Chris's brain, his father still squinting into the bright distance like he'd done at the field. They'd stood there, facing each other. A pair of half-pocketed hands for Mr. Lane, false calm, Chris with fists hip-gripped and ribs fiery. His father had told him before he could regain his breath. The effort of crossing from the cornfield to the farmhouse hitched in Chris's lungs as his father had said it, quietly, his eyes wet as sucked grapes. *"Your grandpa's dead."*

A woman at the farmhouse had stood monitoring the scene with a garden hose, a tray of blood-coloured petunia perfuming the oily air, her chin digging into her pink shoulder as she strained, cocking her head to listen. Grated breaths piled and eventually regulated. Staring at the soil on his shoes, all Chris could think about was planting one of them far up her cottagey ass. She had twisted the spout to Off and dropped the hose suddenly, walking into the mud room as if she could read his thoughts.

Now the car pulled from the McClellan Sideroad across the highway and into a small dirt lot where Chris knew people parked for car pool if they were driving into the city. Mr. Lane killed the engine and they sat there, the hood ornament facing a sea of dried grass.

"Is Mom meeting us? What are we waiting for?" At least he had come, hadn't made Chris finish out the day.

Mr. Lane didn't answer. His front teeth emerged from

his upper lip to bite the bottom one. He glared at the landscape before them, a scant wind rustling the bleached knives of weeds. Beyond, telltale lines of green — corn and tomato fields — cut the sky. Behind them, the bunker of the highway. Chris watched what his father apparently watched, the hard grass folding against itself. Acres of it, roiling, dirty yellow.

A series of telephone posts toothpicked the county. Chris's eyes followed wires like connect-the-dots, as far as he could see. One-o'clock high, a thick sun poured its contents into the car, the air conditioning canned with the ignition. Chris rolled down the window. Light played on the stems in patches, wheat-white and gold. Chris's father's father had once driven him to Lake Michigan to sit like this and stare at the waves. It had been mid-February and they didn't get out of the vehicle, Grandpa Lane hulking in the driver's seat — swirled in the smell of car grease, stale coffee, and spearmint — religiously fixated on the breakers pounding the peppered beach.

Chris's eyes fastened reluctantly on his dad — the deep divot in his upper lip, cheeks infinitely slacker than his tense body.

"What was he like, when you were my age?"

"What was *I* like when you were a kid?"

Chris scraped a grubby nail along the armrest. The memory wasn't much more than a touch, a hand measuring the top of his head against a door frame, his cotton chest when Chris fell asleep against him on the couch in front of the TV.

Mr. Lane's short, thick fingers caterpillared up and down the steering wheel.

They exchanged looks, Mr. Lane's eyes briefly bemused.

"The same," Chris said quickly. "Taller."

The hand gestured, half off the wheel, rolling back to the knuckles, the upturned shrug of a thumb. *There you go,* it said. *There you go.*

Mr. Lane blinked, twice, the smile fading. He pinched the key ring between his thumb and forefinger, jangled it and the engine flipped to life. They pulled out of the lot quickly, as if they'd never been there, the car kicking dust in the side mirror, like the Looney Tunes' Roadrunner when it zoomed ahead of Wile E. Coyote.

ACME, Chris thought, *a suitcase-sized home-funeral kit.* He bit his lip though it wasn't funny.

It would not be the last death, but Chris didn't know this yet. The one thing a person could count on was death; it never ended. In its silence, the Lane house felt like someone had sucked all the air out of it. The four members of the family walked from room to room, waiting to find out when the funeral would occur. Nobody cried. Even Tammy didn't cry. She snuck in and out, as if on tiptoe, looking to Chris for clues. Mr. Lane had said very little since he had picked Chris up from the field. Dusk had turned the house swampy with heat; Mrs. Lane took Shake 'n' Bake out of the oven, nearly dropping the pan as the thin kitchen glove burned through. She bit her cheek from the inside, sucked it into a tight dimple to absorb the pain, extracted her swollen fingers and ran them under cold tap water.

The drumsticks lay on their plates uneaten. Canned green beans swam in water. The chocolate Wagon Wheel Chris had ingested at lunch turned in his stomach. Tammy took her knife and carefully edged the beans away from the instant mashed potatoes. A moat of water and the white and brown pattern on the Corningware formed between the food items as she separated them. Only Mr. Lane picked his chicken clean to the bone. At the end of the meal, the phone rang.

Mrs. Lane jumped up, but Mr. Lane stood slowly. She moved out of his way and he picked it up, but didn't speak. Chris imagined Uncle Bill, standing in Grandpa's apartment among his things. Mr. Lane bent over the sideboard, back to the room, one fist supporting him, grunted into the mouthpiece. "Yep. Yep." When he let the phone fall back onto the hook and faced them, his stony gaze took each of them in separately.

"Saturday." The word was a sentence.

Chris stared at his plate and didn't move. He knew he should stand up and clear them. Under the table, Tammy's running shoe bumped against his leg and rested there, as if she thought it were the stem of the table. He didn't shake it off. This narrow cavity of time was important, more important than what they would fill it with — tomorrow or the next day — how they would act at the funeral, or in any of the days to come after.

On Friday, the morning of the visitation, Chris went into his parents' bedroom for the shoe polish, but sat down on their bed kicking his feet instead. His dad stood at the mirror, clearing his throat, knotting and unknotting different ties, all of which made his face look strange and separate, cinched off from his body. For no reason that he knew of, Chris sat there, staring at his father's back. His shoulders were a stranger's: a pressed shirt.

As Chris stared, the great body fell into itself, crumbled, came apart. Massive shoulders quivered with unvoiced sobs. Chris's legs stopped swinging. All of the sound in the house — the shuffling of other rooms, the talk radio down the hall — rushed toward his father. It was absorbed into his silence, where he stood — shaking.

The car edged forward toward the dark mouth of the tunnel. The radio went stop-and-start. Dolly Parton and Kenny Rogers dissolved entirely. Mr. Lane reached over and flicked the station off. Portals of light whizzed past. Chris counted each of the bulbs attached to the stone wall. Underwater. Under the Detroit River. Mr. Lane rolled his window down a crack. The smoke of a cheating cigarette crept out. Carbon-monoxide lingered in the tunnel, and beneath the congestion, a liquid heat. The passage between the two countries was a reservoir of stale air. *Twenty-nine, thirty, thirty-two, thirty-six, forty . . .* Chris skipped and estimated. He turned his face to the dim interior. The tunnel lights pitched across his parents' expressions in rippling squares of white and grey: his mother pinched in profile, his father segmented by the mirror, the penumbrae of their heads from behind.

The car slowed as it rounded the corner and joined the line with the rest. In increments, it crept toward the slant of daylight where the tunnel ended. A circuit of booths lay on the borderline, red and green stoplights above each — a string of Christmas lights in the July sun. United States customs officers bobbed in and out. *Where are you from? Where are you heading? How long do you expect to be away?* Without emotion, they waved the Lane car through.

It was a three-hour drive and Tammy was fidgeting.

She wore an old summer dress, blue and white with a drop waist. Last year's ruffles made a rumpled V across her new chest. She pulled the seat belt off and rearranged her clothes. She picked at her nylons, pulled them out away from the sweat of her legs, let them snap back. It was her first funeral. Chris's Grade-Eight grad suit already felt tight in the shoulders. She turned to him, plucking at the hem of her skirt.

"D'you want to play the alphabet game?"

Chris shook his head.

The sky outside the window was a pale robin's egg. Beyond the concrete wall of the highway, it was all Chris could see. Detroit protected its neighbourhoods from their tourist eyes, despite the number of times the Lanes drove through it. Chris stared up at the cloudless expanse overhead. Far away, on the other side of the sky, the atmosphere gave way. The blue became airless and black. Chris dropped his forehead against the window, as if he could get closer to that crisp otherworld.

He began to tunnel through it. The layer of air above the station wagon fought him, but eventually he escaped its pressure, penetrated the ether. His shovel scraped. He came up against a coffin where, in Dig Dug, there should only be a rock to stand in his way. Pookas and Fygars paced back and forth in invisible trenches on either side of him. Chris burrowed beneath the chimerical casket, leaving a vacancy where he had passed. The coffin quivered, then collapsed. It plunged through the sky and broke, smashed on the concrete in front of the Lane car. Mahogany thunder rumbled. Splinters separated instantaneously from the varnished box, shot toward the windshield and deflected, clattering, rolled to the shoulder like discarded bones. Brass handles snapped on the cement: small bright boomerangs dinging off the highway divider. Chris's father changed lanes swiftly, easily avoiding the collision. He reached out and flipped down the sun visor without seeming to notice the obstacle Chris had discovered and dropped across their path.

Chris reclined against the seat with some force.

"Don't you think black holes are the saddest thing? There's no matter. They're collapsed universes."

Tammy peered at him, half slithery-eyed, half-quizzical, then resumed squirming, skimming her skirt with her palm as she tucked her legs up underneath her on the seat.

A sideways glance. "D'you want to play now?" she asked.

Chris shook his head. "The opposite of existence."

The highway slowly rose, and yellow fields spread on either side as the car surfaced. Crossing into the United States was no different from driving in Canada, except everything skewed slightly. Someone had come along and adjusted the knob on the picture so the colours weren't quite themselves: rude reds, excessive purples. Trees weren't cut as far back from the freeways. Exit signs were blue instead of green. Every time they crossed the border, he and Tammy were allowed to unfasten their seat belts. There was no law to force them to protect themselves. In America, it was just freer. The Michigan licence plate slogan was "Great Lake State" to Ontario's "Keep It Beautiful." Tremendous seas of fabric rippled over car dealership parking lots, the stars and stripes forever waving, in competition with the little triangular neons farting *(flap-flap-flappity-flap)* down below, over dazzling new windshields swabbed with white: $6995, $5995, $4995!

Beside I-95, the giant Marlboro man angled between the trees in his cowboy hat and plaid shirt, always looking off into the distance. The cars on the freeway had passed beneath him for decades, filling his matte billboard lungs with exhaust.

Chris stared at the back of his father's head.

After the funeral, a fine layer of dirt seemed to have settled over everything. Where had it come from? All of the cars in the lot were covered in it.

Chris eased out of his jacket and folded it over his arm, yanked his tie loose. Across the street on the steps of the funeral home, his parents stood, smoking. It wasn't the first time that summer since they had "quit," yet the thin wisps of smoke expelled from their mouths seemed intentionally proof of something. Of breaking down. It rose up, feathered away. Tammy wandered back and forth in front of them, a blue-and-white dot on the green grass. The cars in the lot bore funeral flags on their hoods, though they hadn't before. Chris wondered guiltily if they could keep them. In another half-second, he had justified it to himself. He would display it prominently, on his shelf, or in some other place of honour — like an urn full of ashes. Solemnity told Chris to fold and refold the jacket that hung over his arm.

In a few minutes they would proceed to the cemetery, a long line nosing its way through the streets, their car in the lead — The Family — traffic clearing for them, the world parting like the Red Sea.

And all the cars in the procession would be dirty.

The thin film appeared to have fallen across hoods and

windshields within the hour they had been parked there. Chris glanced around, searching for nearby construction or some other source. The boulevard stretched in two directions, past tidy white mid-western houses with wide porches and flagpoles. There was only the kicked-up dust of cars going by. Four lanes and a turning lane. It couldn't possibly be enough. Slowly, Chris spun 360, looked up for some answer. There was none.

He broke the pellicle of grit with his finger, wrote upon the Lane car door. Immediately he regretted having done so. Swiping his palm over it, he erased his name, left a clean trench where it had been.

PLAYER 2

The Lane car journeyed home, a blue dot against the green earth, the black pavement. In the dark, the trees were popcorn-headed, explosions on thin bodies. A collection of photographs of boys in suspenders. Little men. That's what Mrs. Lane had chosen to take away. *Let me see . . .* Tammy had whispered, leaning over her mother's chair. A box of black-and-white images with crinkle-cut edges, photographs from 1947, '50, '55 — borders bearing the dates in green ink. Mr. Lane as a white-robed girlish baby. As an eight- or nine-year-old, already solemn, standing next to Uncle Bill, arms around one another's small white-shirted shoulders. As a high school graduate, the gown a thick black shroud. Tammy lay curled in the back seat, across two-thirds of it; Chris upright at her feet. She watched the sliding sky between the blue Bakelite window frames. The car hummed, held her.

She had chosen the strangest things to take from the apartment: a jar of pennies, a decorative Dutch drinking jug from someone's vacation, a thick glass paperweight, a deck of cards. Cool grown-up things, the kinds of things she thought Chris would be likely to fight her for, though he hadn't taken a thing. He would regret it later, she knew.

In the Arrow Books club, it seemed that decades and decades of girls had discovered important family secrets after poking into places they shouldn't. In the third dimension, Tammy the Spy was defeated by Cheez-Whiz-celery sticks and Vernors. The one thing a person could never know was the past: it was gone. Grandpa Lane lived in an apartment; there was no attic, no workshop, no cellar, no barn. Uncle Bill and her father stood on the balcony half the afternoon smoking cigarettes and drinking miniscule bottles of bitters, the only alcohol in Grandpa Lane's apartment. Whatever they said out there hung among the branches of the trees beneath the rail.

"Come over here," Uncle Bill had called to Tammy between one-bite sandwiches brought by Grandpa's upstairs neighbour — American cheese, ham and lettuce with butter on white, quarter-cut the way Tammy liked them. "You see here?"

Through the balcony sheers, his square head was squeeze-faced; inside, he was overly jovial, open. He gestured to the house Tammy had only seen in the photos, a long laneway in fall, her father teen-aged-gawky, none too neat, leaning on the mailbox, grinning, pulling on the metal flag. 1960, according to the edges.

"I was already in Indiana when this was taken, but I got updates, letters from our mother." When he said *mother* his voice dipped, like the word was made of love instead of letters. Uncle Bill was bigger than her father, and Tammy stood between his legs, leaning back against one, where he squat-sat on the edge of the floral sofa.

"He hated that school bus, she told me. There was a girl he rode with who always wore her curlers. She'd take out her comb and fix her hair on the way to school instead of beforehand. One day, he borrows one of our mother's scarves, ties it up over his head . . ." Uncle Bill's thumbs looped under his broad chin, kerchief-knotting the air ". . . gets on the bus, sits behind her, takes out a lipstick, puts it on, takes off his scarf, begins teasing his hair . . . He's mimicking her, poor girl. Must have hated him. But he hated *that bus.*"

Tammy had held the photo carefully along the white frame, peered into stone-grey laughing eyes. It didn't occur to her that the story was third-hand, that it had passed from her father to his mother, now long dead, to Uncle Bill, and now to her. She had only handed the photo back to Uncle Bill, wondered silently who the girl on the bus was.

Lying in the back seat of the moving car, Tammy closed her eyes and replayed the outlines of fixed moments, scenes she hadn't seen. She projected them out into the night, into a blank, moving patch of sky.

She lay, not moving, her body like an electrical cord, coiled up on itself. Tammy hadn't expected this kind of ending. She had come to say goodbye. Sam's arms lay wrapped around her abdomen, her knees pulled up to her chest. Beneath her was the one remaining piece of furniture in the house, the orange and brown flowered sofa. Sam's breath *phewed* out of her.

"I thought it wasn't supposed to hurt," Tammy said. She peered at Sam from the doorway. Sam was "O.T.R." She had whispered it into the receiver preceding Tammy's walk over. "O.T.R.," Tammy had just gleaned from Joyce, was On the Rag, having one's period. It was Sam's first. Tammy didn't know anyone else who had, except Joyce, and their mothers. Tammy hovered at a relatively safe distance, leaned one hip against the doorway.

"Can you wash your hair?" she said. It came out smug, rather than the quirky, sarcastic comment she'd intended. It was one of the *dumb dumb dumb* questions in the Q&A section of the sex-ed. book Samantha had. One of the girls' favourite expressions, whenever someone in class asked something they considered irrelevant, Sam and Tammy would nudge one another and whisper, "Will I be able to go swimming?" or, "Can I take a bath? Can I wash my hair?" — apparently all common questions about the kinds of activities one could continue while menstruating.

"Ha, ha." Sam sat up, glaring.

This wasn't exactly the *Anne of Green Gables* kindred-spirits farewell Tammy had envisioned. Weren't they supposed to do something meaningful, like swear their eternal friendship or exchange locks of hair?

The perfect, flat black skipping stone Tammy had brought along for Sam weighed down her shorts' pocket. Tammy had used a nail to scratch their initials on it, T.L. on one side and S.S. on the other. At Point Pelee the previous summer, the girls had walked all the way out to the end of the peninsula, the southernmost tip of Canada, watched the current swirl around them. Blue surrounded them on three sides. They stood on the narrowest part of the point — a long, brown, crooked finger extended into the unknown, the United States somewhere just beyond their view. Tammy had gathered the stones, and Sam had thrown them. Tammy couldn't make them skip more than twice, and usually they just went *plunk* and sunk on the first hit. Sam threw for both of them.

Mrs. Sturges came in with Mr. Riley and his twin twenty-year-old sons, Carl and Kevin, a couple of sasquatchy guys with big glasses peeking out from under brown shaggy haircuts. Sam had to get up so they could take the sofa out, load it into the van. She and Tammy stood alone together in the room. Voices drifted from the open door: the men grunting and Mrs. Sturges shouting instructions on how to fit the couch in. Tammy looked at Sam, but Sam just pulled at her underwear, and said the pad was a pain in the butt and gave her a major wedgie.

"Does more come out when you stand up?" Tammy asked, her final attempt to make Sam laugh. This time the reference didn't even land.

"Yeah, I guess," Sam said, yanking on the legs of her shorts.

Mrs. Sturges came back inside. She wrapped her arms around Tammy in a big hug.

"You've been a good friend to Sam," she said. "You have to come out as soon as we get Sam's room fixed up." She left a chalky coffee-smelling kiss on Tammy's cheek.

"Mom!"

"All right, all right . . ." Mrs. Sturges kissed Tammy one more time, on the top of her head, then grasped a girl tight on either side of her, shuffling them out of the house. Warren honked the horn, yelled for her to come over and back him out. Mrs. Sturges left them to plant herself at the end of the driveway.

"It's too hot," Samantha complained. She walked away from Tammy and stood under one of the two trees in the yard, though they were barely more than saplings. A few leaf-sized shadows were thrown on the grass at Sam's feet. Sam tipped her head back. "I'll miss my trees," she said.

Thin rivers bled from the corners of her eyes, down the curves of her cheeks. They fell between the freckles on her tank-topped shoulders. The air went out of her. Then, without looking back, she ran and climbed up into the cab of the truck beside her mom and Warren. The horn honked, and the truck proceeded slowly down the road. It braked a full three-second stop at the sign, turned the corner, and passed behind the other houses, onto the highway, on its way out to the Beach.

Tammy transferred the stone from her pocket to the driveway. It landed with the Sam initials face down. Tammy kicked it. It skidded out onto the road. She jogged over to it and stared at the dark, perfectly flat shape it made against concrete. She kicked it again. She kicked it all the way home.

When she got there, she saw in the mirror that Mrs. Sturges had left rusty lipstick on her cheek in a strange, open half-circle. It was the same shade as the Crayola Indian Red pencil crayon. It looked like half a valentine.

When she went to rub it in, it came off on her fingertips. She stuck them under the tap and watched the water run over the colour, marvelling at how quickly and easily it seemed to wash away.

LEVEL 7

Defender

PLAYER 1

Chris started the car and pulled it in and out of the driveway. He backed all the way to the edge of the curb, then pulled forward again, until the nose was within a few feet of the garage door. He angled the mirror and watched the green edges of the grass on either side of the driveway, practised staying perfectly within the space between the Lanes' and the Scotts'. He adjusted the side mirror.

OBJECTS MAY BE CLOSER THAN THEY APPEAR.

Chris watched the flower bed on the Scott side, used it as a guide as he accelerated backward. Yesterday, in the car, his father's neck had been stiff and sunburnt, the grey hairs almost greyer against the red flesh, the rectangular canvas of it etched with lines. How could it have been so sunny on a funeral day? It seemed wrong somehow. His dad had stared straight ahead, said nothing except to announce his intentions: "Grab some fuel," as he pulled into the Shell, or "Grab some grub," before the Blimpie.

Chris caught his own eyes in the rear-view. They were like his father's, only young. His dad must have been miserable, but when Tammy started to cry, he had scooped her up as if she were the only thing that mattered. Chubby cheeks and skinny, hairy legs beneath nylon — she still fit in his lap. Meanwhile, Chris remained tight-lipped and tentative, arms folded, standing close to his mother — close, but not touching. *Trying to keep track of your own emotions and someone else's at the same time must be like trying to fly a plane backward,* Chris thought. He pulled the station wagon back into Drive, edged it forward slowly, until the fender was within spitting distance of the garage door.

J.P. appeared, a pair of swimming trunks hanging beneath his T-shirt, a towel slung over his shoulder.

"Aren't you supposed to be in the corn?" Chris asked.

"Jesus H . . . . whole crew got canned. White thought it'd be funny if we all grabbed Keele and chucked 'im in this nasty-ass ditch. Marc didn't put a stop to it, so Keele — yeah, like Marc woulda stopped it — whipped this corn tassel at him. Brutal. Caught him — *smack!* — right in the eye. Sure you can just imagine Marc's reaction. . . . How was . . . How was your grandpa's party?"

"Ha, ha, yer so bloody funnay."

"You're so totally gay when you do that lousy Jagger imitation."

Mrs. Lane came out of the house, their conversation cut like the ignition.

"If you already had it going, you could've left it," she said to Chris, accompanied by a pointless hands-up gesture. "Hello, John Paul. How are things? Swimming?" Before he could nod, she was yanking open the driver's door, Chris left with no choice but to passenger on over, J.P. only a "Goddammit" in the rear-view as they pulled away. Mrs. Lane agitatedly adjusted the mirror that Chris had set to his own height.

Mrs. Lane zipped the car into the strip mall lot. She walked into Zellers and came back with a huge box in a shopping cart. Chris got out to help her. Inside the brown cardboard was a microwave. It was about two and a half feet wide and weighed a ton. It was going to change their lives. Chris hefted it onto the tailgate of the station wagon, slid it in.

The night smelled like chlorine. The stiff pages of Mrs. Lane's magazine clicked like knitting needles between her fingers as she turned and flipped them. Mr. Lane had the sound down on the television, its dumb jumpy head parked in the corner. As soon as they touched home ground after the funeral, Chris had been on his bike and gone — in search of recharging, an hour or two in a game, and any game would do. But now, a few days later, guilt had delivered him down: he suddenly felt he couldn't leave the Lane house, had to stay close, shakily plucking at pages. Orwellian landscapes gnawed at his cortex, strange and hollow. Above him, his parents tucked and untucked themselves into their chairs. Tammy lay on the floor next to him, also flipping, one of his father's issues of *Time*.

Chris glanced over at her but didn't say anything. A head-loll above him, his mother was hidden behind her women's magazine. *War of the Sexes,* one of the blurbs screamed from the glossy front. Tammy had gone three shades of red when Mrs. Lane picked it up, presumably because it had the word *sex* on it. Chris leaned over, clutched at Tammy's reading material, flipped past the article she was pretending to absorb, kept leafing.

"Check this out," he said. "It's about Jack Kilby and the integrated circuit."

His sister stared at him blankly.

"The microchip."

She took the folded page and studied the picture. Wires on a wafer of glass.

"Back in 1958, in the span of one summer, he built something that would change the entire world. One summer."

Tammy gazed down, words under her elbows, eyes that didn't appear to be processing.

Chris nodded, "The instant exchange of information."

Tammy yawned sarcastically, a melodramatic hand draped across her mouth. She snorted, collapsed onto the carpet. The volume on the television leapt, though it was only a taste test.

Chris dove back into *Nineteen Eigthy-four.*

"What's it about?" she simpered, eyes on the novel, quietly flipping away from the microchip.

"The future."

"But that's right now." She pointed to the title in the running head.

"Big Brother."

With a socked toe, she dug into his anklebone, goofy-faced. *You,* she mouthed.

He steamrolled her, the television volume rising another notch as he did.

PLAYER 2

"I made a friend already," Sam said. "She lives down the street from Warren's. She's really cool. She'll be in Grade Seven this year. She's got a bikini and we built sandcastles together and then smashed them."

"Uh-huh," Tammy said. She fingered the cellophane Chris had left behind on the kitchen table from a Fruit Roll-Up.

"We shared a cigarette out backa' the neighbours' boathouse."

"You did not."

"Admit it," hissed through the earpiece. "It freaks you out how cool I am now. It's just too much for you."

Tammy admitted it was, and hung up the phone.

A layer of pink polish spread across the nail, formed a thick streak in the centre. Tammy dunked the brush back in the bottle and coated the sides, tried to spread the texture evenly. It remained heaviest in the centre. She redunked and recoated until the white of crescent-moon cuticles disappeared. Its hard pink shell was like candy.

Chris stood in the kitchen and sniffed audibly. "That stuff traps disease," he said, not coming any closer. "It forms a base where germs can thrive. They live in oil. In only a few hours they'll be all over your fingertips."

She imagined them swarming, ambushing her. Removing the dripping brush from the bottle, she painted. On the table inches from her elbow, a simple five-pointed pink star took shape, shining. She closed the last brush stroke. The cover of Chris's *Starlog* magazine. His 8th Anniversary Issue: Leonard Nimoy, Frank Oz, Mark Singer, *2010*, *Donald Duck*. The Beastmaster peered through a sketchy portal of polish.

Tammy abandoned the magazine and the Bonne Belle. One game of Defender was the perfect amount of time for nails to dry. If she played carefully — gently — she would not smudge the nails, would not wind up with those hard creases and buildups of paint at the corners, pink pyres.

A patch of sky hung above her spaceship, filling with indistinct white blobs, showing her the space she had left behind or was about to fly into — and all the enemies that filled it. She fuelled and began the unrewarding task of rescuing humans, shooting the alien ships that carried them ever upward. When the ships disappeared, the humans fell, small bold dots in the black. Tammy scooped them up carefully, set them back down to Earth for 500 points. Refuelled and rocketed onward.

The bleating of the new invention signalled a thing was done in thirty seconds time. It signalled a chance to call Jenny Denis, from school, and have her over to make S'mores. Tammy had waited three whole days since Samantha's desertion; it was time to get into the world of friends again.

Jenny confessed she too was ready for a change of friends. "For a while all we did was make prank phone calls," Jenny said of her own former best friend, Ann-Marie. "But prank phone calls are so fifth grade." Tammy agreed. "Now all she wants to talk about is *doing it,*" Jenny said, her voice dropping from volume 6 to volume 1, as if a knob had been turned inside her. She blushed until her cheeks looked like they would explode. Her hairstyle was the kind with a window cut out for her face. "You know, like whether we ever will, or how old will we be? It's really gross."

"Yeah, gross," Tammy nodded. "Samantha was the exact same way."

"Pervs," Jenny said, pushing aside Tammy's Snoopy dog and other stuffed animals. "Ann-Marie said that even though she never would, the best time to do it would be before you ever got your period, because that would be the only time in your life when you wouldn't have to worry about getting pregnant." Jenny picked up the Snoopy and shook it gently so that its ears flopped back and forth. Its eyes were thin, blind black lines of fabric stitched on.

"When I grow up, I want lots of kids though. Five," she said, and rattled off an assortment of names she had already chosen. Jenny's lips pulled back when she smiled, the glint of metal showing through.

"Hey, when did you get that?" The retainer shimmered, alien in the other girl's mouth.

Jenny recounted getting the mould made for it, how it had been like biting into a jaw-shaped tray of pancake batter — but salty as tears and awful. Its gummy hands got down in the crevices, melted around molars, filled divots where nonexistent wisdoms waited, a gooey union cemented, tongue plastered into stone: *surprise!* A maw full of Fiberglass, thickening, wadding, clotting around canines. How it would harden, harden, harden, harden, harden, seal, a bond between gums and cavity, open mouth slammed shut. When the dentist had finally pried it out, she thought that her inscisors would go with it. It captured an imprint of every bump and depression, the retainer fitting snug against her gums. Jenny popped it out and let Tammy look at the firm filmy plastic: an exact replica of the roof of her mouth.

"What if they could do this with your heart?"

"Like . . . cloning?" Mousey brows scrunched as Jenny tried the word out.

"Can I hold it?" Tammy extended her hand toward the plastic in Jenny's palm. The thing was pink, translucent, a three-dimensional map.

"No way." Jenny wouldn't let her touch it. She said that was disgusting.

"I have to take it out if we're going to eat something sticky, like S'mores," she said. "I usually wrap it in a paper towel, so other people don't have to look at it." Jenny wound the perforated white sheet around her mouthpiece. Tammy continued to stare at the lumpy shape it made on the dresser, bound in Viva.

"Do you ever think about your parents breaking up?" Tammy asked.

"Yeah, but I don't think they would. They're always saying 'I love you' and stuff . . ."

Tammy didn't believe her. She picked up an old friendship pin from the dresser and popped it open and closed, running her finger absently over the point. "But if they did, who would you go with, your mom or your dad?"

Jenny wasn't sure you always got a choice, but if you did, she said, she would go with her dad. "Because I think he'd need me more."

Tammy giggled suddenly and couldn't stop. Tears leaked out of the corners of her eyes, and she threw herself back on the bed. "Like you're a washing machine or something?"

"My mom has more friends," Jenny explained soberly, a sadness opening in her plain, happy face like a trap door. "But my dad would be all alone."

"I think my dad has a secret life," Tammy said, straightening up, equally sober. She stared out the window at the lopsided little shed that had been tagged onto the back of the garage. "Maybe even a whole other family somewhere. One day he'll just leave us. We're only his temporary family."

Even as she said it, Tammy knew it wasn't true. It was her mother who hovered, hovered, hovered. Like a jet overhead, leaving nothing behind but a trail of cloud. Or smoke.

Tammy and Jenny stood with their faces pressed directly against the microwave door. They watched through the black screen of window as squares of chocolate and mountainous marshmallows toppled and merged with graham crackers.

"You shouldn't do that," Chris said, coming abruptly into the kitchen. "The waves inside it can seep out. They'll turn your brains into nuclear mush."

"*Screw* off," Tammy said, the word emerging for the first time in front of a friend. The thrill of officiousness and obscenity stuck to her palate as she popped pure sugar between her lips, crushing graham crackers under teeth without twins.

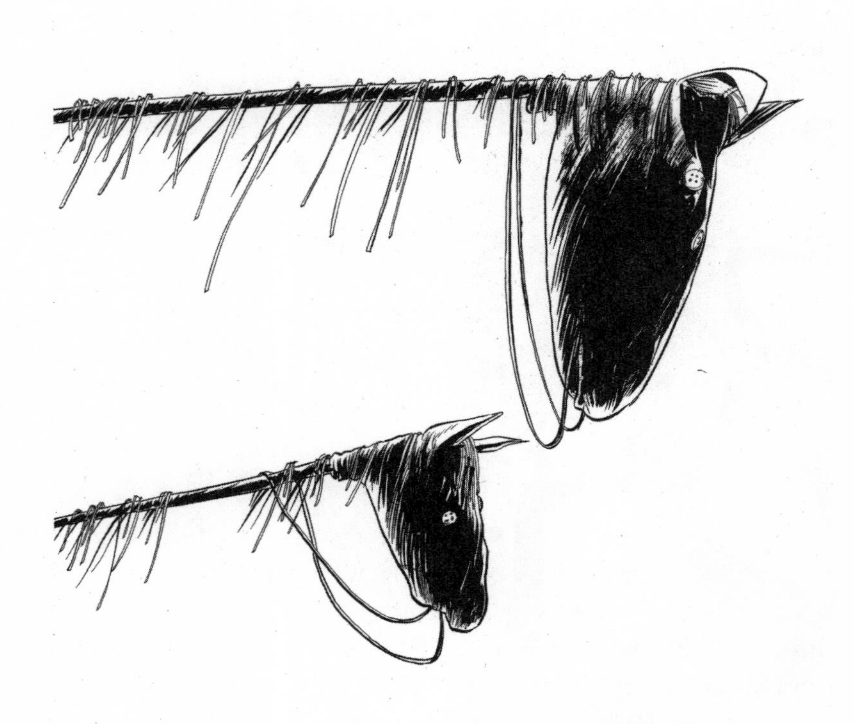

LEVEL 8

Ms. Pac-Man

PLAYER 1

Twiss's: its letters hissed in yellow and purple plastic. At night, the sign creaked on gigantic hinges in the wind. In the afternoon, August, there was no wind, only the music of a distant transformer and the thrum of rubber under Chris's thumb, BMX lying nearly in his lap on the pavement. He spun the tire of the prone vehicle, faster and faster, trailed his finger along the rubber grid. His nail dirtied as he did so, but Chris did not notice.

Across the street from the Gas 'n Go, the building where Joyland had lived was now nothing but a free-standing concrete square, four sides of a two-faced creature. In its heyday during its peak hours, the small windows let in only the most burned quality of light. They were now filled with bristol board, obscenely white, set on either side of the door like eyes that had rolled inward. The door — chain links like teeth across a lip of handle — bore a hand-markered sign that said only, CLOSED. If he were to pick up his bicycle and spin across the road and around the building, Chris knew he'd find the rest of the edifice undisturbed: back wall still sporting the Rolling Stones mural. A tongue pouring out of a fat red gaping mouth. A once-joyous *fuck you.* Chris picked up a stone and used it to write in grey on the grey concrete gutter: WEEK 6. He underlined it and tossed the stone away, resumed spinning his bike tire.

In June, the two side walls had been blank lobes, studded only with garbage cans. Now the beer bottles lined up, markers indicating the weeks the boys had been locked out. A crumpled chip bag beside Chris shifted in the breeze, scurried across the street and joined a small army of newspapers and brightly coloured debris that had blown up against the foundations. The garbage cans had been quickly liberated to form bike ramps for trick jumps in the alley behind the defunct arcade.

The first time Chris had seen Laurel Richards was at Joyland. Unlike the other girls, Laurel was actually playing. At the Kung-Fu Master machine, she jumped and ducked with such ferocious grace it had seemed to Chris even the knife-wielding woman onscreen should have been flinging lotus flowers at Laurel's man. Laurel's short, dark hair feathered around her face, almost boyish, if not for the pale pink lip clenched firmly by her teeth as she concentrated. She worked the controller between frantic fingers, worked it so hard her ass shimmered visibly beneath the aqua-and-white pinstriped nylon shorts.

Chris had moved as if programmed, followed a pattern he wasn't even aware of. Whatever he had been saying to J.P. as they entered the arcade was lost. Chris felt a surge in his system, a momentary blink, then he went into autopilot and followed the most direct path to his destination. Standing behind her would not be like standing behind J.P. or Johnny Davis, and he'd known this before he even got there. While he'd wanted to know her score, he'd also wanted the smell of coconut suntan lotion from her shoulders kicking in with the lurch of her lean body, the sound of her breathing and cursing. It was a wonderful, terrible thing, to stand behind a girl like that.

Chris didn't know how long he had stood there, eyes fixed on the screen, silently tracking the movements of the characters while his body tracked the movement of her hips, the slight swivel and bend of her neck, the motion of her arms that released blasts of baby-powder Soft & Dry, followed by the faintest whiff of sweat and true female scent. How Chris had felt and smelled all that in a place where the girls leaned against machines smoking twice as much as the guys, he didn't know. In the final four weeks before Joyland had closed, Laurel's scents and rhythms were imprinted on him in such a way that he could detect her presence even if he was in mid-game and she was on the other side of the arcade. She'd been like the cherries in the Ms. Pac-Man game. She came onscreen and he could hear the soft bleeping, like a beacon, marking her every step through the maze of ghosts he was constantly running from. If Chris had a quarter for every time he thought about Laurel Richards after that, he could open his own arcade and play 'til doomsday.

Chris stopped the bike wheel with his hand, picked himself up off the ground, righted his vehicle and climbed on. He let himself fall from the curb into the street. On the other side, he circled the building — its dim walls revealing nothing more — and pumped home.

He imagined the black-painted walls inside and whatever was left of his hopes, the ghosts of cut-off denim and bra-straps through mesh tops. In contrast, Chris felt the silence of his own body like a hundred still-invisible levels stacked up. His thumbs clumsy with solitude and lack of practice, at home he was only able to clear the first level. Even then, he felt as though he passed through candy-coloured ghosts that stuck to his hands. Laurel was a blue apparition. He was an open mouth, chasing her around the screen in his head. Within the walls of Joyland, he might have caught something more real, the girl in the ghost, the red smell of ripe strawberries, the pretzel loop of her fist around the joystick.

But he was on the outside, playing over his moves with the precision of one still trying to figure out the next steps. The passageway leading from one side of the screen to the other. The key to the beloved building with its two mouths, one open and one closed. The pattern that emerged only out of instinct and repeat errors. The one his mind could not retrace.

The stripes of her shorts, her short hair, hard laugh, and soft lips.

So went August. Chris lay. In the daytime on his skinny single mattress, the Eddie Van Halen poster affixed on the top wall, and the Christie Brinkley one on the side wall.

Stretched diagonally between them, he learned to listen to the sounds outside the room, to the screams and squeaks of his sister and her prepubescent friends, the *pish pish pish* of his mother's sandals, and the rhythmic jangling of his father's pocket change. Between them, he learned to touch himself modestly, to lay always facing away from the door on his stomach, hand down front of jogging pants (jogging pants for easy access), book open in front of him in case of interruption.

He learned the pillow was no substitute for the design of Laurel Richards' thighs. He learned his hand was faster at video games than at masturbation. He learned that he was a wonderful, terrible lay. There were boards he could clear that he had never seen, power spots he could eat that had no names, manoeuvres he could execute that were unrepeatable. But for all that, he could not keep the most beautiful girl's face in his mind's eye while he played. It was an excruciating way — in the end — to watch his mobile yellow head wilt and die. Alone.

Chris lay. In the nighttime on his skinny mattress. Stretched perpendicular to Eddie, he turned to face Christie. Each of them became dark shapes without distinct features. In pale squares hanging, their bodies became featureless and unsmiling, genderless and uncaring. In the slight breeze from the electric fan, they shivered small paper sighs. Their edges curled. They bubbled and breathed, dark blobs, suspended beings. Between them he learned to touch himself immoderately.

If Chris could draw a picture of what his heart looked like, it would be all hair, jostling over a heavy bass solo. Chris lay on his back, legs bent at the knees, dick coiled backward against his stomach like a garter snake he had just found and hadn't decided if he would wrap it around his hand and chase girls with it, or put it in an immense pickle jar and punch air holes for it.

PLAYER 2

The world was laid out in concrete-coloured rows, rectangles of red and brown rooftop, and succulent blinking squares of water. The cranks for the covers announced holy ceremonies in May, when the Scotts and the Stanleys had exposed their in-ground pools, gigantic scrolls perched on the ends. Now the pools were naked and much-used. From the top of her backyard tree, Tammy could see everything. All she wanted was a glimpse of blue through the leaves, fence boards, and antennae that screened her secret perch from their private parties. The higher she dared to climb, the more she could see.

Her parents called her the Neighbourhood Watch. They'd even bought her a pair of binoculars for her last birthday. Chris called her Harriet the Spy. Tammy had read the novel earlier that spring. She still wanted Harriet's cynicism for herself, her streak of cruel perception. Instead, she found herself affected only by the sad semblances of other people's lives.

People came and went. They came and went. The expressions on their faces were strange, pensive expressions. They did not know they were being watched. They were not waiting for anything to happen. They were without any expectation, hope, or anger. They moved like ghosts in their own lives, their bodies like thin shafts of light thrown up from their shadows. From her altitude in the thick-limbed maple, everyone was small by comparison. Their arms moved stiffly at their sides like Playmobile men, their hands always cupped. Their feet were like Barbie's, not made to allow them to stand upright. Everyone walked hunched over. Everyone carried things from here to there. Everyone came and went. Afternoon and evening. No one ever really looked around. No one looked up.

The Stanleys' lights were on a timer in their front room and turned on and off at the same time every evening. Though the curtains hung like a wedding veil over the window, Tammy could see the entire room. The sheers formed only a pale barrier that gave everything a double outline. She could distinguish the picture frames on the opposite wall, though she couldn't make out who was in the photos. No one ever passed in or out of the doorway at the back of the room, as long as she watched. She named this room the Dead Room, and saying it — even to herself — sent shivers up the backs of her knees. There was something almost too real about it.

With the exception of the Dead Room, there was nothing extraordinary about the Stanley house or its occupants' lives. Rita and George Stanley were an attractive couple, a few years younger than Tammy's parents. They had the pool, where Mr. Stanley did laps with religious zeal. But they had no children, and so were of nearly no interest to Tammy.

On the surface, one would expect the Scotts to be more exciting, with their teenage daughter who had played the lead that spring in the school play, and their college-aged son, Duncan, who never showed up twice with the same old bomber of a car. He had babysat Tammy and Chris years ago, but even at seven and ten, they could tell he was a dork who desperately wanted to appear cool to somebody. Unfortunately, they may have been his biggest fans, and even they didn't laugh at his jokes. His most decent vehicle was the VW Bus Tammy and Chris named the Green Machine. But Dunc Scott quickly went from groovy to geek with the Blue Bomber, an old wagon with wood panel on the side. (On crasser days, Chris called it Ol' Blue-Balled Woody, and Tammy laughed reluctantly, understanding the implication by his half-whisper, though not entirely certain of the meaning.) Duncan followed Ol' Blue with his 1971 Chunky Cherry El Camino. Without the binoculars, she could identify him by his assortment of sound effects, long before he rounded the corner. The Scotts provided a passable modicum of entertainment. But in spite of the glimmering surface beyond the fence, their lives too, held a quiet misery — punctuated — almost emphasized by occasional splashes in the pool.

From an aerial view, Diana Scott, sixteen, bent ballerina-style, not unlike the painted mirrors in the home decoration section of the Sears catalogue. The flattened shape of femininity framed by one's own reflection. The perpetual girl. Her hair loosened and fell over her face, toes pointed like a dancer, arms looped loosely around her skinny, suntanned knees. Tammy expected there to be more excitement in the life of a teenager, especially one who acted and sang, and owned at least three different bikinis. Tammy wanted a never-ending parade of boyfriends and girlfriends to arrive in cars, to storm in tossing red, white, and blue beach balls and snapping towels. But there was only Diana, strutting about the concrete by herself. Sitting on the edge with the occasional friend, kicking their feet slowly back and forth through the aqua light. Again and again, Diana bent to paint her toenails. She drank Pepsi-Free. She put her lipstick on again. She yelled through the window to her mother. Her mother brought out the nail polish remover. Diana painted her toes again.

The day the whole design of the neighbourhood shifted, Chris was monopolizing the television, watching the Olympics. He was nearly as fanatical about running as video games. He made no secret about the fact a guy like him (with a mouth that was too big for his body) had to learn to move fast if he was going to stay alive. It was true. Tammy had once seen Pinky Goodlowe chase him from one end of the schoolyard to the other, across the street, through the park, and over the fence into J.P.'s backyard. She had been sitting on the swings with Samantha when the flight began. All she saw were the white stripes of her brother's sleeves pumping furiously, his head tucked so low it was almost under his arm, like a football. Chris ran erratically as if dodging players that weren't there. His pursuer was too angry to follow his zigzags. Even from Tammy's vantage point, by the playground equipment, Pinky Goodlowe was unmistakable. In the eighth grade at fifteen, he was nearly six feet tall and built like Hulk Hogan. Levis faded to white in the bum, high-top running shoes, and Ozzy Osbourne hair. As soon as she saw Chris start his crooked sprint, Tammy knew that if Pinky caught him, her brother's head would be bitten off as easily as a bat's. But when Pinky was crossing the street into the park, her brother was already hurdling the top of the fence. By the time Pinky was curling his meathook fingers through the diamond pattern of the wire barrier, her brother was probably drinking ginger ale with Mr. and Mrs. Breton.

Tammy had developed a bit of an interest in the Olympics, in spite of herself. While Carl Lewis was the obvious favourite, Chris also had an interest in the female athletes. He kept feeding Tammy interesting tidbits, and she kept acting as if she were supremely uninterested. Later, she would find herself requoting them with great authority — for Jenny's benefit of course.

"Did you know that between 1926 and 1966 women were barred from marathon-running? They thought women were physically incapable, that their health would be placed in jeopardy if they were allowed to compete," Tammy echoed. "In 1966 Roberta Gibb ran, but she had to sneak in."

Chris had memorized the women runners' previous race times as if they were poster girls' measurements. It all came down to American Mary Decker and South African Zola Budd, who was running for Great Britain.

"Well, duh," Tammy sassed, like Chris hadn't pasted up pictures and stats all over his corkboard since Decker won the World Championship in the Soviet Union the year before.

Cross-legged at the coffee table, Tammy markered a marquis on a sheet of typing paper. Inside it, Pac-Man and Ms. Pac-Man kissed. Their bodyless heads streamed with motion lines, as if they had just glided in, one from either side. The only difference between them was her pink hair bow and a long extra line behind her, a notion of greater acceleration behind her blank yellow face. Below the decapitated couple, four ghosts stood, ablaze with their names, like movie stars. Tammy plucked turquoise and yellow markers from her pack and added light lines to the frame, a flashing facade.

She half-watched the race and half didn't. She got excited when events were introduced, but they took too long to finish, and she lost interest. She was marking a heart between he and she when Chris shouted. Tammy looked up in time to watch Mary Decker nosedive onto the grass on the inside of the track, hands spread out in front of her.

"Jesus!" Chris yelled.

Mrs. Lane ran in from the kitchen, where she'd been attempting the art of from-scratch microwave lasagna, one eye trained on the screen of the microwave, and one ear tuned to the TV in the living room. There was a snapping in the room as Chris turned the knob back and forth between the Canadian and American channels, trying to get the best coverage. A strange smell began to permeate the household, and in the other room the microwave wailed.

Tammy fled the scene. Outside, she grabbed hold of the bottom branch, swung up into the green folds of the tree. Branches pulled her muscles out and up past the third fork in the trunk, into the place she had named the Stadium, because she could sit on one branch and use a lower parallel one as a footrest. This lookout point faced the park, far away across six rooftops. In the evenings, she could often see baseball practices, dark figures circling like tiny dots.

But it was still afternoon and the only place to look was down, at the Scotts' pool, where Diana was lounging face down on the blue raft, blue water behind her pitching light up at Tammy. It took a full ten seconds before Tammy realized why Diana was face down.

Beneath her long thin body lay another body. It seeped out from under Diana like a second skin she was shedding. It was male — Tammy knew by the leg hair, plastered in black trails across its shins. The two were lying very still, which was why, at first, Tammy didn't see him. She watched as Diana's long brown hair swung sideways. Their mouths stuck together in an ugly, sinewy tunnel of tongue. Tammy didn't know the boy, and there was something about him that didn't seem real, the way his head reclined, his expression unmoving even as his cheek muscles flexed in accommodation of their union. Diana's body seemed to be sealed to his, in spite of the bathing suits that clung to them, darkly, wetly. It was their skin that bothered Tammy, the nonchalant closeness of it. Diana raised herself from the waist up and Tammy focused on the gold V between them where their navels faced off, subcontiguous. Rising above, a purple bikini top. Below, their abdomens sealed in nylon that seemed superfluous. They were like morphed creatures.

Twigs snapped as Tammy hurried to exit the tree. Partway down, she stopped to see if they were still at it. At that moment, he moved. One hand, spreadeagle, clenched the slick fabric over Diana's bum. The other grasped one handle of the raft. With a sudden twist he rocked to one side and rose above her, thrusting them both into the water with a shriek, sending the floater jetting into the air. When they emerged from the bubbles, she clung to him laughing, their hair plastered like plastic helmets against their heads. Tammy watched hands moving underwater, like little goldfish. The boat floated upside down, bottomside white.

Inside, on her bed, Tammy played the scene over and

over again. As much as she tried to stop it, it seeped in, circling. *Is love so careless?* she wondered. One day there was no one, and the next, there you were, sprawled out on top of one another. Somehow she always thought there'd be more dates, more roses, more time in-between. This was what she had been waiting for, and now it sank to the bottom of her stomach with the heaviness of a candied apple. Through the walls, she could hear Chris changing channels. The ongoing commentary on Zola and Mary. She felt hot and sticky inside. She lay face down on the pillow and pushed her pelvis against the mattress until she could feel the sun move off in the other direction. She closed her eyes, and half-naked bodies merged with the bodies of runners. When she opened them again, it was evening. She could hear the sound of Chris playing the Atari. It sounded like an electronic fireworks, and clapping, like something large and real.

Jenny put down the pink plastic horse she had been manoeuvring across the beige carpet. She moved closer to the television, her eyes on the back of Chris's shoulders. Inky, Pinky, Blinky, and Sue poured from the box in the centre of the screen and milled through the maze, Atari-retarded, not exactly hell-bent on haunting him. Chris steered the yellow head around the dividers, gobbled a power pellet, and crunched two ghosts in quick succession. Tammy's blue horse reared back on its hind legs. It was almost unthinkable, someone feeling toward her brother the way Tammy felt about Bo from *The Dukes of Hazzard*. Even more emphatic was Tammy's crush on Face from *The A-Team*. Tammy had written the actor's name in her best cursive again and again: *Dirk Benedict, Dirk Benedict, Dirk and Tammy.* Jenny leaned in on one hand, closer to Chris and the Atari console. Tammy imagined her going home and writing: *Christopher Lane, Chris Lane, Chris and Jen.*

Unless Chris was present, Jenny didn't pay much attention to the Atari, or to video games of any sort. In the first days of their new best-friendship, Tammy boasted about having been to Joyland and, especially, having been there on closing day. Portioned out and wrapped in whispers, these bits of information were given like love notes, or like small frantic stories about sex. An exchange of information not meant for adult ears. But they meant very little to Jenny, were received like obligatory valentines. If Jenny's older brother had frequented the arcade, he had not passed on its legacy in the way that Chris had. Jenny was that one child of ten unaffected by the trends and passions of her peers. Mouse Trap, Q*bert, Donkey Kong: she had little interest in playing any of them. The matter was simple. There weren't any horses in the games.

"Let's go outside," Tammy declared, standing. Jenny looked up at her blankly. She glanced back at the pointed white shoulder blades of Chris's T-shirt as she followed Tammy out.

As the heads of Chris's hockey sticks emerged from the garage, they became Arabian stallions. The girls galloped up and down the driveway. Every time, the game followed the same pattern. Jen's horse was named Shadow, Tammy's, Speed.

1. They encountered villains. Beneath their running shoes, asphalt sank into the sands of foreign beaches. The girls could outride every trouble, and as they fled, their

steeds' hooves pounded louder than their sneakers, threw up dust in their wake. Each became one with her horse, ribs heaving as the horses' would, hair warm from the sun. The Scotts' front lawn was a green ocean, their backyard, a hidden mountain stream always beyond the girls' reach, much though their horses yearned to drink there and kept returning to the outback, a sparse line of bushes to peek through and nose between.

2. They discovered other horses. Beautiful as their own, but roaming free and wild, Jenny and Tammy coveted them, torn between their faithful animals and these. In the end they vowed to capture and train them alongside their own.

3. They were watched. The day of the horses' capture, they discovered the animals were smarter than they'd credited. The failing effort to seize the horses was being monitored by secret trainers. This was the scenario with which they met Lucas Wolf and Jonathon Rider, who — thankfully — bore absolutely no resemblance to guys Jenny and Tammy had ever seen, and who eventually would become their boyfriends. At this time, there was much riding off alone and hand-holding with imaginary figures, arms thrust out from their sides. Triumphant one-sided fists represented the entwined.

By August, they'd allowed the game to morph.

1. Their horses were actually unicorns that had existed in a disguised state for centuries in order to protect themselves from extinction.

2. The girls retained their pretend potential boyfriends, but under no circumstances was the secret revealed to them.

Even this variation began to grow tiresome as the summer continued to rear its straw-coloured head. The day after the Zola-Mary incident, Tammy miraculously conceived of a new plot. It broke tradition right at the beginning of the game.

1. Instead of a glorious flight to safety along the beaches and into the mountains, they were overtaken.

2. The horses were set loose by the perpetrators, and

3. The girls were gagged and taken hostage.

"Why did they take us hostage?" Jenny struggled against the invisible bonds on her wrists and ankles.

"I don't know . . ." Tammy called from the maple tree where they'd tied her. "They want something from us?"

"They let our horses go."

"Then they must want something else."

The plot always took shape like an uncharted pattern. They could see the twists and turns before they occurred, yet once they followed it, they could rely only on quick manoeuvring to get them out of corners. Jenny and Tammy both knew they were in a corner now, and though Tammy couldn't put a name to it, she was certain they were thinking of the same escape.

The grass at Tammy's feet was tufted and dry as she shrugged. Jenny shimmied closer, crab-walking on what were supposed to be bound hands.

"They want us?"

In the next five minutes, the deed was done, two effective invisible men had entered the garden dungeon, forced Jen's and Tammy's legs apart, and taken the thing they knew so little about. With as much struggle as the girls could provide — "We're bound, remember?" — they lay beneath the maple, about three yards away from one another, watching each other's knees slowly bend outward as unseen hands assaulted. Tree boughs swayed against the sky. The pale green underside of maple leaves flicked against bold blue as Tammy imagined him — a faceless, nameless powerful Him — rising over top of her there. She closed her eyes.

Tammy found out later the Him was Jonathon Rider after all. She had found a new game plan for meeting them.

PLAYER 1

Twenty-four bottles of Bud stood guard over the Breton basement, empties and fulls lined up on the table like opposing football teams. Adam Granger was the provider, everyone's second-best supplier of illicit things. If the boys couldn't find Doyle, they could probably get Adam Granger to buy them alcohol. If they couldn't find J.P.'s brother Marc, they could probably get Adam Granger to drive them to the arena or Circus Berzerk. If they couldn't get any of the girls in their class to go out with them, they could probably get Adam Granger to tell what going out with them was like.

He was eighteen years old and dating Cindy Hambly, who'd been in Chris's class since kindergarten. Cindy Hambly was the one and only girl Chris Lane had ever danced with — *Eyes-like-Lake-Michigan,* according to the last graffitied page of his Grade Seven Science textbook in conjunction with fumbled imaginings. Certainly there were crasser things he could have written. Eyes-like-Lake-Michigan had almost kissed him in a birthday party closet, a game of two minutes, but he'd shifted into shy mode after six seconds and burst through the door before her lips reached further than the nib of one embarrassed earlobe. Unfortunately, Cindy turned faster than an American Flyer miniature train. The little engine that could — and did — the memory now stashed behind a wall of garage junk in Chris's brain. That winter, she had dated David White, who fell from her list after waving his finger around under all the boys' noses. Adam was the solution to the Grade Eight graduation, but, in spite of his guest pass, he'd been turned away at the door. His exclusion had only served to endear him further to Cindy.

Adam had been charged for statutory rape, though not convicted. His previous girlfriend, Amy Leeland, had been thirteen. He got off because, at the time, he'd been seventeen. How seventeen and thirteen were any different from eighteen and fourteen, no one really knew. But he was definitely chargeable now. Why Cindy Hambly's father hadn't torn Adam into bite-sized pieces already, J.P. and Chris could only speculate.

The Hamblys were going through a divorce. Not the loud, messy kind, but the kind that snuck up from behind one day, grabbed your arms and jammed a knee in your back — for no reason, just like that, matter-of-fact — and you suddenly found yourself in a full nelson, your head pressed halfway to your knees and your breathing laboured. Except, Chris and J.P. guessed, if you were married to the person, you couldn't just yell "uncle" and get let back up. When the Hamblys were home, they moved between rooms like robots, their jaws constantly hanging open and nothing coming out, their arms reaching jerkily to change the channel or to press two-dollar bills into Cindy's palm. The boys assumed that if the Hamblys even noticed what Cindy was doing, they were probably just too consumed by their own problems to care. Even at the time, Chris wondered if there was a distinct dividing line. In the same way that parents were oblivious to kids' lives, kids were oblivious to theirs.

J.P.'s brother Marc could barely tolerate Adam. He cut out early, barely glancing at their crude pre-Adamic circle of canned pop and Doritos bags.

"Find something to do without *Fairyland?*" Marc oozed irony. He knew full well that within an hour they would be soused, snorting beer through straws, lying on the thin carpet that covered the basement's cement floor. At least they were using Adam, Marc said, as much as he was using them.

"Bottom-feeder," he called Adam behind his back. Marc would hawk up phlegm wherever they were standing, the green splooge like a snail-trail of Ghostbusters' slime.

"Watch out for guys like Granger," he warned Chris and J.P. with what seemed like unwarranted severity. "They'll steal the girls your age that you could be dating. They'll suck them up and they'll fucken — what's the word? — *effluviate* them. By the time you're my age, those girls will be gone. You won't know what happened to them. If they don't get knocked up and disappear, they'll get worn down 'til they evaporate. I've seen it before. There were guys like Granger, older than me, when I was your age."

In spite of his moral righteousness, Marc was hardly a paragon of virtue. Once he had hidden inside the garage and hit J.P. in the chest with a two-by-four. J.P. had told their mom it was Marc who'd left the tire tracks in the front lawn. J.P.'s sobs were hiccupy, high-pitched but held back behind his teeth — desperate-sounding, like a dog's sharp whimpering — buried deep inside his throat. That was the first time Chris had seen J.P. cry. He remembered when he was eight or nine, that everybody cried at some point — over scrapes, or losing, or not being allowed to have something — and how it had been a defining moment to any friendship. People weren't really friends unless tears had been shared. Whether Marc had more respect for honest girls than he did for honest guys, J.P. and Chris didn't know. Marc's grand theories on What Women Are and What Women Want went untested, mostly because girls were too frightened of him to give him a chance. This was J.P.'s theory. He had never overheard a tittering phone call, yet had often put up with unyielding punishment.

But when Marc said the supply of girls worth having would dry up if Adam Granger didn't stop "dating down," Chris had to admit, he had a point.

Now, Adam lounged against the brown floral couch, massive arms hooked back in a display of wingspan like no one else left in their flock. When not one female had arrived at the party by 10 p.m., Adam looked like he was suffering major withdrawal.

"Shhh-i-i-i-t," he said, his feet like battleships on the horizon of the coffee table. "You guys should be grateful. Just starting your first year of high school. Don't know nothin'. All that pussy waiting for you. Fucken, *everything* waiting for you . . ."

He leaned back, sucked hard on the short brown stogie as if it were a candy stick between his thick fingers. Chocolate-smelling smoke wafted up into his ash-brown hair, and he seemed to turn greyer and greyer with each passing moment. The boys afforded him a silence that could easily be mistaken as awe. They nodded their heads, sipped the bounty Adam had generously bestowed upon them.

"Know what I'm gonna do?" Adam said. He leaned forward, dropped the stub down inside an empty. Smoke rose out in an undefeated wisp. He put one fat thumb over the mouth of the bottle. The brown vapor withered inside the brown glass. "I'm gonna call Cindy. She'll bring some friends for you guys."

J.P. kicked Chris under the coffee table. "Scumbag," he mouthed across the table. Adam was supposed to have called Cindy before he'd come. Apparently he'd been hoping they would coax out some new girls on their own whom he could meet.

Chris heard them before he saw them. The girls. He couldn't tell how many, or who, besides Cindy, because she was the one talking the loudest. J.P. sprinted upstairs to get the door. Chris sussed them out, shuffling about in the foyer taking off their running shoes. Cindy thumped down the stairs. Behind her jubilance, the other girls threw hesitant shadows against the panelling. The light in the front hall pitched a bright patch across their feet, only their white socks visible from where Chris sat. One pair of sport socks with delicious banana-yellow stripes, two pairs of plain white, and one ankle pair of luminescent pom poms.

Freshly shaven knees brought her down to him on the set of yellow stripes. As they descended, Chris processed the flutter of feathers before he saw their faces. Soft pink wisps billowed on thin leather strands around white cotton shoulders and attached to a roach clip, which in turn attached to the short black hair of Laurel Richards.

When she reached the centre of the room, the light fanned out, framing her face in rose tendrils. The sleeves of her white jacket were pushed up to the elbow, bunching her shoulders out with the extra material. Bangles tangled as her hands clasped in front of her black T-shirt, tightly, in such a way she looked as if she was trying to hide the nails Chris had noted months ago were torn ultra-short from chewing.

She looked at him. All the sound had been sucked from the room, as if into a vortex. He didn't trust his voice, so he leaned forward and nodded. He hoped he didn't look like one of those old-time bobbing dolls with its head separate from its body. Even if he did, it didn't matter. She had come.

LEVEL 9

Venture

PLAYER 2

It was Tammy's idea that she and Jenny should ride their hockey horses as far as Mr. Sparks'.

Mr. Sparks lived around the corner across from the park. To ride the horses there was not at all like taking their bikes. Taking their bikes would be an obvious sign they had gone missing in action. Leaving them meant Tammy's parents would assume they were close at hand, not galloping as far away as the park. If they looked for Tammy, it would have been at the Scotts' or the Stanleys', or even the VanDoorens', but definitely not at the Bretons', and especially not at Mr. Sparks'. Tammy did not consider all of these factors.

She simply said, "Hey, let's ride to Mr. Sparks'."

He had just driven by in his Corvette, honking as he rounded the corner. At the stop sign, the window slid down into the door as if melting from the heat.

"Hee hah," Mr. Sparks called, his thumb and finger hooked in a pistol shape toward the hockey sticks between the girls' legs. He winked above the mirrored sunglasses he'd let slide down his nose.

"Hi ho, Silver!" He pushed the shades up again, gunned the engine, and drove past.

Tammy sighed. "Cool car." Intrigued by the decadence of automatic windows, she galloped out into the street and stared after the shiny ass of the white vehicle.

"Awesome," Jenny said. She lifted her hockey stick up and let it fall. The butt of it banged the concrete, tapped to some kind of tune in her head. "How do you think he knew they were horses?"

Tammy turned her horse, Speed, in the direction the car had disappeared. "Hey, let's ride to Mr. Sparks'," she said. Without waiting for Jenny to mount her stick, Tammy was off.

Mr. Sparks was like Buck Rogers if Buck Rogers lived on Earth. He flew past in his white shuttle to unknown destinations. On the TV show, Buck was accompanied by his ally, Hawk, the stoic half-man half-bird with a feather cap for hair. On Earth in the 1980s, Mr. Sparks was a lone man, travelling in his space probe, seeking the lost tribes. Tammy had patiently waited to be discovered, a singular remaining human foraging for friends in the aftermath of the nuclear apocalypse that had occurred, if only in her heart. She imagined wherever Mr. Sparks arrived — the Shell Station to refuel, or the Metropolis Diner downtown — there must be half-clad women with incredibly large hair waiting to brief him on the planetary status and what his next mission might entail.

Even after the show went into reruns, Tammy wanted to be Buck Rogers' colonel, Wilma Deering. She envied actress Erin Gray's crinkled space coveralls. Tammy had only the velour halter-shortset that looped around her neck, the elastic top of which occasionally snuck to nipple-level if she wasn't careful. However, with the help of a borrowed can of hairspray, she was the hair queen on the edge of the stratosphere. Anyone with shoulder-length hair could do a ponytail on one side, but Tammy had once fashioned two on the same side, bunked over top of one another, each with a cherry-red bobble.

"Weirdo," Chris said when Tammy walked into the room.

"Goof." She'd gone outside to sit on the porch, waited for Mr. Sparks to drive by, recognize her as his futuristic equal, and invite her into his space car. He would zip them off to some other city where they would eat hot dogs, play skeetball, and go roller-skating. She was ten then. Mr. Sparks had not driven by on that particular day, nor on any other occasion had he stopped to admire Tammy's radical sense of being, her aptitude for adventure (namely tree climbing), or her ability to stop, drop, and roll. By the age of ten, these were the only survival skills she had acquired, unless Monopoly counted. Now she was eleven and seven months, she assured herself, almost old enough to menstruate, and that meant nearly a woman. With or without Jenny in tow, she was determined to show off her invisible-steed equestrian skills.

"Howdy gals," Mr. Sparks grinned. The corners of his mouth pushed up in mild amusement. His hands went to his hips as he slouched against the compact, curvy vehicle. He wore work clothes: blue dress pants, short-sleeved white shirt, skinny pink tie already loosened.

"We're not cowgirls," Tammy informed him. "We ride Arabians."

"Oh really? I guess you don't wear spurs then."

He winked at her. Heat surged into her cheeks.

"Of course not," Jenny piped in. "We wear Kangaroos." She gave her feet a shuffle to show off the brand of the back-to-school shoes she was already wearing.

"Well, if you're sure you're not wearing spurs, I guess you won't wreck the carpets. You can come in for some grub — say, what do Arabian riders eat anyway?"

"Pizza?" Jenny asked hopefully.

"Mangoes," Tammy answered, her tone an admonishment to Jenny's woeful lack of authenticity.

"Mangoes and pizza." Mr. Sparks smirked, and pushed off the car. He swaggered toward the squat brick house with brown awnings, a place Buck Rogers would never have lived, even before being frozen in ice half a millennia before the twenty-fifth century. "Have you ever seen a mango?" he called back over his shoulder. "I don't think you'd like them."

The girls followed him up the porch steps. His keys swayed and jingled as he twirled them, his big thumb thrust though the ring. Jenny tugged on the back of

Tammy's T-shirt ever so discreetly. Tammy knew what Jenny wanted without looking at her. She knew Mr. Sparks better than Jenny did. This was her neighbourhood. They weren't ever supposed to go anywhere with strangers, but Mr. Sparks wasn't a stranger.

"Don't worry, girls," he said as he unlocked the front door. "Your horses will be fine right here. This is where I tie mine all the time." He nodded to the alcove where the door dropped into the brick, out of sight from the street.

Tammy stood her hockey stick next to the mailbox and Jenny followed suit.

"Will you show us your car?" Tammy asked, determined to detain him before he disappeared forever into the realm of the ordinary — with his bathroom exactly like the Lanes', and his dinette set, and his television.

He smiled. "Of course," he said. "After."

After what? the girls didn't ask. Then he was inside. He held the screen door for them. Jenny and Tammy gave each other a quick *what now?* glance. Then they, too, were inside.

There was a moment, standing with uncertainty in the front alcove, watching Mr. Sparks progress down the hall, past mirrored wall tiles, that Tammy saw him as two people. *Like the episode of* Buck Rogers in the 25th Century *where Ardala returns, captures Buck and clones him,* Tammy thought. Four duplicates of Buck were manufactured, each assigned a different aspect of his personality. Ardala's drive to take over the Earth using Buck continued to fascinate Tammy. Regardless of her motives, how well would she have to know someone, Tammy wondered, to be able to divide their personality so succinctly into parts?

Mr. Sparks was divided in two. He spun at the end of the hallway, and both Mr. Sparks smiled. One was the Mr. Sparks she always knew — broad-shouldered, kind, funny. The other had serpentine squiggles cast over his face — the ornamental gold strands that ran through the mirror tiles — covering one of his dark eyes. He was the one Tammy was unsure of, the one with outdated decor, and a possible murkiness to him that she couldn't quite name. Tammy followed the real Mr. Sparks, and the other disappeared where the mirrors abruptly ended at the far end of the hall.

The room turned out to be a kitchen/dining room. Dishes threatened to jump from the sink on top of the trio as soon as they entered, but aside from that, there was no danger. Jenny and Tammy stood, turning. They looked at everything, as if examining the possessions of a bachelor would give them clues for what to expect later in life. Until this point, they had known Mr. Sparks only as the guy on the next block with the cool car. Now they knew he had a glossy black dining table and tall skinny chairs that flocked around it. At the other end of the room, life went on rather less elegantly, as the dirty dishes could testify.

Everything in the room was black, white, or gold. White and gold linoleum in the kitchen met white carpet in the dining area. Gold filigree crept up, dividing the kitchen counter from the dining room, a plastic partition of swirling vines. A framed black-and-white poster of Elvis hung on the wall at the head of the table. On another wall hung a mirror, the image of a woman in silhouette painted over it. She wore an old-fashioned hat. Her face was turned away from the viewer, as if she too was looking into the mirror, possibly making adjustments. The two items didn't seem to go together, and Tammy wondered if Mr. Sparks had chosen these things himself, or if they had been gifts, possibly from a past girlfriend. With the exception of the dirty dishes, a haphazard stack of *Sports Illustrated,* and some pencils next to the phone, the room was crisp as a motor inn. The girls could still see the vacuum grooves in the rug from the last time it had been done. The plush pushed this way and that in symmetrical stripes, like a freshly mown lawn; the carpeted side hadn't been walked on in some time. It was as if it had been prepared for them, for all of them, waiting for the moment they gained access.

"How long have you lived here?" Jenny asked, reading Tammy's mind. Mr. Sparks had lived there as long as Tammy could remember, but standing among his things it occurred to her that might not actually be very long in adult years. It occurred to her that adults were like dogs; time was different for them. For every one year of Tammy's, the Stanleys' dog experienced seven. If the size of any given animal determined its experience, the adult would perceive only one-quarter or one-eighth the time that she did.

As unthinkable as it was, one day Tammy would morph, begin to run on their time. She would cease to say, "Are we there yet?" She would simply drive the car silently until she arrived. She would stay up late and watch news reports, talk only of the seasons, the weather, shake her head and say how much neighbourhood children had grown. Her time would come to mean less. She pulled herself back from this bizarre daydream. It really was unthinkable.

With the exception of the kitchen counter, Mr. Sparks' house looked like no one had lived in it yet. It could easily have been furnished on whims from the pages of a catalogue, the way that Tammy and Chris sometimes flipped through, picking one hypothetical item per page they would like to someday own.

"Four years." Mr. Sparks set down his keys on the counter next to a pan that contained a bowl, and a mug stacked sideways inside the bowl. On the Formica counter, the individual keys on the ring fell together with a solid *clunk*.

"Yep," he smiled. He held his arms out wide. His fingertips brushed the maple-coloured cupboards on one side and the gaudy divider on the other. "This is it, the man's castle." Tammy had seen her father make this same expression when boasting, and she realized for the first time that this wide open grin was one of absolute pain.

Mr. Sparks turned away and began to rummage in the refrigerator.

"Mind if we sit down?" Tammy asked.

"Go for it."

"This is a really cool table," Tammy said. "Way cooler than anything out of the catalogue."

"Thanks," Mr. Sparks said. His head popped up from behind the fridge door. "I like it." Tammy saw him now through the holes of gold that separated the two areas. "The kitchen I'm less fond of. It was like this when I bought the house and I haven't gotten around to ripping it out. I work a lot," he said, apologetically, as he appeared on the other side of the counter.

Tammy had a sense these were the exact things he would say if she were his date instead of a not quite twelve-year-old swinging her feet so that they kicked her best friend under the table.

"As it turns out, I don't have any mangoes. Not a one," Mr. Sparks said. He crossed his arms over his chest. "In fact, I don't seem to have too much of anything. If you girls think you can stick around, I'll order pizza. What'dya say? I hate to eat alone."

Orange grease-spotted napkins — *serviettes*, Mr. Sparks called them, though they were only paper towels. Paper towels instead of plates. They sat at the dining room table with Mr. Sparks — Ronnie — between them, parked right under the framed Elvis, so that with every bite, the King looked down on them with hound-dog eyes begging for a bite.

"It's funny, usually I just eat standing up at the kitchen counter. Isn't that funny, after spending all that money on this table?"

They nodded their heads and agreed that it was funny.

For the most part, they ate in silence, until Tammy asked Mr. Sparks if he was really old enough to like Elvis. He laughed a little too long and admitted he supposed he was. Jenny kicked Tammy under the table like she'd said something rude. Tammy quickly amended by confessing she liked the Beatles, so maybe age didn't have anything to do with it. In painstaking detail she explained how one could either like the Beatles or the Stones, according to her brother, and that he liked the Stones, whereas she was a John Lennon fan, tried and true. She could even remember when he was shot, although that was before she had "discovered" the Beatles. She wanted to know where Elvis fit in. Could a person like Elvis if she was a Beatles fan?

"I don't see why not," Mr. Sparks said. He let out a heavy sigh, rubbed his napkin forcefully across his mouth, crumpled it up and threw it into the pizza box. A decidedly masculine gesture. Tammy vowed to remember it.

It was not beyond her understanding that she could never date Mr. Sparks. He was, she knew, old enough to own a house and listen to Elvis. The gift she had been given was that of memory, and she committed everything to it. An hour with Mr. Sparks was an eon for her imagination. So when he said, "Would you like to see the rest of the house?" how could she refuse?

The house was a diminutive version of most of the others in the neighbourhood. Helping Chris deliver newspapers, Tammy had been inside most of them on collection day, at least as far as the hallways. Sometimes farther. From the outside, Mr. Sparks' house had a porch, front and centre. It jutted out like a pouty bottom lip. The door indented. Windows like eyes were placed on either side. Some houses on the street were shuttered. Mr. Sparks' were fitted with sleepy-lidded awnings. Brick or siding, it made no difference, the shape was always the same: square. Tammy had realized early that if she could turn their neighbourhood into a black-and-white movie, there would be nothing to separate them from their neighbours. Atari on a black-and-white TV, the switch on the console flipped from colour to grey, grey to colour, colour to grey — so were divisions easily lost between a player and an opponent, a player and the objects surrounding it. Size was the only distinguisher. Houses with basements always seemed to stand on tiptoe above the others on the block. The foundations were built up in some other colour, blue or grey, like wool skirts. Always, 1950s structure met 1970s interior. Even in the mid-'80s, some things remained the same.

Mr. Sparks' house bordered the area of town known as the VLA, and he had obviously purchased his little square of paradise when its previous owner — a WWII vet — died. The interior consisted of four rooms. The kitchen the girls had already seen. The living room. The bathroom. The bedroom. The living room was similar to the Lanes'. A large window peered into the street. Built-in shelves cloaked one wall. Their painted wood held a couple of bowling trophies. Dust greyed the arms of little bent bronze men. There was a complete stereo system and a black velvet painting of elks. Unlike the Lanes', all the furniture was new.

"What do you do for a living?"

"Ahhh." His brown eyes turned liquid with enthusiasm. He clapped his hands together solidly. "Let me show you."

Into Tammy's head crept all kinds of ideas, none of which came close to reality. Mr. Sparks went into the hall, past the wall of mirrors. The girls followed, and he opened a door.

Jenny and Tammy edged toward the doorway. The room was dark, and Mr. Sparks' back blocked their view. He moved ahead and they hesitated, still in the hallway. They could hear him fumbling. In another moment, the room was illuminated by a small brass lamp. The walls were beige, the carpet was beige, the heavy drapes were beige, and taking up the rest of the space was a gigantic waterbed. Concealed to some extent beneath a beige bedspread, brown leatherette framed the smooth bubble. It might have passed for space-age, with its convex surface, its perfect smoothness, its pregnant shape, its ability to quiver to life. If Tammy hadn't been expecting something entirely less ordinary.

He held out his hands, as if to say *Ta-da!* As if the girls could possibly miss it.

"I sell them," he said proudly. Tammy would never be able to think of him on par with Buck Rogers again.

They lay upon the waterbed for some time. The light leaked in like melted maple walnut ice cream through the beige curtains. Beneath them, the bed wavered with the slightest move. If they lay perfectly still, Tammy told herself, she could suspend this moment. She would leave her body and float upward toward the ceiling. The only thing that would bring her back down would be her commander, saying, "Return to ship, read me."

Jenny and Tammy had performed the perfunctory response to Mr. Sparks' enthusiastic unveiling of his occupation. *His real occupation*, Tammy told herself, *not a side project or cover-up identity.* He sat now, in the living room. She could see him through the door. He was flipping through a magazine. A pair of horn-rims had materialized from nowhere. He was definitely more Clark Kent than Buck Rogers now. Christopher Reeve, though not as Superman. Tammy sighed and the bed shivered. The perfunctory response, in this case, had been to request to sit on the bed, and then to bounce on the bed, and then to get up and jump and somersault on the bed. All of these things the girls had done, and Mr. Sparks had seemed quite fooled by them, enamoured of their affection for the beautiful object he had shown them. He had laughed and looked on bemused for a few minutes before leaving them to it.

Now they lay, digesting pepperoni and the wedge of history surrounding their fallen hero. Through the doorway, across the hall, through the living room arch, Tammy could see him sitting alone, as if in a picture frame. He looked bored now rather than lonely. He was an adult, another species. Like in Venture, the video game set in a dungeon of perilous chambers, she realized that once she had cleared a room of its treasure, she couldn't go back in.

PLAYER 1

Another round of beers was opened. Cindy and Adam left to make out in Marc's workout room at the other end of the basement.

"Don't drink all my beer," Adam said over his shoulder as he lumbered from the room.

"Hey." David swaggered over from the air hockey table, Kenny trailing, bobbing like a red buoy on a string in his wake. Between his index finger and thumb, David held a tightly rolled joint. "You want to smoke this with us?"

J.P. spun quickly from the turntable, nearly dropping the albums he was in the process of lovingly selecting. Judas Priest's *Screaming for Vengeance* landed on the floor, hellion cover face up: red sun in a yellow sky, large robotic bird mid-swoop, talons extended. J.P. clutched the Scorpions, Journey, and Quiet Riot quickly to his legs before they could slide to the floor. "Not in here, man," he said. "If my dad smells that shit, he'll kill me."

"'That *shit*'? It's *goo-oood shit,* man. Fucken A." David held the joint aloft. He peered at it as if its very being was proof of its goodness.

"Yeah, man. Fucken A, fucken A." Kenny sounded like a parrot going through a voice change. Behind square silver-framed lenses, beady eyes skipped with excitement.

"Blame it on Marc." David tossed his hair back off his shoulder.

J.P. shook his head. "That'd be worse."

"Backyard okay?" Kenny was eager as a puppy to please. Only Chris knew Kenny still had issues of *Mad Magazine* in his closet, and that he secretly loved Transformers, the half-human half-car figures *(autobots in disguise)*, and was — in all likelihood — already eagerly gearing up for *Voltron*, the cartoon series which would premiere that fall. Things Chris could tell, but didn't.

J.P. put the records down and followed them out, left Chris with his half-finished second beer. Chris used it to salute when J.P. glanced back. It was one of those moments Chris would consider long after. He sat there sipping in silence with the girls.

When he considered his early grade-school years, playing at Kenny's house, Chris's throat constricted. Kenny laser-shot through rooms of purple velvet wallpaper and yellow linoleum. A phaser-voiced only child. His basement was full of *Star Wars* figures; his bedroom brimmed with chemistry experiments; birthdays and Christmases telescoped into something larger than life. In glass beakers, Kenny distilled essences, hydrogen-peroxide frothy, showed Chris the lighter he had stolen from his father for his "experiments." In the bathroom, Kenny once showed him the pink and orange pages of blue magazines whose titles remained disconnected to the orb-like images they bore (*Playboy*, though it featured *girls, Penthouse*, though setting was obviously irrelevent). And other things, Kenny showed him quietly, hushed tone, excited embarrassment fading easy once a thing had been exposed.

Nothing was more mercurial than a yes-man. If they had kept hanging out the way they did, they would have become Dungeons & Dragons guys like the other grade-grubbers in their class, but the overnight desertion didn't make Chris respect Kenny any more. Seventh grade would have sealed their futures, made them halflings in a dark universe of ever-expanding social circles, constantly waiting for ambush. In retrospect, the repercussions would have been gi-normous to the point of celestial. Chris would have been Short Fry, and Kenny would have been Four Eyes forever.

Still. Kenny had become the little dog from the Warner Bros. cartoon, constantly yipping at David's heels, "Where we going, boss? Where we going?" To think that Kenny had once won Science Fair at so many levels, he had gone all the way to Toronto! On the day it was announced, Mr. Keele had come to the school and stood — with his cracked marble eyes — in the back of the auditorium during the assembly, his wide, blue-stripe tie gathered into a tight triangle under his Adam's apple, which bobbed ceremoniously as he wept. He was so happy. Chris could still recall the exact shape of Mr. Keele's hands grasping Kenny's shoulders. He stood behind Kenny in a constant back-clap, as if showing him off to all congratulators to come. Mr. Keele's meaty pink thumbs clutched, pressed joyously right down to bones, as if all of the energy in his body had fled to concentrate in his fingertips —

Amazing, the way there was no shame to his emotion, how, even afterward, no one said a word against the display. Grade Six. Two years.

Chris tore the label off his beer in one abrupt motion.

"Hey Smart Guy, that means you're a virgin," one of the girls called from the appropriated stereo.

Chris looked down at the intact, damp document in his palm. Glaring at her, he wadded the label up. The wet papery peel flecked away white between his fingertips.

Skin friction-viscous, red with rubbing. Memory had a way of uncurling at inappropriate moments. Smart Guy was the nickname J.P. had given him to replace Short Fry. Earlier that year, everyone in their class had made homemade tattoos on lunch hour, used protractors, and sealed the scratches with Liquid Paper. Chris was the only one who wouldn't do it. That day they called him sissy, fag, and nerd — the girls too. A week later, Smart Guy sprang from their lips with the regularity of a cuckoo popping out of a clock. They all had infected wrists and biceps. Flesh swelled fluorescent around the white, flaking letters. They were forced to show their mothers, and their mothers were forced to buy prescription salves from the drug store. It really pissed them off that Chris had known better.

Chris and Laurel locked eyes. He made a circle with his thumb and forefinger, pinged the remnant of the balled label across the room at Debbie's back. Laurel's lips inched sideways toward home plate, a smile.

In addition to the stereo — instantly seized and subjected to the crotch-grabbing squeals of Michael Jackson — the girls took control of the air hockey table. Its sleek white surface breathed, held the thin puck, hovering, expectant. Slam jam. She shoots, she scores! The air hockey table was one of the big draws to hanging out at J.P.'s. It also didn't hurt that Mr. and Mrs. Breton had gone on vacation, and naively left him in the care of Marc for four days. Sheila and Debbie assaulted the table ends, their bracelets and giggles obstructing the slots. They plunged around the chrome corners indelicately, the asses of their shorts jutting with each sudden jab or block. Julie designated herself some kind of referee; her only real job was to drop the puck for the first play, and act during subsequent disputes, as when it launched off and landed atop the big, brown vinyl bar dinging among the beer bottles. Laurel was sitting alone on the couch, digging her hands into her jacket pockets, even though it was at least seventy-five degrees Fahrenheit in the house.

Chris knew that if he didn't speak to her now, he would only wind up interviewing his Christie Brinkley poster later.

Five Qs for Christie Brinkley

Chris Lane has been sent to interview America's top model — in bed. She's about to reveal her deepest secrets to him. The glamour girl smiles and leans forward. One nimble thumb circles her own nipple.

CHRIS LANE: What makes a woman like you hot? Tell

us, what does THE Christie Brinkley think about at night?

CHRISTIE BRINKLEY: Mmm, if video games were played on vinyl records, you could make them skip. . . . You could play them backwards. . . . (Head tilting with pleasure, thumb and forefinger caressing.) Jump between boards as if they were musical tracks.

CL: Oh yeah, bitchin'. (Continues to stroke self.)

CB: Analog is but an imitation of the world — an imitation of the thing as it is recorded. The game is digital. A mathematics of programming, of circuitry. (Inserting finger into mouth, withdraws glistening.) The game is perfection. There are no skips.

CL: Why am I such a cretin?

CB: I can help you.

CL: I'll bet. . . .

CB: Easy, just relax. (Tosses hair, cups breasts fully in her palms, drawing them up to her chin.) The machine is preprogrammed. It will always continue.

CL: Shall I . . .?

CB: Oh yes!

CL: Yeaaaahhhh. Oh baby . . .

CB: I'm not your baby, Chris. You're not even real. I'm real. You're a dot on the screen.

CL: Christie? Christie?

CB: Sorry, Chris, I have to turn you off now.

CL: Just one more question?

CB: Sorry, Chris, no more questions.

(Reluctantly CL falls asleep, concluding the interview.)

Under the coffee table, Chris balled his toes into fists.

"Don't you want to play?" He tipped back the rest of his beer and tried to seem too cool for words.

Laurel shrugged.

"Do they have games?" she asked, and he felt an immediate affinity, as though they were operating on the same level.

The Atari was in Marc's room, and normally J.P. and Chris had to ask permission to use it, though Marc played once every two weeks to their daily habit. But Marc had gone out. Chris pushed open the door to Deep Purple. The one and only song Marc had taught them to play on his guitar, "Smoke on the Water" seemed the unnamed anthem of that room. "It's about a *bong*, man," Marc had hissed, whisper thick with giggles, while J.P. and Chris fought over who had better mastered the opening chords.

Black and blue waves ridged the folds of the closed

curtains, lending the room a Sears-brand psychedelia Mrs. Breton could not have intended. Chris switched on the overhead. It emerged instantly, pale and globular, like a bulging parental eye between the layers of Marc's chaos. Forty-watt light filtered through the room like old smoke. It hung between the blue shag and the rock flags which cloaked the ceiling in elongated cloth bubbles, their edges thumbtacked into plaster. Narrow rivers of white stucco separated Black Sabbath from Van Halen, and Ozzy from Def Leppard. Against the dark wood panel on the far wall, the classics held court. The Stones. The Doors. Floyd. Chris stood aside for Laurel to go first into a room steeped in otherworldliness, the aroma of older-brotherness: Brut cologne, transuded cannabis sativa, and thick, sandalwood incense burned to cover both the illegal and the human smells. Laurel entered, then Chris, breath meshing with that small and stagnant space of awe.

Chris closed the door, hesitated, left it open just a crack to avoid seeming bold. Laurel's eyes travelled the walls and littered floor. She ignored the only place in the room to sit down, the dishevelled bed. She ran her thumb over the remnant of a Chewbacca sticker, torn diagonally, gummed and worn into the veneer of the top dresser drawer. Chris felt uncomfortable suddenly, as if all of it were his, because, of course, he had brought her there.

"Wanna see something?" Chris reached across the dresser with what he hoped was authority. He picked up an intricately carved wooden box. Flipping up its lid, Chris exposed the proud leaden object. Its oblong shape consumed the length of the box. Chris picked it up, separating it from its home of green felt. The metal was cold to his grip, its series of sturdy silver ridges. He passed it to Laurel, the glass eye and detailing face up. She handled it with contrasting delicacy.

"It's heavy."

"Join the dark side, Luke," Chris said, eyes never leaving Laurel's hands as they traced the contours of the swordless handle, the handcrafted light sabre minus the light.

She straightened her arms, held it at waist level, then quickly ripped it through the air, palpitating a tone deep in her throat. *HmmmWhoooooosh*. The imitation was impressive but her face twitched with embarrassment and she passed the *Star Wars* replica back to Chris.

"J.P.'s brother made it. In shop class. That's why it's a little rough. He's also got throwing stars from a ninja catalogue. But he hides them." Chris rolled the sabre in his shirt to erase the fingerprints. He placed it back in its box, not worrying about the way his T-shirt rode up over his chest as he continued its use as a rubbing cloth.

When he turned back around, Laurel had settled with an understandable amount of hesitation on the edge of the bed.

"What do you want to play?" she asked, leaning forward, nervously, toward the twelve-inch TV on the pop-can-covered desk.

"Your choice," Chris said.

Laurel reached for the open shoebox where the games were kept. She ran one finger down their spines: Video Pinball, Pac-Man, Yars' Revenge, Journey, Missile Command, Warlords, Breakout, Frogger, Defender, Vanguard, Pele's Soccer, Golf, Bowling, Space Invaders, Centipede, and the bitterly disappointing E.T. Their names jumped out in green, yellow, and red as Chris followed her path. She skimmed the black and bone-coloured cartridges, flicking them forward and back against each other, quietly rattling. Her bracelets trailed, falling together on her wrist, *click click*. What would she pick?

"No kung-fu?"

Laurel took off her jacket to play. It lay on the pillows at the head of the bed like a white, lifeless version of her. The shoulder pads hunched the neck up, the sleeves still bunched at the forearms and crossed across the missing chest. She moved the bracelets from her right wrist to her left, so they didn't click while she played. Now Chris knew why the other girls didn't bother playing. Too much prep time.

She'd chosen Venture. She cleared the three rooms on the first board before losing her player in the Serpent Dungeon, partly on account of having entered through the wrong door and having faced three snakes instead of two. Still, she was passable, and Chris respected her for picking Venture. If not the hardest, it was definitely the game with the most obstacles. It fell into that category where — with so many elements in motion — watching other players was key to developing strategy.

Chris had a feeling that if they kept playing, and if he kept talking, she wouldn't kiss him, which was strange, because Chris had been waiting to be alone in the same room with Laurel Richards since spring. He'd thought she didn't even know his name, yet no one had bothered to introduce them when the girls had arrived. Panic broke inside Chris as the hall monster began to form outside the Two-Headed Room. What if it was so obvious he liked her that Cindy or someone had told her? Inside his T-shirt, a droplet of sweat made its way down the centre of his chest to his belly. Chris dodged around a dead dungeon monster and made his exit. If it bothered her, he reasoned, she wouldn't have come here in the first place, and certainly not up here — to Marc's room — with him.

"Do you play at home?" he asked.

"Nah, my mom won't get me one. Says I'll get addicted like that guy, Mickey what's his name, and never go outside again."

"Mickey Newton."

"Yeah, him."

Mickey Newton's greatest accomplishment was shoplifting an Atari 2600 from Zellers back in 1980 when it was still a coveted gaming system. Mickey was twelve then, two years older than Chris, but Chris had heard the rumours ever since. By wearing Mr. Newton's big vinyl parka with the hood up, instant hoodlum-hero status had been achieved.

Chris had learned many things at Joyland by watching Mickey. Firstly, Chris ascertained that anonymity begat fame. He'd never gotten an introduction to guys like Mickey Newton and Johnny Davis. He didn't need one. He knew who they were. He observed their ways, and one day, he too became good enough for them to know who he was. In the same manner, one day Laurel had appeared in Joyland from the other side of South Wakefield, and Chris made a point of finding out her name.

Like Johnny Davis, Mickey Newton was above entering his initials on the machines. A simple row of Xs became his high-score signature. ZZ blazed from Johnny's vacated games (short for ZZ Top). Younger, ambitious video-game guys took note, struggled to find witty ways to represent themselves. Occasionally, they resorted to the most unoriginal: abbreviated obscenities typed in the space provided for winner's initials. Meatheaded Pinky Goodlowe was the exception, tapping the control stick over the onscreen alphabet until PKY filled the dark space. David White became Black — BLK — for Black Sabbath. Kenny's signature was YES. With misplaced loyalty, he continued to use it through the spring of '84, even after the band of the same name had sold out its art-rock roots and "Owner of a Lonely Heart" clung like a wart to the pop charts for a solid twenty-one weeks. Chris had flirted with DEF, but by early '83 he'd decided the best signature was none at all. A row of dashes. A blank line stood out from the screen at a glance, even from across the arcade, like the dangerous flat line of a heart monitor. It had become Chris's legacy as he moved up in rank, rounding the corner and climbing up the metaphorical staircase with an involuntary ease.

Mickey vowed he would have victory over Johnny Davis one day as the South Wakefield champion of Galaxian. The declaration was Mickey's first mistake. His actual downfall was his mother's removal of the Atari, not because it was hot, but because Mickey had stopped doing anything else, including eating. Rumours circulated that the good woman continued to bring him bowls of Kraft Dinner that went untouched. J.P. and Chris visualized a platoon of plates, ketchup gradually hardening as Mickey played on, cracking infinite numbers of game patterns without witness to his genius, until one day she pulled the plug and sent him to his aunt's, or some other never-before-seen relative, who happened to live remarkably close to St. Beckett.

St. Beckett: the closest city with an institution. The

name of the city alone had come to stand for looney, cuckoo, bananas, the funny farm. To Chris (and indeed to nearly all his peers), a person couldn't go within twenty miles of it without it meaning he was *loco*. All this Mickey-lore had occurred the previous year, before Ray Kassar sold $250,000 of his own company stocks, before Atari had crashed and burned, the entire industry heading into a nosedive. Chris had heard a few whispers that Mickey had returned to town. Apparently, he was really pissed to discover Joyland had been shut down.

Chris recounted these details to Laurel with an authority he did not have, as though he and Mickey had been best friends, Chris the one and only witness to his genius and his madness.

"Since you can't play at home, you should come to my house some time. I mean, if you want, you know, maybe."

Chris had located Laurel in the phone book, the name *Richards, K.* in blurred black and white, the stern evidence of her birth. Once Chris had ridden to Cassandra Crescent where she lived, passing quickly on his bike before the mouth of her building. *The Sunset Villa* was stencilled on the side in faded blue looping letters. A four-storey C-shaped structure with stairs and a balcony running the length of each floor, doors opened out onto the balcony instead of an inside hall. California motels in old movies couldn't salvage its appeal, or its peeling pink paint. In the brown-brick bungalowed lap of South Wakefield, the villa's misplaced glamour had degenerated before either Laurel or Chris were born. One of two apartment complexes in town, it sat on the south side of South Wakefield, and Chris's mother said nobody decent lived there. Only Laurel Richards. Chris waited for her to say, *Yeah, sure, I could ride my bike over, it's not that far, that'd be really cool.*

She didn't reply. With mascara-damp eyelashes, lips slightly ajar, she watched the screen where he moved in and out of danger.

He was spending pointless time shooting things, corpses that would kill him if he touched their dead edges. They left blobs in his path to the treasure. He could hear the hall monster growing outside the Skeleton Room and he felt his heart speed up. A choking-hissing-swooshing sound.

"I hear that sound and I know it means instant death."

Laurel rocked onto her knees. "Come on," she said, "You can still outrun him."

Sometimes, no matter how hard Chris jerked the joystick, he didn't stand a chance.

Other times, fate seemed to be on his side.

Winky moved slowly. The red ever-smiling head that was Chris progressed in a straight line toward the exit as the hall monster arched diagonally through the wall, a thunderous growl paving its path. Straight for Chris.

He made it out just in time, clearing the third board.

"Woo," Laurel slapped his shoulder. Her hand settled momentarily in the space beside his neck. "All right!"

Chris arched into her touch instantly. His reflexes took over, moving him toward the thing he meant to move away from. His neck caught her hand between his face and shoulder, held it captive against his cheek. Laurel didn't try to withdraw it. Her brown irises were indistinguishable from the pupils. An excited blue light shone in them. Chris realized too late that it came from the screen and the new game board. Jerking his head up, her hand was free. Her fingers trembled as she brought them up, hovered over his left ear. The touch, a small white shock. Before he could react, her chin came down, and that was how Chris realized Laurel was taller than him: sitting on their knees on Marc Breton's bed, her lips steadfastly inching his open. The controller fell from his hand, and he could hear the electric jolt of a hall monster banging into him. All the blood in his body rushed into his blue jeans.

Her tongue circled his mouth. He didn't know when she gained entrance, or why he hadn't thought to do it to her first. This was the part he'd never been able to practise. He felt her begin to withdraw. His hands jerked toward her, caught in her feathers, tangled among the short strands of her hair. Chris realized his eyes were wide open. He closed them. He let his lips loosen, felt the alive thing inside her face move into his again. He followed it back, and found the warm thick cavity of her mouth, the wet quivery wall of tongue that had retreated and curled up there behind her teeth. All the while, he could feel the rushing blood.

"Shit, the game! The game!" she yelped. She pulled away, made a grab for the fallen joystick twisting on its cord halfway between the desk and the floor.

She was so frantic for it that Chris grabbed the controller and played the last man directly into the Spider Room, where he died an instant death by means of red, shivering spidery electrocution. The beauty, he thought, was that only with Laurel could the game be as important.

She twitched into a giggle fit. Her shoulders shook. V-shaped breasts quivered beneath her black T-shirt like small private entities all their own.

"You were doing so well!" She fell sideways on the bed, rubbed tears from her eyes.

He didn't know what possessed him. He flopped beside her, her jacket lying there, a pillow for his head. The saccharine musk of drugstore perfume surrounded Chris, the empty sleeves of the coat beneath his shoulders to hold him. The real Laurel turned to him, leaning close, the same smell on her.

"Chris . . ."

He could almost taste the soda on her breath again, NutraSweet and lip gloss. A surge of joy crested Chris's ribcage and rushed downward.

Her spontaneity turned serious. "Christopher," she said. She edged intentionally closer. They both looked down at the space she had closed, an inch of blue bedsheet between them. She propped herself up on one elbow, her face a finger away from his face, as she placed one digit upon his lips.

"Chris, I love . . ." She bit her lip. "I love — the way — you play."

That was what she said. What Chris heard was, "I love you."

She put her hands on him then. Though Marc's smell still clung to the covers, Laurel's chalky sweetness drew a cloud around Chris's head. She shoved his T-shirt up, ran the palms of her hands across his scrawny chest.

"Unh . . ." he said, when she hit the nipples, a part he'd never known had so many nerve endings. Then Chris couldn't say anything else or he would have grunted directly into her mouth. Laurel's shirt slid up against his stomach, an inch or two of her skin against his. He knew right then he should just shut up, that if he wanted this to continue, it would, but only if he didn't speak. He lay very still, willing her. His hands were trapped, one beneath her, the other pinned by her arm. Uselessly his hand froze on her back below her bra strap. He kept kissing her, and hoped.

Laurel's fingers moved to the waistband of his jean cutoffs. A second later she was inside. Fly undone, blue Kmart briefs exposed, she rummaged beneath the material. Her hand wrapped around him clumsily, and Chris groaned. Her tongue effectively silenced him. For a few seconds Laurel fumbled, got her bearings, then began to jerk him somewhat harder than he would himself. Chris still couldn't move his hands. In another minute, it would be too late.

She stopped abruptly, edged her shorts down her legs. Their sock feet tangled as she lay down, pressing Chris further into the mattress, the white lining of her jacket coming up crackling around his head, a peripheral halo. Laurel paused, a strange look in her eyes as though she was waiting for something. Then she reached down and grabbed Chris half around the balls and half around the shaft, attempting to yank him toward her, Stretch Armstrong–style. Aware of the impossibility, Chris still said nothing. She scooted down his stomach deliciously. Above Chris, her body became a stethoscope, amplifying. All he could hear was his heart pounding. *Dum-dum, dum-dum,* the dull song subsumed his skin as well as his head.

Laurel freed more of him from his jeans, and with further adjustments, Chris was in.

Consciously, he put his mouth against her ear, kept it there. It was the only normal part of her, the only part that felt definite. Below, he savoured nothing but a warm, silent hammering. The room and pressure closing around him.

Don't jerk into her like an overeager dogboy, Chris said to himself, wanting to laugh and not able to.

Four seconds, and already she was sliding away from

him. Chris tried to go with her, to come out on top. They wound up side by side. The two children lay still for a moment, looking at each other. Her eyes were frightened and determined. Up close, her face seemed less formed. It had the malleability of adolescence, though Chris did not recognize it for what it was. A narrow forehead, ample flaccid cheeks by comparison, and rounded blades of nose and chin that would grow longer and more angular with age. Chris saw only smoothness, a dark freckle here or there, annular eyes, girl.

He reached up her shirt then and felt her. Beyond the elastic of her bra, her breast was smaller and softer than he expected. It wavered in his hand like egg yolk.

Inching his hips forward carefully, Chris felt himself becoming fluid, and thought for the first time about the danger of what they were doing. *Two more seconds,* he told himself. *Just two more seconds.* She pulled his face against her shoulder. The cotton became wet with his breath. She pulled him tighter and tighter against her until Chris couldn't have left if he'd wanted to. Laurel moved his body, her breathing rising around him like fog.

Chris didn't hear the door open. He'd never fully closed it. He didn't see the person in the doorway. The first indication Chris had that they were not alone was when Laurel yelped. The second was a beer bottle flying over his head. It hit the wall behind the bed and shattered. Spray erupted over the two of them. Rivulets of glass poured down the wall, across the pillow in Chris's hair.

"Get — the — fuck — out!" Marc whispered, the words almost inaudible in Chris's shock. From where Chris lay, J.P.'s older brother was an evil force towering over them, at least ten feet tall and capable of sucking all the blood out of the room with those four whispered words.

Chris left Laurel's body only because she sprang away from him. Apparently he could come out as easily as he'd gone in. The evidence of what they'd been doing lay against his left leg.

Before Chris could move, Marc had him by two handfuls of T-shirt, ripped him from the bed.

"You get that shit in my bed? In *my* bed?" Marc knocked him against the wall. A crack of heat heaved through the back of Chris's skull.

Laurel flew across the room to the dresser, her shorts suddenly up, her shirt suddenly straightened. She tremored there for a second; Chris saw her hesitate, then more heat.

Marc pinned his throat with one elbow. "What's this?" he asked, reaching down between them.

Not that, Chris thought. "Don't —" he choked. "Fuck —"

"What? Don't fuck? Don't. Fuck." Marc laughed. His paw swiped around between Chris's thighs, caught his dick unintentionally, then lunged against it, bagging him. Chris crumpled forward but Marc continued, ungreased the wad that had landed there in blissful surprise during his own, far-less-welcome entrance.

"Don't fuck. You're damn right you don't fuck, not in my bed. Here's what you can do with this." His hand was warm and rough. He brought it up to Chris's lips. Mashed smeared fingers against them. Chris bit down and wouldn't open. Marc's other hand prised Chris's nostrils. The room slowly blued. Laurel screamed, and then J.P. appeared in the doorway. Chris's eyes watered; blood welled beneath his lips; his mouth reluctantly opened. The hand smashed in, congealed salt smudging Chris's teeth and chin.

There was no place to go. If he went back to the party now, he would run at Marc, attack him, flailing, essentially sign his own death warrant. Slowly, Chris's BMX wobbled past A. J. Mitchum Fabricating, the South Wakefield faucet factory, and the cannery where his mother spent days stuffing strips of pork into the beans. Smoke rose against the night in plumes, feathered sulphurous stains against the sky. The town was never asleep, but its insomnia was still and submissive. Chris was too ashamed to cry. At the very back of the cannery parking lot, the cement gave way to a cornfield that had been burnt and left fallow that particular year. Beyond it, Chris knew there was nothing but the highway on the other side, other fields, and infinite rows of telephone-pole webbing. The land was flatter than a sheet of glass. Chris let the bike clatter against the concrete, echo through the empty lot. He stepped off the cement.

There were so few lights he could count them. If the sky was dark, the horizon was darker. A thick black line blotched by the occasional tree.

He turned in three directions. Black line. Black line. Black line.

He put his hands in his pockets and took a deep breath. When he pulled them out, a quarter leapt with them, landed on the mud in front of his feet. Tails. Chris didn't stoop to pick it up.

Behind him, the small town had managed to cut the horizon, set up factories of light, which quickly, violently bleared.

LEVEL 10

Donkey Kong

PLAYER 1

The uneven crescent in front of the building was littered with children — they rolled out of nowhere. Two kindergarten girls on a Big Wheel barrelled toward Chris. They both had sloppy pigtails, one brunette, the other blonde. The brunette hunched on the back, fingers gripping white to the plastic seat as the blonde propelled them forward. The blonde screeched backward on the pedals just before she collided with Chris's front wheel. Stones scattered. He glanced up nervously at the stucco castle before him. *The Sunset Villa.*

"My friend wants to know if you'll marry her," said the blonde, jerking a thumb at the one in back, who appeared to have little choice.

Chris's forehead furrowed. "Sure," he said. "One condition."

He was informed, between giggles, that Laurel lived on the top floor, #48C. They led him around back, pointed to the aqua-blue walkways that segmented the bubblegum pink building into horizontal fourths: plastic flower boxes and dirty, daisy-shaped windmills; beer cases stacked up to the windowsills. Some of the windows had floral bedsheets up instead of curtains, but Laurel's didn't. Beside the door identified as hers, an oversized patio umbrella crammed against the rail and the wall. Its fringes waved in the wind, little white knotty fingers.

"Shame shame, double shame," the blonde screamed at her friend as they fled around the front of their building.

Chris scraped his bike against the stucco, leaned it without locking it. He climbed the steel stairs that bridged the back apartments, each footstep ringing. When he reached the first landing, he stood with the imprecise drumming of blood in his veins before he turned and clambered down again. If he could have written a whole song using just the words *chicken shit,* it would play on an endless loop, clicking into place and turning over like an eight-track as he rode away. He grabbed the bicycle and broke fast through the hard ruts of weeds in the railroad yard — avoiding the small peeled eyes in front of the building. White-knuckling the rubber tread of the handgrips, he thought of Doyle's sofa girl for the umpteenth time. Laid out, exposed. Unaware of someone watching. Somehow, it didn't seem so unusual now.

"I'm not coming over." Chris sat at the table, phone propped against his ear, the foundations of a card house on the table before him. His fingers trembled as he added a new layer. "Not as long as that imbecile lives there." An A-frame of cards leaned against one another, wavered, and stayed.

"Is he there? You didn't just repeat that. Yeah, yeah you did. In front of him. Well, swift one." Chris added a new pyramid.

"Haha," he said, voice flat. "It's so funny." Without provocation, the top level collapsed. Chris swiped one hand through the bottom row.

J.P. sat in Chris's desk chair, legs out on the bed, sweat-socks crossed at the ankles. His lanky legs wore a thick dark sweater of wires. He punched down the keys of the Casio, having sampled the sound of himself belching. The resultant chords burped through air.

"So how come she let you?"

"I hate that thing." Chris cursed, gave him a look. J.P. knew Chris had gotten it for his last birthday. He'd hoped for a guitar; even an acoustic would have held more dignity than the mini Duran Duran. Uber-gay. "Turn it off."

"But we could make beautiful music together." J.P.'s lips shot out like Mick Jagger's, half-kissy, half-sucky. He made a slurping noise, which Chris ignored, glancing down at the pocket video game in his hand. J.P. straightened his feet out and nudged Chris with them.

Chris kept playing the game.

J.P. nudged again, digging his toes in.

Chris slid toward the edge of the bed. "Don't be a goof."

"You're pussy-whipped," J.P. spoke into the Casio. "Have you phoned her since?"

"I don't want to talk about it."

"Puss — puss — pussy — pussy-whipped —" the Casio bleated as J.P. fingered the keys. Three octaves of pussy. Chris glared at the thin white plastic keys beneath the dirty crescents of J.P.'s nails.

"Cut it out." Chris tossed the game aside. "She probably thinks I'm a creep and a perv, and a wuss to boot." Chris's voice rose and cracked. One arm came up repeatedly, the hand at the end of it bunched. They had both avoided any mention of what had happened afterward: a scramble and a toss-out amid J.P.'s protests and David White's wisecracks. Adam Granger didn't bother emerging from the basement, the workbench either less sacred to Marc than his own bed, or else simply unnoticed.

"There isn't anything to tell."

J.P. kicked Chris off the bed, his legs suddenly straightening, power unprecedented.

The room wheeled. Corners and ceiling ended in an abrupt crack when Chris's head made contact with the floor. Chris twisted his feet loose of the sheets that followed. He stood quickly, axis off. He sprang up, body still sideways, not navigating, but rather, falling at J.P. Full force, he hammered fist into nearest body part — in his vertigo, shoulder rather than face.

J.P.'s hand bisected Chris's chest, pushed him backward, fast and easy. Chris springboarded back up from the bed, stopped under J.P.'s glare.

"You should be careful." J.P. said, the threat enough to cause Chris's breath to hitch. J.P. rubbed the spot where Chris had pounded him. His eyes slitted. "Her mom and dad were first cousins, you know."

Chris's ribs filled with fire. "You're starting to sound just like your stupid brother."

J.P. didn't say anything. He tipped his head back, gazed up at Chris where he stood. Calmly, he pressed several notes on the Casio in slow progression. A simplistic one-handed death march sounded through the room, made up of one-word vulgarity. "Pussy — pussy — pussy — pussy — pussy — pussy —" Chris's head throbbed.

"At least you don't have to live with the guy . . ." J.P. said finally, snorting. He turned his head and spat through the screen on Chris's window. A bubbled white strand hung between the thin black squares, before it dribbled down on the outside.

PLAYER 2

Tammy's hockey horse lay limply in the driveway where she had dropped it after returning from Mr. Sparks' house.

Mrs. Lane was in hysterics. Contradictory commands sprang out. *Where've you been? Get out of my sight! Don't even think about going anywhere!* She gripped a Bic lighter in her fist, as if she would strike Tammy with it, set her aflame. Tammy took the most reasonable option under the circumstances.

"It's your own fault," Chris told her when she tried to take refuge in his room. "They're worried you'll wind up like one of those kids in the McMartin School. You can't go knocking door-to-door all the time. Shit happens. Molestation, Satanism, sex rings," he expounded in response to her blank look. "Don't be a retard." The door closed in her face.

Tammy descended the porch steps, sat facing the driveway. Blue tubing snaked through the grass around the Scotts' house. Water spilled onto the curb, sloshed down the street, dropped through the slats of the sewer grate. Through the window screens of the Lane house, her parents' voices jumped over one another, occasionally landed atop each other and became muddled. Tammy leaned her head on her elbow, watched the pool water drain away.

She sprang off the porch and picked up the stick, threw one leg over it, and trotted around the house into the backyard. Two rungs had been hammered into the tree trunk, a small compromise in the name of Tammy's new friendship. A pulley had also been rigged — with Mr. Lane's help — for hoisting books up to the Stadium in a basket, her Walkman and homemade cassettes. She climbed in silence, up into the seven o'clock humidity, the dusk thick with gnat colonies and people calling their kids to come home. The branches bit into her bare feet, her abandoned flip-flops like small blossoms at the base of the tree. From the top she could watch the pool next door being drained and refilled. Partway up the trunk, she stopped.

The curtains were open and the lights were on. Chris jerked around his room, from the dresser to the bed, back to the mirror, to the desk. The bedroom window was high. His head and shoulders floated in disconnect, a blue alligator shirt open at the collar, at his clavicle, the spark of a gold chain from Zellers he had taken to wearing.

Hunched, one hand cupped his ear, though he wasn't wearing the headphones. He twisted then turned back, a scowl marring his mouth, as if he were trying to hear something. His pacing cancelled out interaction with anyone outside of the empty room. In silent petulance, he passed out of Tammy's line of vision, his head down.

In another frame, her mother was rinsing the supper dishes. An angry fork scraped ceramic. Mr. Lane slumped against the counter on the opposite side of the room. His face was like a brown, popped paper bag.

Tammy wrapped her arms around the tree trunk. The bark pressed into her cheek. She stayed that way, letting the imprint work its way into her skin. Then she felt around the trunk for the small grooves, like lines in somebody's back. When she found them, she curled her fingers in and began to shimmy upward, bare feet curled around the coarse cortex.

For three days the pool remained empty. From the top of the tree, the hole seemed even deeper. Ladders hung impotently from the concrete, bottom rungs extending only partway down the blue liner. The deep end plunged away from the shallow — lopsided and dry. In the bottom of the crater, next to the small black plate, two leaves had been sucked together. Their dark wet shapes overlapped on the pale bottom.

The liner was coming out, a new one going in.

In carpenter overalls, Mario ran up and down the platform. Jump the barrel or climb to safety? Options were limited; swiftness imperative. At the top of the screen, Mario's girlfriend, Pauline, stood patiently beside Donkey Kong. In the arcade version, the word *Help!* wavered over her head. Atari was a cosmos of restrictions. Tammy's man grasped the ladder, single-runged, too late. The barrel bombarded him. He spun and died. Her second player began again at the bottom of the construction site, repeated the trek up the beams to the building's roof, where the magnificent digital ape stood beating its chest. On the third floor of scaffolding, Mario snatched the hammer and began to smash the barrels as they rolled toward him. Tammy smiled. In another second, without warning, the hammer disappeared. Just when she was feeling most powerful, she found her player crushed, returned once again to the bottom of the screen.

On the second board, there were fireballs to avoid. But Mr. Lane came over and reduced the screen to fuzz with a flick of his finger before Tammy could make it that far.

"Quit playing this —" he gestured abruptly "— stuff. You're free. Just don't wind up in someone else's kitchen today." His gaze softened as it fell on Tammy's face. Mrs. Lane called his name from the other room. He smiled, briefly, the corners of his bottom lip tucking under. "Get outside before we change our minds."

Workmen, large and beer-bellied, rolled around the edges on their knees, workpants gapping with bum cracks. They shouted out measurements to a younger guy. His ash-brown hair feathered back from his face, but was cut short in a square line at the back, giving his thick white neck the look of an entire country. When they went away, they took the old liner with them in the back of their truck, folded up sloppily, sticking out the gate, like a used maxi-pad rolled in toilet paper, the wet seeping through the tissue. It trailed a thin line of water down the street. Tammy climbed on her bike and followed it all the way to south South Wakefield.

LEVEL 11

Donkey Kong Jr.

PLAYER 2

Charcoal streaked the air. Porch parties and barbecues echoed through the streets. A couple of kids not much younger than Tammy ran from a plastic turtle pool to their porch in underpants and T-shirts. They flapped their hands and howled. A steady *clink clink* replied as older hands exchanged beer bottles. Screen doors slammed. A jumpy feeling grew inside Tammy as neighbourhood moms began to lean over porch and balcony rails to call their kids in for supper.

She shouldn't be here.

She should be home.

She looked at her digital watch. Five-thirty was supper without fail at the Lane house, even in the summer. She pedalled slowly up the street, set one foot down at the stop sign, scanned for movement. After the truck had pulled into a small compound with blue siding and wire fencing, the men had been quick to abandon their workplace. The younger one had headed in her direction — walking so snailish, Tammy had been forced to duck into a park to wait before following. Now she had lost him.

She crossed the street and dropped her bike at the curb. She hooked her toes into the wire diamonds of the fence and stood tall.

At one end of the railroad yard, stacks of rusted blue oil drums sat shoulder-to-shoulder. Unlinked cargo cars squatted, some gleaming, others graffitied with desperate messages that would roll across the province and be read at crossings, cargo loaded and unloaded behind those words, in industrial yards in towns both like and unlike South Wakefield: *Brent + Candy* emblazoned in dripping black. Alongside it lay a long metal flatbed — *Eat Shit and Die* scrawled across it. Though the second was written in green, the letters had the same deflated-balloon look. Tammy wondered where Brent and Candy were now. The other end of the field offered nothing but tracks fading into the horizon. Then, a feathered brown head popped up from behind the flatbeds, hoisted its owner up onto the platform, and began to walk the length of the *Brent + Candy* car. He had shed the top of his uniform, now nothing but a white muscle shirt over an obvious mat of chest hair. He was talking to himself. Tammy could tell because he raised one hand and lowered it, shaking it up and down à la Paper-Scissors-Rock.

His shoulders were like bowling balls, and when he turned his head to stare off in the direction of a pink apartment building, Tammy made a positive I.D. by the thick white expanse of his neck. The successful spy quickly mounted her bicycle and sped clandestinely back to the safe house, control.

In her mind she had already taken to calling him the Rabbit, though he was more of an ash-brown ape. The term came from the *Big Book of Spy Terms,* the rabbit being the target in a surveillance operation.

A small pair of portable field glasses had been liberated from the Lane garage. Their twin eyes had been squeezed flat, compact. They lay on the bottom of Tammy's wire bicycle basket; a brown paper bag (rations) hid them from the top. Tammy had scheduled a lunch break, then a status check of the bubble-pink building that had drawn her impulsive target yesterday. The playground was a cover stop, had Tammy the depth of espionage wisdom to realize it.

Children screamed like seagulls. The bright wavering dots of their T-shirts stretched between the chains of the swing sets. Their running shoes kicked up the sky. Their heads were thrown back. The longest hair dragged in the sand. Tammy headed for the ship-shaped wooden climber in the centre of the park, bumping across the grass. Its strange emptiness ambushed her with gratitude, and she stood on the pedals and pumped hard and fast. She carefully scaled one end, its starboard side a ship's netting. The spiderweb of chains shook beneath her shoes and pinched her fingers. When she reached the top, she swung over the rail and settled on the log catwalk. She took out an apple and began to eat.

Thirty yards away, teenagers tangled beneath the trees. A skintight girl of jeans in spite of the heat. A shirtless boy of wristbands. The length of her arm became the boy's; he perused from the tank-top strap down to her wrist, stopped at her hip, sidled closer, snakelike, to make contact with his body, lips. Tammy turned and stared across the park at nothing in particular. The merry-go-round. The bobbing birds held up on industrial coils of wire. The glider on its taut cable, stopped halfway down the tailored incline. Its handles stuck out from its head of gears like a pair of large curved ears. Crunching down on her apple, she wished the couple would go someplace else.

Tammy had kissed a boy — just once — Joshua Grenwald, the final day of fourth grade. She had lost her nerve at the last minute and kissed his cheek, up high beside his ear. Then she had run off across the playground. Sex was an "adult connection, a closeness between a man and a woman." That was how Mrs. Sturges had described it to Samantha, and how Sam had described it to Tammy. When Sam repeated it, she always rolled her eyes or raised an eyebrow when she intoned the word *closeness*. If it was an adult thing, Tammy reasoned, how come she had never seen adults doing anything even remotely related to it? All they ever did was hold hands. Teenagers were kiss-o-matic, groping in the grass, wandering South Wakefield with fingers stuck in one anothers' back pockets. Tammy couldn't remember the last time she had seen her parents kiss.

Suddenly, a soft shuffling. She was not alone on the

climber. Tammy turned and surveyed the location. Kids still pumped furiously on the swings, faraway twitters. The sand below her was barren. Her eyes fell on the cabin at the far end of the climber, tucked beneath — a small enclosed area, four feet cubed at most.

She froze, consulted a mental spy guide. Burned, burned, burned. To remain still was stupid. She was out in the open; whoever was inside could see her through the peepholes. So long accustomed to being the passive probe, she could only hope now to become a double agent. From CIA to KGB. With what she prayed would look like confidence, she pitched her apple core through the air toward the garbage can. It fell short, landed in sand. She traversed the catwalk, slid down the fireman's pole, and peered through one of the holes in the wood into the cabin.

The entire area was taken up by an enormous man. His white T-shirt glowed in the dark half-light, arms folded across his broad chest, and in one of his hands, a tallboy of beer. A running-shoed foot propped just under the eyehole Tammy peered through. They stared at one another. It was him. The Rabbit. The ape-rabbit.

Tammy said, "You're too big to be in there."

He didn't say anything. He took a sip from the can, eyes never leaving hers.

"Don't you know that's where little kids go pee?" she said.

Immediately he struggled up, hit his head on the wooden ceiling, crawled slowly out the tiny doorway.

"You're the pool man," Tammy said, tentatively. "I saw you from my tree. You were taking measurements for my neighbour's pool."

He squinted at Tammy as though he thought he might

recognize her. "Sh-i-i-i-i-t," he drawled, and quickly corrected himself. "I — guess so. 'Smy dad's company."

"You shouldn't drink beer in the park."

The guy shrugged, brushed back wings of bangs. He blew up his lips with a breath for no apparent reason. "Got any more advice for me?"

"Maybe." Tammy leaned back against the wooden bow. If she were with either Samantha Sturges or Jenny Denis right now, they would have already flown to the opposite end of the park. But Jenny was on vacation. And it was the third time Tammy had encountered the Rabbit in as many days. A sense of purpose filled her, pricked her skin like the splinters in the huge wood beams of the climber. She gave the ship wheel a vigorous spin. "What's in that big pink building you stand outside?"

The Rabbit's eyes narrowed. "Why do you follow people?"

No one had asked her this before.

The question sent a thrill of secrecy through her, and the answer — though she did not possess the wizardry to verbalize it — widened the gap between them, giving her a special upper hand.

As they stalked across the railroad yard, Tammy's bicycle cut a line in the grass. She took four steps to each of his. The pink and blue building bloomed like a scar on the horizon. A girl lived there. The girl. His. The Girl and the Rabbit.

The Rabbit gestured vaguely. "I could take her away from all of this."

"How?" Tammy asked. When he didn't say anything

— simply extended his hand — she passed him the spy glasses. “She’s a kid and you’re a grown-up.”

He laughed when she said the word *grown-up,* a dead engine sputter, and swore. “How old are you, like, twelve?”

Tammy drew back her shoulders with importance. “Thirteen,” she lied. A year and five months shrivelled up and crept into oblivion.

His eyes were hidden by the miniature binoculars, which, in front of his round face, were even littler. A small smile hung itself on the corner of one stubbled lip.

“You don’t know her.” He didn’t seem to be listening. He lowered the field set. “She’s not like other girls her age. Believe me, I should know. She may look fourteen, but inside . . .” His hand made a poetic twist in the air Tammy interpreted as his lack of language to do her justice, though it could just as easily have been obscenity. He turned toward Tammy and grimaced, an upside-down smile, face full of bewilderment, possibly fear.

“She’s an old soul. Like me.” He tapped his sternum with the baby blue binoculars.

Forgetting her earlier fib, Tammy said, “I play soccer with girls her age.”

He shook his head, unconvinced. He swore again, the sound of it inoffensive, comical, zephyrean. He had a broad, open face that was likeable.

“I’m Pauline,” Tammy said. “What’s your name?”

He extended one meaty paw to shake hands. She hesitated, took it. In comparison, her hand was thin, disk-like, inconsequential as a coin between his fingers. “Adam Granger.”

PLAYER I

Padded leather hugged his ears, and Chris ducked with the weight of the headphones. He closed his eyes and let the music form a wall between himself and the rest of the room, where Tammy lay reading on the couch, her head in their father's lap, the television now blaring silently.

The finger-picked opening of the Scorpions' "Still Loving You" spilled into Chris's ears, shook him to the core. The whispered first verse built into straining climax and Chris grasped the tape cover in his fist, blindly. His chin thrust out, Tilt-a-Whirling to the song's beat. Behind his lids, Laurel transformed into the mysterious woman from the black-and-white cover, a half-nude evening-dressed fantasy in his arms, skin shadowed at its softest points, dark head thrown back, lips showing the trace of a smile as he lay the most chaste kiss upon her throat. Between the dirge of Klaus Meine's vocals and the surge of Rudolf Schenker's guitar, Chris clung to the image, crossed and uncrossed his sneakers, slouched down into the velour recliner.

The music climbed, then faded from one ear. Chris opened his eyes. He unhooked the headphones, jiggled them. He settled back down. The song smoothed.

Absently, Mr. Lane began to stroke Tammy's hair. His thick fingers fluttered over her brown head tenderly.

"I will be there, I will be there," a voice murmured in Chris's ear. His left ear only.

Mr. Lane stared at the television. Tammy turned a page. His hand stilled. She glanced up, backward. He didn't notice. Her head wriggled, a command. He looked down. They exchanged glances.

Schenker ran up and down the strings as if he were swinging from them. Chris pushed the working side into his ear with his fingertips.

Mr. Lane smiled, lay his hand across the crown of Tammy's head, continued stroking.

Chris snapped the tape player off, pulled the headphones out by the cord, went to check the adapter in the stereo. He yanked the cord out again, tossed the headphones forcefully into the seat he had vacated.

"They're not working well anymore," he said.

"Already?"

Light pitched a patchwork of vines across Chris's closed face, the white and green of the curtains Mrs. Lane had chosen for his room earlier that month. Chris had shrugged, *I don't care, I don't care,* to each suggestion from the catalogue, sitting on the scourge of the old comforter while Mrs. Lane grandly tore down the juvenile wall covering — a paper museum of antique cars — small shreds of it sticking like ghosts. Perhaps she had been urged to redecorate after brooming the sock knots and popcorn kernels of Kleenex from beneath the bed, but Chris had no proof except that Tammy's room had gone elaborately untouched. Now the light was thick and willowy through the cotton-poly, and Chris turned over. He ignored his father's command to get up. Mr. Lane must have leaned through the doorway, watched his son yank the pale blue sheet over his back and head with a hand more alive than his noggin.

Chris awoke later that morning to the sound of breaking glass. Across the street, the VanDoorens were transporting materials from one truck bed to another, a wash of fragments falling. Immediately Chris went to the Atari, ignoring Tammy's pleas to watch *The Price Is Right.*

"Ten minutes," he told her, and collapsed into the easy side-to-side of it, a state of simple hand-eye forgetfulness. Time was allowed to pass unnoticed outside the borders of the screen. Ten minutes buckled into twenty, twenty to thirty. Eventually, Tammy won by squawk factor.

Defeated, Chris jumped on his bike and rode to the donut shop, where there was a Donkey Kong Jr. In Donkey Kong Jr., the game roles suddenly reversed; Mario became the villain, a captor, and the ape a trapped, tormented creature needing to be saved by his son, a diapered hairy version played by one Chris Lane. He stoicly gripped the controller. The baby gorilla frowned, face full of emotion.

By this time next week, Chris would be scuttling through the halls of the high school like all the other ninth graders, searching desperately for room numbers. A couple of the older guys he knew would send him to the opposite side of the school for a room they knew was just around the corner, others would give him an affectionate and thoroughly undeserved gotchie pull in the bathroom between classes, maybe even gas pedal him like a gradeschooler: tip him upside down, use his ankles like a steering wheel, accelerate a cruel sneaker against his crotch. He could already imagine it with clarity.

"Faggot" would follow him. There was no doubt that J.P. had deliberately deleted Laurel's role from the scene in Marc's bedroom. Given the lack of information forthcoming from Chris, the cum-eating episode had already superceded what came before it, he was certain. *Chris "cum-eater" Lane, come over here.* He could hear the easiest and kindest of taunts; the unkindest he didn't want to imagine. After-the-facts could be uglier than actuals. Smart Guy and Short Fry were lifeboats now.

Almost more imposing was the actual idea of faggotry. Chris had never known a real-life gaylord, though they'd been weeded out like McCarthy reds on the playground. At some point between Grades Four and Eight, everyone had had his week in the role of the faggot, whether it was a one-recess boycott or perpetual gym classes of last-player-picked and hard-whipped dodge balls to the balls, hockey stick slashes to the nuts, no doubt bruising tennis-ball bright. Alone among clapping hands and backslaps. Did Kenny Keele count? With his JCPenney catalogue haircuts, his incomplete baseball-card sets, secret beakers full of urine and food dye, he was perhaps the furthest along the queer metre. The Robin to Chris's third-rate Batman. And if Kenny was gay, undoubtedly Chris couldn't be so far removed . . .

Sure, he assured himself. Sure he liked girls. But he also liked wanking it.

He swung hand-over-fist upward. Former hero Mario had sent traps down the vines, their teeth clamping hungrily toward Chris, Chris the next-generation ape in this post–Donkey Kong version. Down and up again. He was having his third bad game in a row. He knew that when danger was near, it was faster and easier to slide down the vines than to try to outclimb it. Yet he kept trying to get above it, dying needlessly. *Even in the world of video games,* Chris thought, *gravity applies.*

Adam Granger came into the donut shop with Cindy.

She headed up to the counter, opening her jean purse. As he passed, he gave Chris a jab in the kidneys. Adam's eyes were full of chlorine, though neither of them smelled it.

Chris acknowledged him with a nod, proceeded to the second board where he had to scale the chains, avoid the birds, force the keys upward to unlock his papa, the mighty gorilla in a cage at the top of the screen. Chris pinged one of the birds with an apple.

"Whatever, whatever —" Adam was saying to Cindy. "Something chocolate. Maybe sprinkle. Oh yeah, sprinkle, sprinkle, sprinkle."

Chris's eyes flicked sideways for a fraction of a second. Adam's hand had settled on Cindy's back pocket. Immense fingers protruded from a fingerless black leather glove.

Chris purposefully let himself kick the bucket, the baby ape falling to the bottom of the screen, waving his arms in a flailing parody of death.

"Granger," he said, practically squeaking.

Adam pivoted slowly.

"You got any?" Chris lifted his fingers to his lips quickly.

Cindy singled several quarters from her shoulder bag and slid them across the laminate, and the three of them left together.

Without discussing it, the teenagers headed down the street toward Joyland and into the back alley. Adam led the way, lumbering, feathering his hair with his fingers. Chris trailed one hand along the wall. Stray bumps of mortar flicked his fingernails. The colours of the lolling open mouth lingered under his flattened palm.

Adam held the joint in his mouth and attempted to

spark it up. He flicked the lighter a few times, took a quick, forceful toke, managed to illuminate the tip. The paper glowed and shrivelled slowly. He held his breath, face a tight line with the effort. He extended the joint to Chris. The weed deposited a burning across his palette. Chris sucked hard on it anyway, flint floating through his throat. He held it down and stared at the fat red mouth on the wall. Adam snickered around his own mouthful of smoke. Cindy sat down on the ground and peeled open their donuts.

Chris's stomach knotted. He was a new Chris. A Chris who did not care. Instant-satisfaction Chris. Anti-introspective Chris. Cool-at-all-costs Chris. He took another drag and tried not to cough it out.

"Hey." Adam nodded toward Joyland. "Donkey Kong. 'How high can you get?'" It was a reference to the original game, the apes that appeared in between each board, the slogan spelled out across the screen as the player moved up a level and continued climbing. Chris burst out laughing, the smoke lost. He leaned against the wall choking. Choking and giggling.

"Has it hit you already?" Adam asked.

Chris leaned against the building and laughed. "I don't feel anything." There was only one reason for him to be there, and it had nothing to do with getting high. "Granger," he said. He passed the joint back.

"Hey . . . you ever . . ." Chris cleared his throat. "Y'ever knocked someone off his bike and just . . . pounded him?"

Adam paused, doobie halfway to his lips. Through half-stoned, skeptical lids, he seized Chris up.

"Sure." He inhaled.

Then the air came at Chris, thick and throbbing. He felt the spot his ass made where it leaned against the wall. He knew it would be covered in a layer of white dust whenever he pulled away, but he didn't feel he could move. He would stand right there in that same spot forever. He loved everything about that spot. He loved everything. He had never been so happy. He laughed until his eyes teared up.

"Oh shit," he said. His voice was loose and far away. "Shit, shit, shit." He wiped his eyes and looked down at the hands he had wiped them with. They were dusty from running them along the surface of the wall.

Cindy looked up from the parking block where she sat, laughed through lips ringed with chocolate.

"Hey . . ." she said. "Hey Smart Guy."

PLAYER 2

Ahead of her, the building exposed a bulbous splash of colour above its concrete knees.

Tammy picked her way through the Yellow House's backyard. Every kid to the east of the VLA subdivision had learned that if one walked between the Yellow House and the Rock Garden House, the hedge at the back of both properties could be hopped, landing the explorer, approximately, at Joyland.

Today, Chris was the rabbit. Prompted by his annoyance at losing the television, Tammy had slowly trailed him, a simple, reticent revenge. His destination — the donut shop — proved dull. She had been on the verge of entering to persuade him to buy something for her, when her original rabbit appeared from nowhere. He pulled up in the rusted pool-duty pickup truck — *Granger Inground* emblazoned on the side — and a slim blonde girl with hoop earrings and jelly shoes jumped out. It was Cindy Hambly, who had been in Chris's class since kindergarten. She walked past a stunned Tammy without acknowledging her. Adam was on the other side of the truck, his back to Tammy where she sat on a parking block, bike leaning against the shop sign. It hadn't taken a genius to deduce their destination when the three of them exited together and headed down the street, Adam abandoning his vehicle, Chris leaving his bike locked where it stood against a parking metre.

Doubling back, Tammy reduced the danger of being caught. *When in doubt, always double back*. Her brain had begun a parade of such basic adages, for this was the first time since she had witnessed Diana Scott's kiss that anything had come of Tammy's low-key loitering. The encounter in the park with Adam Granger had happened so quickly she'd had no time for basic spy prep. Now she knelt, wiping her sweat-lined palms on the grass of the Yellow House. Furtively glancing over her shoulder at its dark windows, she missed the joint as it made its first round. When she peered through the branches again, careful to keep head low, she saw only Adam Granger smoking. Chris was laughing at something he had said.

How they knew one another, and why they were there, smoking together, Tammy couldn't decipher. But it was bad. Breath swung through her ribs. Why was Adam with Cindy, when only yesterday he'd told her about the girl who lived in the Sunset Villa? Cindy Hambly lived on Bienville, directly behind Running Creek Road, one crescent over from J.P.'s. And why was her brother hanging out with them at all?

Behind Tammy came the scuffle of a hose tugged across concrete. Someone had emerged from the Rock Garden House through a side door, still out of sight. Tammy half-army-crawled, half-bolted, took off down the Yellow House sidewalk running.

LEVEL 12

Joust

PLAYER 1

Laurel pushed the cart through the wide, refrigerated aisle. A woman with skin the colour of sliced ham stood next to her, behind the open cooler door. She had one of those mouths that didn't quite close. Through the half-misted door, fat bulged her bright pink stretch pants as she bent. She picked up a carton of eggs, opened it to check for cracks. Her watery arms wavered. Laurel's mom. He wondered what her dad was like, whether it was true what J.P. had said.

Chris looked away. When he glanced back, Laurel was

staring straight through him. He lifted his hand in a little wave, but she didn't blink. The glass door between them fogged.

Mrs. Lane turned into the cereal aisle and Chris manoeuvred the cart after her. Tongue dry, he held up a box of Capt'n Crunch. He clung to it, juvenilely, in reverence of the other capt'n, the first phone-phreaker. Mrs. Lane shot him a look, and the capt'n's blue hat fell back into line beside the Sugar Pops bear and the Booberry ghost. She handed him a box of Life to put in the cart (packaged in Don Mills, a name as flat and strip-mallish as South Wakefield). Catching his disdain, she defended the choice with commercial sarcasm. "Well, *Mikey* likes it." She moved to the end of the row and began examining the coffee filter selection. She picked up a package of Size No. 4 (a stellar name, Stellarton) and held onto it. Without looking up, she asked, "Did you know that girl?"

Chris shrugged.

When they reached the checkout, he saw Laurel two lines over, sticking her head up like E.T. Over the chocolate bar racks he watched her crane her neck, black hair push upward above her thin curved brown throat. The red eye under the countertop wavered across the bottoms of packages, bleeding a momentary stain of light into them, instantly seeing their value.

Chris loaded the paper bags into the cart, wheeled it out fast, his mother still dealing out bills.

Tammy once told Chris, in a misplaced fit of trust, that she imagined God as an old man with a beard. She'd gone on to confide that when she had done a particularly bad thing (like not paying attention in class, or imagining stinky Tina Brown's head exploding during the swelling climax of the Canadian anthem or — worse — during the Lord's Prayer), she remedied her own sins. In the shape of a cloud, a gigantic hand emerged from the sky at her instigation. She imagined it sweeping across the land. She would watch through the long windows as it swooped through the schoolyard, made of wind, grey curling digits. The feathery hand billowed through all obstacles, came to spank her.

What Chris was supposed to do with this information he was never quite sure. Tucked away, like the rest, it became fodder for jokes and teasing, especially in front of their friends.

"What are you afraid of?" Chris would say, "Hand of God going to come along? Better hold your pants up."

Corporal punishment was a great source of hilarity. Among all kinds of yanking and shaking and smacking, there was no such thing as an old-fashioned spanking. Only two boys in Chris and Tammy's entire grade school had received the "Strap." One was David White. The other was a guy a couple of years ahead of Chris, who later faded from South Wakefield as easily as Pinky Goodlowe's older brothers. Pinky himself had had tons of trouble. There had been a time in fourth grade (before he had grown so huge), when Mrs. Mackie would walk by his desk, grab him by the collar, haul him up, and whack his blue-jeaned ass several times, hard and in quick succession — often without provocation. David became another of these targets, eventually sent to the vice principal's office for the legendary Strap. Throughout the middle years, he bore the story with pride. He had accomplished something so terrible, no one could ever hope to reach his level.

On this particular end-of-August morning, it was he who put the pieces of Chris's semiprivate plan in place. Standing behind Joyland waiting to meet Adam, Chris was soon descended upon by David and Kenny, Dean and Rueben. Chris heard them before he saw them, a long way off, Kenny wailing something ahead, David answering only by skidding his BMX across the pavement, issuing a sandy screech, perhaps leaving behind snaking trails of black. When they popped around the corner of the building, Chris had half a mind to pull an instant, imaginary Samurai sword from behind his back and lop them to pieces. Instead, he did his best nod-and-ignore: just hanging out behind the old arcade, nothing special, what you up to? A nod could say all that and more. Dean slowed his bike and Rueben jumped off the back pegs where he'd been standing. His belly rippled beneath his orange T-shirt.

"So, we gonna kick that white fart's ass?"

You could put the whole world in Rueben's mouth, as per usual, Chris thought. *White fart's ass?*

"Heard you got yourself a mercenary, Lane," Dean said. He slicked his hair back under his hands, reknotted the elastic at the base of his neck, the bike wheel turning off to one side indifferently as soon as he let go of the handlebars. He swivelled it back around, and leaned against the wall without getting off, perched high, shoulder pressed against the brick. How twin brothers could be so drastically different, Chris had been attempting to figure out since sixth grade.

"Schwatzaneggah," Kenny riffed. "Arnold!"

David jumped off his bike, flipped it upside down on the pavement, gave the tire a spin and deserted it that way, standing on its handlebars. He dropped to the parking block and, squatting, began marking the ground with circles using a stone. He untied the red bandana from his jeaned thigh and mopped sweat from his forehead, before fastening it there, humming the Stones' "Start Me Up" faintly. The collar and sleeves had been ripped off his T-shirt, and a Playboy bunny emblem glinted in the white divot of his clavicle. Under its leaden head, a bowtie wrapped its silhouetted cartoon esophagus. David's skin showed through the large blank hole of its eye. He moved sticks and stones around with a kind of clunky authority.

"Skinny motherfucker getting uppity," David said, looking up at Chris with a grin. "I got your back. At least you scored the lady before the shit hit the fan." David extended an open five. Laurel would disappear between their hands. Turn into a single stroke of applause, a light slap. Chris knew it was gross to celebrate it that way, that his mother would choke. Over David's shoulder, Kenny's face was that of someone who hadn't been invited to a party. Chris reached out and slapped the open palm, David pretzeling into a variety of knuckle-locks before letting go, eyes fixed on Chris's.

Adam showed up late. At least he had had the sense not to bring Cindy. Sweat crawled through the maze of hair on his mammoth legs and curled it into thin brown rivers. Brut aftershave drifted across the small circle. David was already outlining the plan with the help of the makeshift markers. David and Chris met head-to-head over the circle of pebbles, knocking knowns and unknowns out of the stone-rubbed spheres and trajectories on the cement, easily as marbles (a game none of the boys had ever mastered). While they talked, Adam Granger hovered overtop of them, stretched his arms out over the backs of their shoulders as if they were in a football huddle. His shadow was shortened — thrown in a fat blob by the morning sun, across the cement under their feet.

The next day was Registration Day. Marc had been working on his Barracuda all summer. It was his intention to have it ready to drive into the student parking lot on his first day of Grade Twelve — half a week away. He had driven it out in the country to a guy who was supposed to do good, cheap paint jobs. Tomorrow, Marc would still be like them, still riding his beat-up ten-speed with the tape unravelling from the curved handles. Like them, he would pedal over to the high school in the afternoon to stand in line and fill out forms, receive his class schedule, get his picture taken for his student card. He would wear a black muscle shirt to show off the barbell shoulders on either side of his head. Wear a stupid grin across his pasty face.

David outlined it all like a movie segment, some kind of shakedown, excitement weakening the plotting as he got ahead of himself. "And then, Lane, Lane, I'll hold him, and you drop kick 'im. And then, I'll say —"

Dean lost his reserve, sprang from his bike, descended on Rueben with a flying forearm smash, spokes and tires clattering to the pavement behind him. The two of them jockeyed around, Dean fitting Rueben snugly into a Camel Clutch, Rueben all grunt.

"— and then you'll say —"

"Look, I got my own way of dealing with Breton," Adam declared, adding rather grandly, "If you don't mind," like it was a simple matter of manners, all of David's cut-downs unnecessary. Unvoiced promises of future twelve-packs and mickeys of rye led David to agree far quicker than Chris had expected he might. He had just been laying down the bare bones, man, just the bare bones.

Adam's sticky arm lay across Chris's back with the weight of wet cement. When he tried to shift away, Adam tightened it. In the heat, Chris could feel the clammy cold in Granger's skin, and a wave of nervousness set in, scrambling from Chris's spine on down. Marc would kill him when this was all over; there would be one moment of vindication and then Chris would be dodging him for months. Granger, at seventeen, had an armour of muscle, a fortress of wheels. He would never be caught walking home alone after school.

"Look, where's J.P. in all this? You don't really think you can just send Lane here up to the doorbell while Granger hides in some bush, do you?" Kenny spouted at the three of them with exasperation. "I mean . . . here's J.P., and this is J.P.'s brother. You can knock Marc off his bike maybe, but you can't kick his teeth in or anything. You just can't do that in front of a brother." The Only Child had spoken an unbearable truth.

Kenny's gaze flicked Chris's way. They stood, hands on knees facing one another. At his raised voice, even Rueben and Dean quit their scuffle and sobered up.

"He won't," Chris said. He nodded to Adam, their faces almost close enough to touch. Adam's irises were snuff brown, splintered like amber, and black knots of pupil were caught in the centres like flies. "You won't, right?"

The barbs of Adam's eyebrows twitched. He unhooked his arm from Chris and David's backs, held up his hands, *What-me?* style.

"Kid — sh-i-i-i-i-t," he drawled. His deliberate slowness gave doubt room to bloom. The words rolled off his tongue heavy as silver. Chris could have taken a marker and written his name in the space between the syllables. Then Adam reached down and absently scratched his balls beneath his Adidas, as if the whole thing meant that much to him. "Nothin' — but — kid — shit," he muttered, and hooked the testicle-tainted hand around Chris's shoulder again, gripping Chris's bare arm firmly.

Chris flew over the streets as if his tires weren't touching the ground. He thrust through hollow air. The night spun like a quarter on its edge. Streetlights skimmed by, snapping into motion with him. His nylon jacket — not his favourite, not the jean jacket — puffed out on either side of his body, billowed in the wind, crackled like a pale blue shell. He fell into the feeling of careening. Putting his head down, he rode on.

When he stopped, he did so suddenly, body going vertical, full force on the brakes.

Looking up, he fixated on the platforms of her building. He stood there, listening to his heart in his chest, his breathing regulating. She was just some girl. He didn't know anything about her except her favourite game. That, and how she felt from the inside. He imagined the body as an enclosed system — a perfect case — all its circuits and synapses snapping within.

The lights around the apartment building gave a purplish glow, turned the night into a bloodstain. When Chris ran his tongue over his upper lip, it was hot and sticky — salty, like tears. He stood for another minute, listened to his breath rise up, shakily, like wings beating.

PLAYER 2

Tammy stared at the screen, its turquoise light infused with wisdom, excitement. The television could so suddenly become aglow with text, code. She knew this from watching Chris. Letters and numbers placed in specific order between brackets.

Tammy understood brackets. They surrounded thoughts that were unnecessary. In novels she had often found that brackets contained the best information, the humourous additions. Asides. She liked that word, *aside*. On days when Chris had been playing ball hockey with J.P. and they couldn't use his sticks, Tammy and Jenny had lain together on Tammy's skinny twin bed, facing one another. Each had clasped a paperback of her own. After every page, Jenny would trail one finger down the right-hand margin scanning for hyphens.

"This page has two —" she would whisper, for no particular reason. Jenny loved hyphens. Tammy, brackets.

Tammy stared at the blank TV screen. Jenny was away on family vacation — Niagara Falls and Marineland.

The Lanes had been there last summer. Tammy had hyperventilated in the House of Frankenstein. In its narrow maze of black walls and mirrors, a real guy opened a real door and said, "Unh," waving a flashlight or a club — Tammy was not sure which. She knew there must have been a light beam or a camera somewhere whose path she kept walking into. She banged against the walls, and the walls began to close in on her slowly. The narrow passageway appeared narrower, narrower, narrower, mean and dark. When he opened the door again, she wanted to grab onto his black coveralls and cry, because he was human, at least, however automated his "Unh!" routine. Where was the exit? Where was the next doorway? Everything seemed like a doorway, but when she put her hand out, her skin only made contact with mirror, reflected back at her the space she was walking out of. There was nothing to walk into. Chris had raced ahead, laughing. He was in the sunlight by the time her breath began coming hard and hurried through her chest, the wind in her like an angry thing trying to claw its way out.

Chris had been bored by everything — including the Frankenstein house. Everything except the arcades. Later, in consolation, he had told her, "Think about that poor guy opening the door all day, again and again. I bet he makes four dollars an hour to say 'Unh!'" Tammy had laughed through her tears, though just a few minutes before she had had no choice but to stand in the dark and scream. She screamed until the woman in the booth let Chris back in to fetch her. He had dragged her out by her elbow, hissed in her ear, "Shut up! Shut up! You're out already. It's okay. I've got you," his breath simultaneously loaded with spit, affection, and embarrassment.

Then they had all walked behind the Falls, and Chris had acted bored again. Bored and wet. He had wanted to get a Polaroid of himself in a fake barrel going over a painted plastic Falls, but Mr. Lane had said it cost too much, and that he and Tammy should take one picture — together.

"Bloody hell," Chris had said. *No, that's not right,* Tammy thought. Syntax Error. It was Chris's pre-British era. It wasn't Mick Jagger. It was "Jesus Christ."

"Jesus Christ! Can't I do anything without her?"

On the fake wood cart before Tammy sat the computer, the Lanes' vacation this year.

**** COMMODORE 64 BASIC V2 ****
64K RAM SYSTEM 38911 BASIC BYTES FREE
READY.

Tammy stared at the screen. Ready. Was she? For what?

Grade Six, and the final week before it. That day, they had posted the lists at the school. Every year, Tammy and Chris had walked down together to find out if their teachers would be the ones they expected, to see who had passed and who had been held back after all, and especially, whether there were any new names. New names were like snowflakes. They hit your tongue, sparkling and cool with promise, even though by the end of the first semester, these new people would be regular and grey. But there was not even that perfect, day-to-day dulling to look forward to. Not one. Everything was the same, but different. Samantha's name hadn't been there. A long row of letters formed a string of useless information.

There was this, the Commodore, and the blinky square — the "cursor" — waiting for a new language.

Tammy typed LOAD, pressed play, watched the screen go blue. Listened to the screech of — what was it? data? information? memory? understanding? — something loading. She waited for the machine to find whatever it was that it was looking for.

That night, Tammy lay on her skinny mattress. She traced the patterns in the wood grain of the panelling above her with her fingertip. This one was a dog. It watched over her in dreams. This shape, a bird. *Oiseau,* she had named him years ago, because she liked the sound of it. *Oiseau* — separated only by an S, its perfect string of vowels was like a hole opening in her mouth she could fly into as she said them. This part of the wall was an island. It stuck out, horizontal, when all of the other knots and ridges ran vertically. Tammy imagined the island as a place she could go as she fell asleep — a place to stand in between sleeping and waking. Tonight, the wall seemed juvenile.

The rumble of the electric fan was amplified. Earlier, she had heard her father in the bathroom running water. Through the walls it had sounded like a deluge, a rushing *shushhhhhh shushhhhhh,* but it had not put her to sleep. Now, no doubt, he was asleep himself. The night seemed both hot and cold.

She had a mental image of Adam Granger sitting in the park. His huge hands and loose, lumbering bear-paw trundle of a walk. His eyebrows that raised after everything he said (Samantha had nothing on him), as if they were just waiting for Tammy to agree and wouldn't go back down again until she did. The small thistle of hair between them. Adam Granger, with his eyes like cinnamon and his tongue like a twig, snapping in the silence. The tuft of brown that stuck out over the collar of his white T-shirt. His stubby neck, downy as turkey scruff. His wide shoulders and determined stance (especially at the bottom of Laurel Richards' stairs). His ideas about love. Love.

The plug-in nightlight was a small taupe egg on the wall beside Tammy's bed.

If they could talk — like real people — what would Adam Granger tell her? Somewhere, Tammy assured herself, there were real people having real conversations, different from the ones she was accustomed to having. This much she had gleaned by observation. As distant as the world could seem, there must be people out there breaking it into bite-sized pieces, filling it up with words.

Would he tell her that? That love could come out of something broken? Take a new shape. Emerge into something else entirely. Like a thing cocooned or a thing born. And if he said that, what would she say? She wouldn't say anything, she decided. She would ask him questions. Questions like: Couldn't love also work in reverse, like when Mork and Mindy had their baby, and it aged entirely backward? Couldn't love begin big and become small? Tammy knew that something in the Lane household had begun to crack. Soon it would lie at their feet, an entirely different thing than it had once been. Small grey figures would emerge from the wreckage. Although Tammy felt someone should warn her parents (just as someone should have warned Mindy before she decided to mate with an alien), it was not going to be Tammy.

She worked her tongue around inside her mouth, felt along the seam of her palate where Jenny's retainer showed a steeper incline than Tammy could fathom. Tammy tasted the curve of her gums, the angle her molars occupied in her mouth. She found she lacked the proper language. Inside, everything was in code.

PLAYER 1

That morning, Chris walked into the clown's mouth. Its red lips were square at the joints with its plastic lipsticked grin. Big eyes arched white against its peach forehead. The beady pupils inside were an incomplete ellipsis. Through the low, narrow store space in front of the Joust game, stood the legendary Mickey Newton. His shoulders elbowed from his familiar crablike stance. His head bobbed back and forth in quick jabs. He had a sideways way of going at the machine, as if he were trying to dive into it. The Second-to-the-Master. Returned.

Circus Berzerk suddenly seemed even smaller. The eight machines faced each other like girls with dolls at a tea party. Chris bit the corner of his lip, crept up to stand behind him.

The bird Mickey rode was veering across the screen. It careened downward, landed atop a Bounder. The opposing bird and its rider transformed instantly into an egg. Mickey ate the egg, collected his due in points. He rose up again in pursuit of the Hunter and the Shadow Lord. His wings emitted a constant electronic *whooosh — whooosh*. He banged the Fire button continuously to stay afloat. He collided head-on with the Hunter. Bird-rider ensembles reeled backward, sharp as tires squealing. He tried again. Success. He scooped up the egg. Mickey wasn't the type to allow the egg to languish and eventually hatch open (whereupon the rider would emerge, miniature and grey, wait for his bird to fly in, pick him up, and resume battle). Mickey grabbed the goods as he saw fit, knocked off the Shadow Lord like he was a sparrow. At the end of the wave, Mickey collected an extra 3000 survival points.

"Watch it, Short Fry," Mickey said. He whacked the button recklessly, forced his player to rise up, jerkily, then crash down on a buzzard-rider-cum-egg. "Don't want to take out your teeth with my elbow." His now-sixteen-year-old chin jerked forward. His eyes didn't leave the screen for a second.

The ball of the controller was still warm. The bird rose above the platform. Chris felt it ascend from his palm, push against gravity, plunge its two-dimensional head across the top of the screen and exit left, re-enter right.

David kicked the corners of the machines lightly with a sneakered foot. "Fuck this shit," he said. "Fuck this shit. Let's go."

Chris let bird and rider plummet into lava. A gigantic molten hand unfurled, pulled them down into the red, lapping section at the bottom of the screen. Chris deserted the machine.

Kenny's back was a small cotton sweat stain beneath the rippling strings of light. *If you make a thing happen,* Chris thought, *everyone suddenly wants in on it.* Sometimes, when he was particularly perturbed by something, Chris broke the words into individual sentences in his head. *If. You. Make.* Kenny pushed another quarter into Ms. Pac-Man, as if he could live vicariously through it. *A. Thing. Happen.* Kenny thrust the yellow head back and forth, muttering "Fuck! Fuck! Fuck!" every time a ghost chased his plushy animated ass across the screen. He couldn't say the word enough.

Everyone. Suddenly.

Rueben and Dean showed up, wearing scowls.

"We're not coming. We're not doing anything," Dean said. "We'll be the first blamed. We just don't wanna —"

"But we want —"

Wants.

Rueben would be lookout, he said.

In.

David kicked the Ms. Pac-Man machine harder, and Kenny lost his man to distraction.

On.

Circus Berzerk spit them out, a regurgitated ragtag army, lightheaded beneath the flashing bulbs.

It.

Ball-capped and snickering, the gang grabbed their BMXs, Chris's arms rubber-loose, fists roach-clamp-clenched around the bike grips, guts pinned down like laboratory butterflies to his backbone, legs cycling like circular jellyfish away from the rest of him. *In on it.*

David and Kenny popped wheelies, a tired experiment resurrected to see who could pull the best one and maintain it, riding a couple of metres at a time on one back tire. Dean wove in and out, wheel wiggly. Rueben statued on back nubs, held onto the plastic seat by his fingernails, his bovine body still for once, unquivering, laughter quelled. Chris brought up the back of the pack, eyes on his running shoes — still too white for the first day of school, no matter how he'd tried to scuff them.

The streets topped, wobbled, spun, the details of them seeming to slow with speed. Chris felt it — felt it inside, felt it as the holding down of a spinning record. The needle sunk to silence, then — letting go again — bobbed back up, all noise. He felt *it,* though *it* didn't have a name just yet. *It* was the way time came off its wheels. Chris observed the activity in the streets as if he had never travelled them before. He drifted across four lanes of St. Lawrence Street without looking. Pill-capsule cars and vans throbbed in blue-veined lanes, but delayed for him, his eyes on the back of Kenny's grey T-shirt, its shifting set of wrinkles. The bells in the chicken take-out tinkled under Lego-red roofing as a girl of ten or eleven raced out to an idling car where her mother sat waiting (face pickled behind air-conditioned glass), the paper bag not yet acquired, bills sticking up from the girl's fist like some unrequired bit of punctuation — a physical question mark. Her other hand split into symbol — V-ed — numbers. A nod. She turned to the car for answer and back again so quickly, her shoulders transformed into the blades of a fan.

Chris cruised on, the sidewalk cracks ushering a soft *thwack* into the motion of his vehicle. This one — *thwack* — where he'd played Break Your Mother's Back a hundred kindergarten times. That one — *thwack* — where Kenny had bet him girls could pee standing up. This one — *thwack* — where he'd sat curbside with Tammy for previous Canada Day parades. That one — *thwack* — where he'd sprawled the night they closed Joyland. This one — *thwack* — the last before the gravelled section ahead. The significance of them slowed down too, became more about the bulk of tar or putty, the yellow neck of the hydrant, the black teeth of the gutter, than it was about history. Quietly, *it* ticked, half-sublime, half-sick.

You can feel a thing before it happens, Chris thought. His mouth filled with warmth, the dry salt of perspiration and fear. Thoughts arrived without words, a series of fast-play pictures made up of visual *perhaps's* and *possiblys*. Chris yanked on his handlebars, leaned back, left his wheel to lift. When they passed his corner, he ducked his head, as if his mother or father could see him from the living room window. Then, so as not to look like a mama's boy, he gathered the cracks from his tongue, leaned to one side and spat.

Kenny dropped back. His eyes were insecure, rattish.

"Are you really —" He squelched it when Chris looked at him.

Kenny's hair was parted on the far right and swooped across his forehead. A salesman's haircut in miniature. No matter how he'd tried to grow it, its clerkish quality remained, a counterfeit of neatness. He looked like a thirteen-and-a-half-year-old salesman, but a salesman nonetheless. He would jerk his dick under his desk all the way through high school, join the army at eighteen, and in a faraway country, in two vicious minutes and without knowing why, he would rape a fifteen-year-old girl. He would never tell anyone, nor would she, and no one could possibly know. But Chris knew it now. Knew it without knowing how. The incident had its own green tinge, flecking the brown of Kenny's rattish slitted eyes behind the lenses of his glasses. He was weak, and he would always be weak. If Chris saw the girl lurking in the future, he couldn't acknowledge it, could only compile it into one word and sticker it across Kenny's pale stuttering presence: *weak*.

"Are you really —" Kenny stammered beneath Chris's appraising gaze. "What are you gonna do?" he managed.

Chris shook his head, pumped the pedals hard beneath obstinate blue jeans. Soared ahead.

The cardboard in the windows of Joyland had begun to peel. One day soon they would fall inward, slough off. The masking tape would let go, its tongue suitably sticky with the grit of old paint and sill dust. It would decide it had had enough, lean back, allow its bib-like self to crumple to the empty floor. When the boys pulled their bikes up alongside the old squat, though they had just been there the day before, Chris noticed for the first time that the outside sign had been removed. He wished for a second he had thought to steal it — then the thought was as lost as the sign.

Adam Granger lounged against the back wall of the arcade, his nose in secret consultation with his knees. He straightened up when he heard them, his face pinched white and red.

"Look like you're about to lose your lunch, Granger," David said.

Adam used his T-shirt to wipe the sweat from his forehead. His belly was thick and pale, a brown-hair swirl in the centre, like a spiral around his bellybutton. Against the tongue of the Rolling Stones' mural, even Adam was small — one of those red-and-white mints they gave away in restaurants with the bill.

He pulled back his elbows, forming fists, and shook his head, his whole throat jostling with muscle, the cord along one side of his neck taking the opportunity to introduce itself to the gang of onlookers. His neck issued a preparatory cracking, and his hair flicked back with reinstated confidence. He shrugged his shoulders, bringing them up like they were equal to his head. His blotchiness faded.

"I've been waiting to pound this fucker for a long time," he said.

Chris stared at Adam's face. Everything in the universe slipped a little bit. Chris glanced at David, then Dean. Kenny's eyes flicked his way for a second. The boys all paused, perhaps to consider what they did or did not know of Adam.

What they knew didn't matter. In ten minutes and forty-eight seconds, Adam Granger would be dead. They did not, could not, have any idea of this fact. Even Chris

— whose powers of prophecy were quietly developing at enormous speeds — could not guess it. If Chris had had access to his best friend's brain, were able to can-opener J.P.'s skull from across three blocks and through the maple brick exterior of the Breton house, Chris might have grasped why, at this particular moment, Adam's neck and restraint appeared to simultaneously crack.

In the bungled cosmos of Grade Nine — yes, even Marc Breton's was bungled — there lived a girl named Genevieve Cartier. Genevieve had the great luck or misfortune of being assigned Marc Breton as a science partner. Marc's affections swelled whenever Genevieve was near, embarrassingly so. Each day, hours in advance of third period, he began to defuse them with the precision of a trained agent.

In first period, Marc filled his notebook with the derogatory remarks he might make — but wouldn't — to Miss Cartier. In second period, Phys. Ed, he exhausted himself in the mind-over-matter mechanics of sport, pouring every ounce of strength into demobilizing his classmates. He devoted half of his lunch hour to cold showers, and the other half to avoiding the older, behemoth versions of himself, sauntering the halls in search of any young Oedipus who might topple them from their positions if not quickly and properly dispatched. By third period, Marc was ready to collapse. Tenderly disabled, he would sprawl across the desk, watch Genevieve through lowered lids, imagine he was sleeping next to her — somewhere, anywhere but in the science room. The routine kept him from speaking to her, from saying what might have, surely would have, been deemed "stupid." Second semester of Marc's freshman year passed without incident, with scarcely a breath or sentence between them, save what was absolutely necessary. Their relationship was unspoiled, a series of brushed hands in the exchange of assignment sheets, their language primary — yellow, blue, magenta. The gulf between hypothesis and conclusion filled with silent, point-form observations. Genevieve's notebook ballooned with smiley faces and green felt-tip exclamation marks. Their careful balance would be broken by the beginning of tenth grade.

There would never be a written history of bush parties. If there were, it might include an adequate mention of the night Genevieve condescended to attend one of the more famous in a series of South Wakefield bush parties, hosted by one Somebody VanderSomething, a sheepish boy whose parents were farmers and who was known more by his plot of land than by his name.

Cartier, Genevieve, b.1966

Related: Male Violence

(jen´e vev´ KAR tyā´) Cartier's role in the historical summer of 1981 was peripheral rather than primary. She made famous this common quote, "Will you do it for a beer?" (see Case, 24, and/or 2-4) Under gigglish command (see female behaviour, stereotypical) of classmate Danielle Desrosiers, Cartier was able to convince Lieutenant Adam Granger to approach civilian Marc Breton, forestall him in his merrymaking, and pose an untranslatable query. In the parlance of the day, "_______ wants to know if you will go out with her," had its grounding as both a serious question and a joke, depending on the circumstance. Given the general

> stench of the messenger, and perhaps several crude improvisations by Granger, Breton believed the offer to be false. Without any plan of action, he stood and pushed the guffawing courier (as oral histories dictate) "flat on his ass." Mutual acts of shame and violence began immediately, issuing in a new period of competition and disregard between the formerly friendly acquaintances. Cartier, by all accounts, left the party immediately following the incident, never to return to the land again. Cohort Desrosiers stayed on to engage in an unrelated act of deflowering (see Cherry, Cracking the Big V, Loss of Innocence, Virginity) inside a decrepit school bus whose reason for being there no one was ever able to explain.

In the grand tussle of memory, neither Adam nor Marc could verbalize exactly what had happened. However minor the rudiments of the dispute, its germination was ensured by alcohol and social standing, growing into long-term avarice, and coming to full blossom on this final thrust of summer, after several years in the making.

Whatever gentleness had lurked in Marc's heart for the girl named Genevieve, it would never be articulated. His affections manifest themselves only in the clean bruising of Adam's face and ego. When classes resumed in September, Marc would avoid all references to the incident (or ensuing incidents) between the spigots in the science lab. There, apathy plotted itself into the drab pencil lines of Marc's new and unusually prim partner. Across the room, Genevieve's forbidding face would glow in the tremulous blue of the bunsen burner. The continuity of emotion remained — moments of private, personal ascension — but it held in the guts of its silence a glass-plated, magnified swim of resignation. A sad swabbing of cotton balls. A directed stream of light for prismed refraction. The red pendant of a mouse's stomach on the long grey chain of its entrails. Even J.P. did not know these details, knew only the names that accompanied them: Adam Granger (often), and (once or twice) Genevieve.

Chris knew only instinct, what was conveyed in the briefest of glances or missteps of vocal tone. Adam and Marc were soldiers of similitude. Whatever had begun as Chris's own agenda had slipped away.

The plan was far simpler than any of them wanted to admit. Chris and Kenny had done away with all unknowns — reduced it to something foolproof and easy.

Mounting their bikes, they whirled over gravel, around the corner, loop-the-loop past the park. The cul-de-sac where the Bretons lived was a pale loose mouth. Running Creek Road straight as a ruler, just there, around the bend, on the other side. Dean and Rueben took up posts on the corner, where they could see all the way down St. Lawrence Street. The other boys fanned out quickly. David and Kenny hid behind the hedges on the left. Adam took shelter to the right. A chancrous rust-smitten van was parked conveniently just beyond the crescent's lip.

Chris threw his bike on the lawn. His only job was to tell J.P. he was heading over to the school for registration. He shouldn't do it — he knew he shouldn't — it would only cause more trouble later. It was too late. The door opened.

"Hey man."

Chris swallowed. "Ready to go?"

"Good a time as any."

"Your brother coming with us?" Chris had got it out. His first line. *It sounded good,* he thought. *It did, didn't it?* He congratulated himself — an inaudible flurry of self-doubt and backslaps.

"Yeah, right." J.P. scoffed.

"I thought he could drive us. . . ." Chris fumbled from the porch. The words hummed on his lips, burned into an invisible swelling, as if a fist had tried to force them back in.

"He doesn't get his car 'til tomorrow. Besides, you got your bike right there." J.P. took off his ball cap and swatted it against his leg.

"Hold on." J.P. disappeared down the hallway to Marc's room. Too late, Chris realized that on any other day he would have followed him in.

He stood just inside the doorframe under the flat-line smiles of Mr. and Mrs. Breton. Suspended at eye level, the 16x20 print Windex-shone. A dark wooden frame against the dark wood panel. In it, younger versions of J.P. and Marc stared at Chris with adolescent penny-candy grins. Marc's hair was unruly as J.P.'s, his scalp not yet sheered mean, his paunch not yet muscle. It had only been six months since he shaved it, and now Chris couldn't imagine him any other way. Even J.P. seemed alien here. A family-photo fervor had tucked in on itself, snuck into the crimped seam of J.P.'s sweatshirt hood, pulled tight. Empty on his back, its faceless face rumped his shoulders with a red bubble. His neck burst from it, taut and beaming. One hand bulged the pocket below the bright white culprit string. Down the hall, Chris could hear them, their voices through the wall.

It was taking too long. He glanced back over his

shoulder, Adam's bike tires obvious beneath the van.

"Get out of my way, limpdick." Marc brushed past him, left an arrowed trace of elbow under Chris's ribs. Marc made his way out of the house, the screen door a swinging pendulum back and forth. J.P. stuck his hand out, stopped it, open. In the next year, in partial response to the next three minutes, J.P. would develop a slouch and a stupid shuffle, begin chain-smoking like Johnny Davis. He'd graduate on his smile, go to university for one week, then drop out. He'd sever remaining relations, move across the country, take a job in a restaurant, eventually manage it. He'd meet a girl in a bar and marry her before he had ever seen her without her makeup. He would wake in the middle of the night to masturbate. He would shovel food into his mouth like it was the only thing worth remembering. By forty he would be fat, his former self unfathomable, the retrograde ghost of a man. J.P. replaced by John Paul, John B., and Mr. B., the manager. He would die a clogged young tragic death. Heart attack. One of his three teenaged children, the girl, would cry. The boys would knot their tongues into their ties.

J.P. gestured for Chris to pass him, Adam's apple bobbing like an egg. It was so easy to see the way things happened, before they happened. It wasn't a supernatural power. It just *was*.

Chris's footsteps jolted into his legs as he bounced down the porch steps. He could feel it. He could feel *it*. Behind him, J.P. had already disappeared into the past. The world lay before Chris — a labyrinth of concrete and trees — and figures and objects appeared, which he could move away from or toward. That was *it*. The world had gotten unnaturally flat. Chris moved out into the green patch, his physicality not much more than a white dot following a black dot.

From where Chris stood, already Marc looked smaller. He threw a hairy thigh over the crossbar of his bike in a smooth, easy motion. Coasting down the driveway, every gesture entrenched with strange arrogance, Marc's shoulders broke out of the long black muscle shirt as he leaned back. Chris grabbed his own bike and launched onto it. The motion quelled the transit already occurring in his guts, as if his body had finally caught up.

Marc's hand fumbled assward, perhaps to grip the back of the seat as he rode. Shirt hem flapped above relaxed-fits. He instantly tucked it back in place over a hard lump of hairbrush. He neared the mouth of the crescent. *Tick tick tick* of the tire.

Chris rose up on the bike, his ass hovering above the seat as he careened forward, air clotting in his throat like cotton. He couldn't say whether J.P. followed or not, whether David or Kenny were appropriately stationed, whether Dean and Rueben had abandoned the mission entirely or were currently parked on some distant piece of curb, watching. When Chris looked back, this one moment would —

Tick tick tick.

— rubber wheel its way home without incident, would press the handbrakes before —

Tick tick tick.

— follow-up, would open its mouth and say —

Tick tick tick.

Chris's throat and head infused with heat. Invisible fingernails on the back of his neck. Marc groped at his back pocket again.

— the thing was oblong and silver and —

Tick tick.

— the thing was —

Tick.

Marc's front wheel shot past the snout of the van. The bike tire whistled over the concrete. Chris opened his mouth to yell — to make some sort of unplanned gesture, sign — stop it. Marc's hand wrapped around the thing in his back pocket, which Chris saw very clearly now. It was not a comb because — in spite of the Bretons' foyer photograph — Marc had a quarter-inch buzz cut.

There was a swerving of bodies and bikes as Adam descended. On the other side of the circle — what seemed a long way away — David and Kenny rolled out to watch. Silence battered Chris's ears. He braked.

Adam reached out, got a hand on Marc. Swiping a meat hook around his neck, Adam pulled to topple him from the ten-speed, managed a good jab. His fist cracked against Marc's face in a splinter of knuckle and skin. The bikes seemed to float. Marc reached backward again — even as he began to waver, even as his head snapped. His fingers ratcheded the thing from his back pocket.

It was a handle. Even before it came completely into sight, Chris knew that it was longer than a girl's hand and as heavy as cast iron. Marc's back pocket slowly unsheathed the thing — the intricate sabre replica, suddenly a basic piece of lead pipe.

It was all Chris could do — to stand there and see, to know the thing before it happened. He opened his mouth. He opened his mouth. He opened his mouth. There was no sound.

Chris realized he hadn't moved, wasn't moving, was in fact the only one who had stopped dead. One leg raised on the pedal, the other flat on the ground, Chris watched his premonition bloom into reality, the colour of blood on concrete.

Marc's bike clattered to the ground and he pitched with it straight into Adam, his hand thrusting forward suddenly. The glinting nub of metal smashed into Adam's open mouth. A loud crack shook the air — the shock of teeth and bone exhumed from skin and gum. Before the red bleared downward, Marc had brought his fist back for a second blow.

This was where Chris yelled *Stop!* This was where Chris became the hero. This was where the world slammed a gigantic brake and Chris avenged all the wrongs of the universe in less than a second.

This was where Chris stood still — breath flapping in his chest like it would tear clean through him — and watched, watched the sky tip over, watched the other boys sink into recognition as they also slowly stopped, each putting a foot down tentatively against the ground. A thick fire reached a thick hand through Chris's throat, as he watched helplessly, his messenger quickly disabled.

The hilt of the *Star Wars* sabre landed with a dull thud against Adam's temple. Adam toppled into a swatch of red. His forehead palpitated with fleshy matter, burst like an overstuffed cushion. There was a warm, soft gush — a rush of things Chris would later claim he had not seen.

The world between Chris and Marc wavered as Chris caught Marc's arm. Marc jerked back hard, the metal flying out of his grip. It rang across the concrete as his knuckles grazed haphazardly off Chris's collarbone. Chris reeled backward. Marc's face was like a hammer, one small, bright freckle of blood clinging to his cheek. He glared at Chris without seeing him, jerked away. Marc picked up his bike, swerved the front tire around one of Adam's bent legs. Shakily he swung himself over the crossbar, and rode away without taking his hands off the handlebars.

LEVEL 13

Berzerk

PLAYER 1

In the timelines of Chris's sci-fi novels, cause and effect remained lateral. Everything would move in a horizontal manner, back and forth across the page. History would hold a spear, and everything would embed itself upon that straight-line steel like a shish kebab. Love, deceit, mechanical error — these meaty treatises were penetrated by time, one act added after another. But in Chris's video games, there was room for upward movement. On each and every board, his icon ran to and fro, moved in and out of rooms or states of peril, and eventually proceeded upward into a new playing field. So enter the interlude music, the board between boards . . .

He had felt *it,* sensed time shifting. Now he waited to see where it would deliver them.

Chris had never known that being stuck in a room could be so excruciating. He had always been sent to his bedroom as punishment. In his room he had all his stuff. This was something else entirely. The boys sat on a bench, partitioned off from the main room by brick and thick glass. None of them spoke. In the end, the silence was broken by Marc, far away, down the hall.

They could see him as he was brought in. J.P. stood up and went to the window that looked out on the hall. The rest of them remained seated.

David jabbed Kenny in the ribs. Kenny didn't respond, except to purse pert lips. His chin, as if in compensation, melted like wax into his throat. He gaped at Chris, as if unaware he was being prodded. From his left side, Dean glared at David, pushed over on the bench away from him, into the space J.P. had just vacated. Dean's thumbs crisscrossed in his lap, the members of his folded hands that would hit the space bar of the old electric typewriter he would lug to university, while everyone around him dormed their PCs and Smith-Corona 8-line screens upon graffitied desks templed with beer cans. Dean would avoid their student pub with its "Downstairs Thursdays" dance parties and its "Wednesdays Hump-days" $2.50 pints; their bookstore selling crest-emblazoned-clothing; their corporate-sponsored student centre; their cafeteria's endless mill of sandwiches smeared with mayonnaise, turdish french fries and gravy. Eventually he'd leave their puffy-lettered intellectualizing behind — six credits short of graduation. He would return to the area, marry a girl from the reserve, be asked to take a post in the South Wakefield high school he had not yet stepped into, cultivate a Native Studies program whose courses he would never be technically qualified to teach. He would be hired on as an advisor, talk one teenager out of suicide, steer three away from early careers in alcoholism, and countless others away from incidents like the one he had just witnessed. But his greatest pleasure would come when his fifth daughter won her first South Wakefield fishing contest. Dean shifted further to the left, his thumbs tightened around the air between his hands, closed over what little Chris could see of life between his palms.

On the other side of Chris, Rueben, broad and brown, stared straight ahead, bouncing his knees so that the whole bench jiggled. In its shudder, Chris could feel the desert shifting, the mushroom sun of Nevada. Rueben would drop out of school as soon as it was legal, drive across North America in all directions, smoke everything that crossed his path, and enjoy everyone who offered themselves to him. He would arrive in California at sunrise one pink morning, live there for a short time, then in Vancouver. He would act as an extra, and eventually shine as a commercial actor for a popular laxative. Later, he would return to South Wakefield to take care of his mother. He would apprentice as a plumber, make a decent living. He would be infinitely grateful his commercial never aired in the area, cancelling the possibility of a crude and unmerciful connection between these two career paths, which surely would have resulted in a flood of poor jokes.

Kenny had been the only one to keep his cool after the blow. The rest of them had stood staring down at Adam.

Wretched David, ever-cool, even tried to help him up, saying, "He's fine. It's nothing." In two years' time, perhaps in some stalled reaction, a new man would emerge. Chris had felt it in the brevity of David's words. Quite suddenly, he would set belligerence upon a shelf one day, crush the shrimpish child in him, begin sleeping flat on his back and waking to a hundred sit-ups, a self-imposed regimen. He would graduate as a police officer, shoot one possibly innocent/possibly deranged-and-dangerous man (charges dropped) and save two children from drowning. Several years later, there would be a third child (a toddler) whom he would pull from an oil pit (dead) and no one — especially not Chris — would ever guess the weight of its half-tarred blue head in his hand, the recurrent image of its toenails dangling, the love in it wasted.

Meanwhile, Kenny had run straight into the Breton's house for the phone, hadn't thought twice about throwing open their front door and dashing through their hall. Now, the shock reversed its effects: David scoffed behind J.P.'s back; Kenny zoned out. And Chris . . . all Chris could think was, *how had he known?*

Chris shuddered. It didn't seem to matter that he hadn't particularly liked Adam, or that he had only known him for the span of one summer. The suddenness of their lives seared like the welt at Chris's shoulder, which he rubbed, tentatively, beneath his collar. Where Marc had struck him, a small thistle of pain beneath the bone.

There were things he still didn't know, things about Adam Granger he would never know, but for the moment, these facts were as minor as the vibrations of the bench trembling beneath Chris. The wall behind his head staticly clutched at hairs.

Escorted by two officers, Marc walked past them. He yielded like a wax figure, face ruddy. A white fist-shaped mark had begun to puff where he'd been struck — four distict spots, the knuckles imprinted in a clean manifestation of their now-deceased owner. It took Chris a minute to process the sound that came out of Marc. He was choking on it, an octave too high, as if he had sucked helium from a valve. The dreadful squalling seized the station. It was stopped short by teeth that refused to open, refused to let the poor noise go.

J.P. put a hand up to the glass, as if to knock on it when Marc went by, but as he came closer, J.P. stiffened. He stopped short, his hand a half-inch away from the partition. His brother passed.

Chris put his head down and lay an arm across his stomach. Beneath him the bench thrummed. A spike of bile jolted in his throat. He willed it back down. Already he knew — in his brain, he knew — that they would be sent home soon enough. A few questions, a stern talking-to. J.P. would be fine. Even Marc would be fine. It was a clear-cut case of self-defence.

But that didn't matter.

Unwilled, it came to mind, set to repeat. A terrible theme composed of heat. Hand scrabbling backward. Handle unsheathed. Muscles plunging into red. Clattering pseudo-sword rolling across concrete. Hand scrabbling. Handle unsheathed. Muscle plunge. Clattering. Scrabbling — unsheathed — plunge — clattering. Scrabbling — unsheathed — plunge —

Someone was dead. His idea, however backward it had gone. *His.* Sweat fled his forehead. Fell to floorboards between his white runners. A faint pink residue still clung to the brand new rounds of rubber. From shoe to floorboard, imprint of dead boy blood.

Chris began a series of breathy hard-kicked hiccups, but struggled to swallow them, one by one, back down.

Outside the holding room, the hallway clock continued its parade of hesitant steps. If he knew a thing, what made him incapable of stopping it? Chris swallowed, swallowed, swallowed; each gulp chalked *it* up to a glitch.

PLAYER 2

Tammy sat down on the stool in front of the pushcart and rested short red-nailed fingers on the keys, tentatively, as though she might receive an electric shock. Blank grey TV face. The wood wall clock pointed its two arms in the same direction, the heart-shaped tin hands momentarily butterflied. The short one had almost hit XI, the long one at X. Ten minutes 'til *The Price is Right*. She reached around the televison's back, found and flicked the switch box. She had time to try just a couple of things out.

The computer spoke, chunky-syllabled.

The arcade version of Berzerk had talked — blurted out, "Intruder Alert! Intruder Alert! Stop the humanoid!" Running from one room to another, the player attempted to shoot the robots before the all-powerful smiley face of Evil Otto appeared, effortlessly bounced through electrocuting walls in pursuit of the player. But by the time this audio made an impact on Tammy (at a Chuck E. Cheese in Michigan), she was intimate with Chris's imitation of the machine. The machine original cried a mere imitation of her brother.

For a television to converse was something else entirely. The black ridges of its speaker mouth were usually a dumb portal, open to whatever actor's voice had been tuned across its pixeled head. This thing that would normally blare Johnny Olson's voice — his repetitive call of "Come on down! You're the next contestant on *The Price is Right!*" — had suddenly found the ability to read aloud whatever Tammy typed onto its fluorescent face.

The machine had the vocabulary of a second-grader, could only spell words that were foreign or unrecognized. Slang. People's names. Anything beyond two syllables, the computer walked into a psychological wall. "Hello, T-A-M-M-Y."

Occasionally, Mrs. Lane's head bopped up and down past the window. The grating of Mr. Lane's scraper on the garage supplied a guide to their locations. Tammy monitored her mother, as if her mother were Evil Otto stationed outside the house. Inside, Tammy navigated the things the computer did and did not understand.

"S-H-I-T-heaaaad," the computer clipped without anger or emotion. White letters on a blue background. "Suck my dictionary." The screen glowed. The blue-green light was tropical and sweet.

The clock on the wall burst open. Above its brown leafy dial, a door opened and a tuft of feather sprang in and out. Twelve. The *cuckoo* was skewed and metallic, followed by the quiet ringing of bells.

A whole hour had passed in nuggets of ad-libbed profanity. She'd missed all of *The Price is Right.* There was nothing on now but *The 700 Club.*

"Screw off."

Tammy rocked back and forth on the stool, folded a

leg across her lap and pressed one heel under herself.

"Eat me," the speaker belched without the slightest quiver — a phrase Tammy had only seen painted on walls.

She clasped her hands over her mouth.

"Eat me," the computer said again, and "eat me," its voice never changing.

Between the four lavender walls of the bathroom, an assessment was quickly made regarding how such a thing was done. That cow head in the diagram. The *vagina*. One, two, three. That was how they went, in pale pink circles on glossy white paper, slim black vector lines leading to their names. *Clitoris, urethra, vagina*. Easy. One, two, three . . . . It didn't feel like anything. Tammy shifted. Tammy shifted. Tammy shif — then she felt it.

It gave way like a jet of hot water.

When she looked down, she had not achieved some state of pleasure. She had broken her hymen, a firewall wafer of skin.

Its descent drummed a shock through her and she froze. The muddy lot of it sunk into the fabric of her clothes. Her limbs went shivery. She didn't catch her breath, it caught her, jabbed a fist in her chest. She hiccupped, made a mad grab for a swatch of toilet paper. Against the white cotton, the blood was like oil, like car grease.

Tammy sat stiffly at the computer. She typed the most banal of phrases into its cold blue face. "T-A-M-M-Y is greaaaaat." On the couch behind her, Mr. Lane sat with his mug. His shirt was hooked limply over the arm of the couch. Next to the back door, his shoes were spotted with paint.

"Hoo boy," he huffed, "it's a scorcher out there, it's a scorcher."

She had no idea if her mother had told him. She entered womanhood, two years and a lie early, sitting tight-kneed around a Kleenex.

"Going to the drug store," Mrs. Lane announced from the kitchen doorway, worrying the car keys from a side pocket in her purse. Tammy cringed into the keyboard.

That was when phone rang.

Mrs. Lane answered. "Yes," she said, "yes" and "yes" again, a jolt in her voice.

When she put the receiver down, she began to tell them. Her mouth moved, but there were no words. The room had freeze-framed. It began to slide out of place in a transition of neon as Mr. and Mrs. Lane moved from one room to the next.

A fight, the Bretons, an older boy, Chris. Dead. The words formed a wall around Tammy as she stood very still next to the doorway. Her head throbbed with the bits of data. She dropped to the living room carpet, clasped her arms around her knees, pressed chin to shins, rocked, Kleenex in her crotch forgotten.

She knew without being told. She shivered. It was Adam, the Rabbit, the pool man. It was the girl in the Sunset Villa, the girl he shouldn't have gone to see. It was the cigarette behind the arcade. It was a long series of *it*s without a proper file for information storage. The nubby carpet gnawed from beneath her socks, beneath her nylon shorts when she tipped back, beneath her. She was back on the ground, the carpet squirmer, this time more foetal than frottaging. Across the den, the piano's foot-rubbed wood stared at her. In the other room, her parents stood in the dip in the lineoleum where a marble or a Hot-Wheels would stall, behind a door with a crack wide enough to slip a doll's shoe under.

She didn't take her bike. That would have meant going the back way, past the kitchen window. Without it, she was unencumbered, slipping quietly out the front door, the screen easing shut between pinched careful fingers, the head of the handle memorized for all time in those few seconds. Its ridged palm-sized square of silver teeth.

Tammy took a few slow steps, then ran, grass padding the sound, the thud of hard August mud beneath purple Kangaroos. She beelined across the VanDoorens' lawn. From the corner of Running Creek she could see nothing, no yellow police ribbons, no ambulance cherry glinting. She flew over Mr. Sparks' shrubbery like a steeplechase steed and snipped the head of a tiger lily off its stalk as she landed on the other side, still galloping. She landed in a blotch of blood, eventually. Her sneakers passed across it before she even saw the stain.

It was here, here. She looked all around the crescent, the Bretons' house like a strange gold tooth, and all the white houses surrounding her still smiling with roses, still yawning garage doors. No one was there, rushing about, weeping, distraught, gossiping. Nothing out of the ordinary. Tammy turned in all directions, then looked down at the single remaining piece of colour. She had no way to document it. The evidence.

Sudden, automatic, a sprinkler turned on, hissing, spun like a gear in a jewellery box with the ballerina pulled off. With its intrusion, Tammy jumped, the colour smearing beneath her shoe.

She bent down, touched it. Immediately self-conscious, glancing at glinting windows, she pretended to tie her shoe. She took a pebble from the scene, pushed it down inside the lip of her sneaker, sprinted home again on top of its jagged stone eye. The blood on it brought her blood to the surface, a small blister rising inside the perfect arch of her white sock.

PLAYER I

Chris saw his father before his father saw him. Across the station. Through the glass frames in police reception. In profile, Mr. Lane had the presence of a pit bull. Years of weight training had left his short body broad and mean, his shoulders wider than he seemed tall. In comparison to the towering officer, he appeared dwarfed, but no less spry. He had the broad, muscled hands of a machinist. One rested upon his hip, the other on the counter, crooked, fingers flexed. Chris imagined the strained conversation through the half-brick half-glass wall that separated them.

"I'm here for my son."

"Which one is he?"

"Christopher Lane. Lane, L-A-N-E."

"Lane," the officer called when he came to get him. But Chris was already on his feet.

As they walked down the hall and out the front doors,

Mr. Lane's basketball shoes squeaked against the fake marble. They didn't speak. On the stairs outside, Mr. Lane stopped. He grasped the large brick wall that ran around the landing and down the wide steps, half-sat upon it, his body visibly shaking.

Chris stared down at the three stripes on either foot that thrust out in front of Mr. Lane, paint-pocked Adidas.

"Chris?" There was a rough question mark in it.

Mr. Lane folded the matchbook backward and pulled the match out from between the two flaps. It flared with a bright *psssst*. He stared at Chris above the cigarette that stuffed his mouth. The end of it glowed, and he held the breath in for a long time before blowing the smoke out. It drifted across to where Chris stood waiting. Around them, South Wakefield was alive and iridescent, sky and grass, rich blue and green, obscenely Norman Rockwell.

Mr. Lane's fingers curled into a fist that knocked firmly upon the top of the stone ledge. Chris stared at it, knowing what he had earned. Mr. Lane glared across the parkette in front of the police station. His mouth opened and closed. He rapped his knuckles again against the stone, loosening a small chunk of skin. A small ragged red circle remained and the tip of the filter glowed. That cigarette was all that stood between Chris and his father. It burned and blew its way out again.

PLAYER 2

Mr. Lane strode across the porch steps as if he couldn't get away from Chris fast enough. Tammy watched her father through the sheers. In front of her, Mrs. Lane also stood watching. Her fingers bunched and unbunched a tense white handkerchief, acquired during Tammy's brief absence.

Mr. Lane stopped suddenly in front of the living room window, looked in at them. Chris — who hadn't raised his head since exiting the car — bumped against him.

Mr. Lane's hand came around, settled on Chris's shoulder for just a second. Mr. Lane's mouth loosened as his eyes fastened on his wife, what Tammy knew, even from behind, was her mother's pinched, skinny mouth. Tammy's father clapped Chris on the shoulder, wrapped his fingers around the tendon, perhaps to steer him into the house, perhaps for comfort. She had no idea that it was the first time they had touched in over a year.

He gripped Chris, solidly, as she had seen men do to one another earlier that summer at her grandfather's funeral, broad palm stranded between affection and violence. Even then, it had struck her that they were bracing one another for something so large they couldn't quite wrap their whole hands around it, or stand to touch it in any other way. Isolation, anger, pain. Things grown men did not have words for, but could only clap out of one another temporarily.

Chris stumbled under his father's touch, his eyes meeting Tammy's through the window, dull with sullen absence. For the first time in her life, more than a few feet and a wall or a sheet of glass divided all of them.

Flap, flap. Flap, flap. She watched her brother swallow under the weight of it.

Then the hand rose up and flew away.

The moiré pattern of the sheer curtain cast a strange haze across the picture. Even as Mrs. Lane reached to sweep it aside, Chris's face wavered. His dark eyes skipped between Tammy and his mother before they dissolved into static. Both sides of the screen blipped and broke into infinite fuzz.

Bonus

PLAYER 2

Tammy the Spy cruised down St. Lawrence Street, dipped into the crescent where the Bretons had lived. There was a new family there now — just since the weekend — and she took every possible opportunity to try to catch a glimpse. Today, the windows were dark. A large rubber skeleton hung on the door. The plastic ripped apart, serrated and stringy. Dark wood showed behind its jangled bones. Its yellow neon ribs sent a quake of happiness through Tammy's chest. A white elastic thread held up Tammy's heart. She looped her bike in a circle, three times. It meant they had kids.

In early September, Chris and Tammy had watched a tow truck cart away Mr. Breton's chipped crash-derby cruiser. The Lane children were sitting on the curb together, an old tennis ball making a grey-green journey in and out of Chris's palms. The police-painted black-and-white hood rumbled up alongside and passed them — disappeared down the road, the signal beside the burst headlight blinking as its porter lumbered around the corner onto St. Lawrence Street. The ball stopped, and Chris was gone, off and running, into the house. Tammy sat on the curb with the tennis ball in her brother's place. She bounced it gently against the concrete and didn't look over her shoulder at her brother's bedroom window.

Mrs. Breton had taken J.P. to live with relatives in Quebec. Apparently, she and Mr. Breton had been on the verge of splitting anyway. The incident had allowed everything to fracture.

Separation was like that, apparently. One day everything seemed fine. The next day, people were gone. Tammy shrugged it off like a bad dream. There was no point in thinking about it; it just *was*. Her parents were still solid. She stopped waiting for the fission. Instead, she dodged in and out of driveways, swerving her bicycle to and fro over the abandoned road.

J.P. had shown up just before he left. Tammy was home alone, and hadn't felt right inviting him into the house. He'd stood there shuffling, until she slowly crossed the threshold and sat with him on the porch steps in her sock feet. They stared at the neighbourhood. He took his ball cap off and on. He'd written his address on a piece of notebook paper he'd tucked inside. It fell out of the hat into his palm, like a magician's white rabbit. He unfolded it and refolded it and gave it to Tammy.

"Before it happened —" he faltered. "Tell Chris I didn't rat," he said, but then he stood up quickly, and loped off. He didn't look back when he called, "Goodbye, Short Fry, *junior,*" over his shoulder.

Tammy watched the points of his shoulders through his mesh shirt until he rounded the corner back to what was still, however briefly, his own crescent. Tammy guessed the space between his shoulder blades was the length of her hand, and after he was gone, she sat looking at them. She took the address inside and pushed it under Chris's soccer trophy. When he came home she would tell him it was there. He would unfold it once, look at it, then put it back without saying anything.

Marc hadn't gone back to school in September. Instead, he had driven his Barracuda to the city, where he was able to get in at one chemical plant or another. In another half year, Tammy would point to the picture in Chris's yearbook — the one Marc had shown up to have taken, ten minutes after bludgeoning another boy.

"I knew him," she would say, in proud, scared whisper, to her friends, though it was only half true. "My brother was *there.*" In black and white, Marc's mouth would be lopsided, between smile and grimace, his eyes vacant. Like everyone else in the book, he would be reduced to a name in ten-point font while he went on living another life. In this case, forty miles away.

Tammy thought about the Rabbit often. In her dreams, he was rounder, a kind of white sphere of a human hurtling through space. He came out of the dark, and Tammy whirled around. Like the spaceship in a game of Asteroids, she felt herself bombarded by something hard as rock. One night she woke to find his ghost in her room, standing at the foot of her bed, his round shoulders and white neck. She lay very still, afraid to ask what he wanted. When she'd gathered the courage to sit up and open her eyes, she saw it was only her new fall coat on the back of the closet door, a pitch of light through the chink in the curtains. She lay back down, turning her face to the mattress, breathing cold, unsure why the sweat wouldn't stop.

The pebble remained tucked into the mouth of a doll's oven, and in shame, Tammy never spoke of it or removed it, its intimacy frightful, far greater than any she had definitions for. The doll's oven would be sold for a quarter, years later, by her mother at a garage sale, and when Tammy asked about it, some time in her early twenties, no one would be able to recall. Another little girl would discover the pebble, put it in her mouth. When her mother asked *did she have something in her mouth?* the girl would swallow it, and it would disappear in the usual way.

Inside the Lane house, Chris was bopping up and down in the recliner — head heavy with the sounds of the boombox in his lap. Around the headphones, notes from Asia's "Sole Survivor" leaked out. Chris had been playing it with religious fanaticism since J.P. and the Bretons had moved away.

Grade Nine had welcomed Chris into an anonymity of hooded sweatshirts and brown bag lunches. So far as Tammy could discern, being a South Wakefield legend was like tossing a stone into water. The ripples spread ever-outward — lapping, little tongues at the edges of everything — but the stone itself sank. Tammy watched Chris sit on the bottom of this new experience, a cheap set of orange foam headphones plugging his ears. He'd reverted to his earliest incarnation of Chris. Chris the Smart Guy. Chris the Short Fry. Chris the Uncool. The third week of school, the optometrist had assisted in the reassignment of this social order — written him a prescription for glasses. The living room lights glinted in the lenses, as Chris raised and lowered his head. Thick brown frames served as miniature detention houses for permanently closed, music-blind eyes.

Tammy announced her presence to her parents and went outside again. They nodded. Their faces were like flat dark stones in the wavering light of the television.

The bark of the tree was rough against her fingers. In the cold, it was difficult to grasp the branches. Getting all the way up to the Stadium would be impossible. Tammy settled for the Second Fork. She pulled her Walkman up in the basket. She had made a mixed tape of all her favourite songs. It began with The Beatles' "Blackbird," and followed with Simon and Garfunkel's "I Am A Rock," "El Condor Pasa," and "Bookends." Then it jumped ahead a decade or so to Yoko Ono's "Goodbye Sadness." Tammy's new favourite colour was grey. It was a good, quiet colour. The colour of the skin of trees.

"Dogtown" drummed through the wires. It seemed to Tammy only natural to explore an affinity for Yoko Ono, the object of John Lennon's affections. *Season of Glass* was Yoko's first album after John's death. Tammy had found it mysteriously in her parents' collection. A photograph of John's glasses graced the cover, bloodied, uncleaned since the day he'd been shot. A misty cityscape was visible inside the empty lenses, and a half-empty, half-full glass of water. It gave Tammy chills.

Below Tammy, the Scotts' pool lay sheathed in plastic. A few puddles punctured the flat black tarp that sealed the water underneath. Dunc Scott was away at school, had packed up his El Camino and driven off weeks ago — stalling at the stop sign and then restarting — disappeared down St. Lawrence Street toward the highway. Every morning Diana Scott withdrew in a car that came to pick her up. Tammy would see her run across the yard, feathery hair sprayed stiff, not moving as she ran. At night, its shape re-emerged as she was dropped off. She had finally claimed that exciting teenage life that Tammy had been waiting to bear witness to. And yet, there was so little to watch.

It was five o'clock. On cue, the lights came on in the Stanleys' front window. At 5:15, the Stanleys' pale blue K-car turned the corner and plunged down Running Creek Road as though there were some reason to hurry. Tammy knew better. It reached the Stanley house, and George got out. He shut the door of the car and ambled up the driveway. Inside, his shape passed once before the window, a double outline of the man. He became a faint dark spot behind the curtains, then disappeared into the folds of the house like something fading out. Mrs. Stanley — Rita — arrived a few minutes later. She fetched the dog and steered him down the street and back at a brisk walk. Then their door shut. It would not open again all night.

Down the block, a blue bicycle teetered around the corner, topped by a green windbreaker. Though the bike moved very quickly, the rider seemed precarious, distracted by something — maybe a pant leg about to get caught in the chain. As the speck grew closer, Tammy saw it was a boy — she could tell by the way he rode — someone she had never seen before. She leaned out, squinted down, angled her body between the branches.

A soft, exasperated look flushed his face, as though he

wasn't sure where he had ridden to. He was round and twelve in his puffy football jacket. Immediately, Tammy liked that he would ride so fast, then slow down to catch his breath, losing all the time he had worked to gain. She leaned out a little farther on the branch, and as she did so, it shook, let loose a small leafy gasp.

The boy pressed his brakes.

Something powerful went off in Tammy the Spy, just under her skin. Turbulence, radar, a warning signal. The boy did something completely unprecedented.

He stopped and looked up. He spotted her immediately.

She flattened herself against the trunk of the tree, as if she could become invisible again. He stared at her, then smiled. A slow, gradual, pure smile. He raised a hand. It quivered back and forth like a brown leaf on a branch, then he stuck it back in his pocket and rode away. She exhaled deeply: she'd finally been seen.

PLAYER 1

The eave had been replaced, and a lightbox slotted above the new white metal trough that encircled the building. The sheet of blue plastic that had become its face declared in white lettering: VIDEO PALACE. A double door had been carved out, presumably to let in more light. Through the glass, Chris could see the white movie stands, boxes hooked between their thin metal fingers. Row on row.

Something swatted Chris's thigh. Johnny Davis replaced the ball cap on his curly Breton-like head.

"Short Fry," he said. He leaned against the side of the

building, skinnier than ever, cigarette clutched between his teeth. Chris paused, and his parents went on ahead.

"Johnny."

Johnny sucked on the cigarette, one hand hovering there, trying to decide if it would take the thing out of his mouth or leave it in.

"Goin' inside?" Chris asked.

Johnny hunched, grinned around the cigarette. He expelled the smoke. "Short Fry . . ." he said. "It ain't what it was."

Chris nodded, and nodded again. That was it. All Johnny Davis would ever have. The end glowed, instantly replaced with ash. Chris ducked inside without glancing back.

A new bell sounded — electronic — as he crossed the threshold.

"Popcorn?" A girl in a uniform shirt greeted him. She scooped readymade popcorn out of a big plastic bag — the kind that cost a dollar from Bargain Harold's. On the little table in front of her, paper lunch bags overflowed. Chris glared at them.

An immense pristine white counter had been installed at the back of the store. Pink and teal stripes raced diagonally down the wall behind white-framed posters of '50s stars with updos. Under Chris's feet was a thin new mat of blue carpet. Suddenly, it was hard to say exactly which machines had been where.

Chris dodged a woman with dangling-ball earrings who leaned past him. Her hair was a fluorescent tangerine hat on her head. She looked like the New Wave version of his mom. She tipped a movie box into her hand, and he stepped back.

He approached the looming counter where Mr. and Mrs. Lane were busy obtaining a piece of blue plastic emblazoned with their family name and a membership number.

He stood behind them, off to the side, with them but not. Behind the counter, the girl moved, made the small stiff gestures that promised absolute efficiency to the customer.

"Have a nice night," she said in rote to the man in front of Chris as he carried three plastic boxes away. *Have,* Chris thought. *Have. A. Nice. Night.* As if it was a thing a person could choose.

PLAYER 2

Two bold dots drifted through a grey universe. In front was a girl in a pink windbreaker and a turquoise skirt dotted with black stars. About a block behind her, just far enough to go unnoticed, followed the boy with the blue down vest and black sweatshirt. She strode ahead, as if something was waiting for her. In the back, the boy's hood was up, his head seal-like. As he shuffled forward, one hand clutched a pair of glasses inside the Y pocket on the front of his vest. At separate points, they sailed across St. Lawrence Street and headed behind the Joyland/Video Palace to the railroad track.

She had brought him here, led him. In one of her hands, a quarter. She'd always wanted to do this, set it on the tracks and let the train run over it, to see what would happen. She was just balancing the coin on the rail when a boy's head edged around the building.

"You better not stand way up there," he yelled. "Train'll drag you all the way to Detroit." It was Chris.

"What are you doing here?"

He shrugged. "I followed you."

Her eyes narrowed, "I *know* that."

Chris didn't properly answer.

They sat on a parking block and waited. The coin balanced on the rail, glinting.

Behind them, the Rolling Stones mural had been painted over with white. A knowing eye could still perceive the ghost of outlines through the rollered two coats. Video Palace was closed for the first time since it had opened: Thanksgiving.

Chris chewed his lip and Tammy watched him. Without unpocketing his hands, he ducked his head to one side, wiped his forehead across the shoulder of his vest, and resumed chewing. A thin line of wet darkened the blue nylon. Tammy didn't say anything. She watched his face waver, then right itself. In the unwritten journals of Tammy the Spy, Chris never cried; he just sniffed back.

"It's all so big and dumb," he said, as if they had been talking all along.

Tammy had been practising the art of nodding her head. But this time, she surprised herself.

"I met him once," she said, simply.

"Don't lie," Chris said. He glared at her and then stared off in the other direction. "I mean it," he threatened, his voice tight, "I mean —"

He took his glasses out and put them on, removed them, and cleaned the lenses on the fleece that hung from beneath his vest like a pouted lip. He was a dumb hero. His killer-for-hire had been killed; at Chris's inadvertent instigation, sent eternally away from his little sister, who had been in graver danger than Chris ever had. The universe had interfered, a future photo of Tammy now captioned differently than it might have been. She would graduate, not only eighth grade, but twelfth, university, and beyond . . . She would be bright, happy, unbothered, altogether innocent and tough. He could see the other picture of her, the one that belonged to someone else, some other girl for whom life had been harder, a girl with eyes like cold wet rocks. Chris hiccupped (sobbed?) once — kicked at the gravel beneath their feet — and swallowed, as if he could be rid of the details he didn't want that easily.

"Did you really meet him . . . if you really did . . ." He didn't look at her. His fingers trembled as he folded and unfolded the bows of his glasses, put them back on his face. He sniffed back suddenly then, and spat it out behind them, his mouth finally unclenched. "It's just as well that he's dead then."

"Don't say that, Chris," she said. She whispered it, like she was afraid someone would overhear her.

"I'm glad."

"— Don't."

Tammy didn't know how he could grieve for someone one minute, and be so cruel the next. She picked up stones and threw them, one by one, into the long grass in front of the tracks. Between her fingers, the gravel made chalky impressions. Stones dug into her palm and she squeezed them hard in the one hand, throwing with the other. She squeezed and squeezed until she could feel the inside skin become hot and white. Eventually she let the pebbles fall to the pavement, let the blood throb back into her palm.

Before Chris could say anything more, the red lights began to go. The gates came down on St. Lawrence Street. Chris and Tammy stood up and watched the dirty shoulders of the train chug slowly toward them, metal on metal. A huge *ka-chunk ka-chunk*. He shuffled his feet around on the cement, as though they hadn't been saying anything important just a minute ago. When it passed, they listened to the clanging, waited for it to stop.

Chris sniffed and nodded, gave a *1-2-3-Go*. He rushed forward to the place their quarter had been, bounding on legs that were finally, silently, catching up to those of his peers. Tammy scrambled up the slight embankment after him, noting the spring and the force with which he quelled his emotions. It wasn't fair, after all this time, that he could reveal things to her — or start to — and still be so much a mystery.

They found the coin, fallen off, between the ties. It was flattened into a large, unidentifiable object. Chris turned the misshapen thing over.

"Well," he said, handing it to Tammy, "now that you've seen what it looks like, what are you going to do with it?" And ultimately, that was the question.

Late afternoon fall sunlight. Nineteen eighty-four was ending. Winter lay ahead; already it was trudging toward them. Soon, the stores would be piping out carols, individual aisles like broken limbs plastercast with tinsel. Looking into his sister's palm, Chris could see that far, but no further. The heavy metal shape sandwiched there pulled the power out of him.

Even pooled, their understanding was limited. In the world outside South Wakefield, the Year of the Spy would soon begin. But Tammy had hung her binoculars in the garage for the season. They had no idea what the future would bombard them with. No idea that Molly Ringwald and Max Headroom lay in wait. No idea that Kid 'n Play and Delite were sitting alongside Guns N' Roses and Nirvana on the cusp of the next decade. No idea where the next streak of joy would come from — a french kiss or a friendship — driving tests, diplomas, or human collisions — Super Mario Bros. or Legend of Zelda. It was as if the pixels that hadn't been projected yet were hovering somewhere, perhaps in the blue sky overhead. Like spirits positively or negatively charged. Like ions. They had only the past, their shared joys and sorrows. There could be no idea of the beauty of the future.

Acknowledgements

The Ontario Arts Council, Toronto Arts Council, Michael Holmes, Jack David and everyone at ECW PRESS, Nate Powell, Don Sedgwick, Shaun Bradley, Clive Thompson and Derek McCormack,

and to Brian Joseph Davis.